# GALACTIC INSTABILITY

## ROGUE ENTERPRISES
### BOOK 2

JOHN WILKER

Rogue Publishing

Cover art by: Ana Voltz

V 1

ISBN: 978-1-951964-35-1

# CONTENTS

News Cast                                    1

PART 1
Chapter 1                                    5
Chapter 2                                   15
Chapter 3                                   24
Chapter 4                                   41
Chapter 5                                   53

PART 2
Chapter 6                                   63
Chapter 7                                   77
Chapter 8                                   88
Chapter 9                                   99
Chapter 10                                 112
Chapter 11                                 120

PART 3
Chapter 12                                 129
Chapter 13                                 142
Chapter 14                                 153
Chapter 15                                 162
Chapter 16                                 171

PART 4
Chapter 17                                 187
Chapter 18                                 195
Chapter 19                                 207
Chapter 20                                 221

PART 5

Chapter 21                                    241
Chapter 22                                    258
Chapter 23                                    272
Chapter 24                                    289
Chapter 25                                    299
Chapter 26                                    310

Thank You                                     329
Offer                                         331
Stay Connected                                333
Acknowledgments                               335
Other Books by John Wilker                    337

## NEWS CAST

"Good morning. I'm Megan, and this your GNO Morning Briefing." The newscaster ran a hand through her blonde hair, revealing one of her conical audio receptors.

"And I'm Xyrzix. The Obotlum sector voted yesterday to withdraw from the Galactic Commonwealth," the blue-skinned newsman said, compound eyes blinking. He continued, "The vote came after months of public debate and hearings. The separatist movement spent a great deal of time and credits on ensuring the vote went against the Commonwealth."

"This makes Obotlum the third sector in two months to vote to withdraw from the GC," Megan picked up. "Like those sectors before it, the Governing Council member representing Obotlum cited recent increases in taxes to rebuild the Peace-keeper Navy as one of the main reasons her sector voted to leave."

Xyrzix turned to another camera pickup. "This latest development adds to the tensions within the GC Governing Council, especially as new systems and sectors are still applying for membership." He turned back toward Megan. "Speaking of...In between what we're calling politely raucous debates in the council around the separatist issue, a new system has been admitted as an associate GC member."

Megan smiled. "For those unaware, associate membership is used when societies are deemed worthy of admission to the GC but not quite ready for full membership. In this case, the world in question is still finalizing its first planetary governing body."

Xyrzix bobbed his head. "I believe they also have not colonized any other worlds, residing solely on their home planet." Megan nodded. Xyrzix smiled, his compound eyes glinting in the overhead lights. "On behalf of the crew here at GNO, and I hope, the wider GC, I welcome the people of Urt to the Galactic Commonwealth." He turned to his cohost. "It is, Urt, yes?"

Megan looked down at her tablet. "Yes...Oh, I'm told it's pronounced Earth."

*PART 1*

CHAPTER 1

The *Ghost* dropped out of FTL enroute to Jdarum Two. The bridge's primary display updated to show the pale brown disc of the planet ahead. One of the smaller sub-displays showed a tactical view from the small ship's sensors. There were only three other ships in sensor range, none close enough to be a threat.

An alarm sounded.

"What the—?" Wil said. He tapped his command console, watching text scroll across the screen followed by a glowing outline of the ship. He looked at the ceiling. "Gabe, why did one of the sub-light engines just go offline?"

From the overhead speaker, Gabe said, "If I had to guess, it would be because you ignored my recommendation to replace the primary power bus coupler, and it has now melted."

Wil scowled. "Can you fix it?" The speaker was silent. "Gabe?"

"I think he hung up on you," Bennie offered.

Wil turned to his Brailack friend. "Shove it."

Cynthia sighed. "We have money in the accounts. Why didn't you just repair it?"

Wil's cheeks reddened. "I forgot."

"You have a wristcomm; it has a reminder function," Bennie said, holding his arm up, wristcomm on display.

Wil reared back. "It has a reminder app?" Everyone on the bridge sighed. "Why didn't anyone tell me that?" He held his own arm up, tapping the screen of his wristcomm, flicking through menus.

"Because you're a grown-up," Bennie retorted.

"From a planet that doesn't have wristcomms," Wil snarled.

"Babe, you've been out here for nearly a decade," Cynthia said.

Wil spun his chair around to face the back of the bridge. "Traitor."

She smiled at him, her tail swishing languidly under her chair.

The ship shuddered once. The ceiling chimed. "The starboard sub-light engine is back online. I advise against vigorous maneuvering."

Wil beamed. "That's the only kind of maneuvering I do."

Zephyr looked at him. "We know. The walls are not as thick you think."

Wil blushed anew. Composing himself, he looked up at the ceiling. "Thanks, pal. Promise to get that..."

"Primary power bus coupler," Maxim offered from his seat at the tactical station.

Wil pointed at his friend. "Yeah, the primary power bus coupler. We'll get a new one as soon as we get home."

A grumble noise came from the ceiling.

Wil looked over his console, confirming that the flashing icon over the starboard sub-light engine was no longer blinking before pushing the sub-light throttle forward. "Always something."

The *Ghost* accelerated toward the planet ahead.

Maxim nodded toward the planet on the primary display. "What do we know?"

Zephyr tapped her console, bringing up an overlay on the display that showed all of the planet Jdarum's details: population, exports, current affiliations, and much more.

Wil turned. "Looks like space Wikipedia needs an update. No longer part of the GC." Zephyr glared at him.

"Probably can't keep up with all the systems and sectors pulling the plug," Cynthia offered.

Bennie added, "Wonder if anyone is laying odds on how many end up bailing on the Commonwealth?"

Wil tutted. "You little degenerate."

Bennie beamed.

A soft beep called Cynthia's attention back to her console. "We're being hailed," she said, looking up from the console. "Jdarum Space Control," she added.

Wil nodded to her, then looked at the ceiling as a speaker chimed. "Cargo vessel *Do You Like Piña Coladas*? Please state your business."

Bennie looked up from whatever he was doing when he heard the name of the ship. Turning to Wil, he raised a hairless brow ridge. Wil winked.

"Jdarum Space Control, we're just making a delivery. We've got a hold full of harvester parts." Wil turned to Maxim and mouthed, *Right?* The big man nodded.

There was a pause, then, "Understood, *Do You like Piña Coladas*. I don't see a form 230 on file. Did you submit that?"

Wil cocked his head and turned to Zephyr. "Of course, we did. A form...Two..."

"Thirty," the voice offered.

"Right, a 230...Definitely." He raised an eyebrow to her and got a shrug back.

"I don't see one on file, *Do You Like Piña Coladas*." The

voice on the speaker sounded like it had explained this form a hundred times.

Wil put on a smile. "That's weird to be sure. We'll make sure to file one next time. Please accept my apologies. I'll make sure to flog my executive officer." He turned to Zephyr mouthing, *Sorry.*

Bennie was watching him. He whispered, "They can't see you."

Wil waved a hand.

"Sorry, *Do You Like Piña Coladas.* All inbound cargo must be accompanied by a form 230. No exceptions. New regulations, you understand."

Wil sighed. "Wait just a second, Space Control. Uh, maybe we have it here?"

"Are you asking me?" the voice replied.

"Just hold on," Wil barked. He slapped the mute switch on his console then spun his chair around. "Babe, can you see if you can work some magic here?"

Cynthia sighed. "What magic? We don't have that form. Are you expecting me to magically produce it?"

"I have faith in you." He winked.

Sighing, she turned to her console. "Moron. No, no. Yes, hi. This is, uh...Cynthia."

"Smooth," Bennie drawled. Not turned to him, Cynthia raised a hand making a rude gesture.

The bridge fell silent as Cynthia spoke to the Jdarum Space Control operator. Finally, Max stood up. "I'm going to help Gabe get the cargo ready." Without waiting for a reply, he left the bridge.

Wil sat listening to Cynthia. It didn't sound like she was having any better luck than he had. He flipped the autopilot on, got out of his seat, and went over to Zephyr's station. "Anything hinky?"

She looked up. "Hinky?" Her station had many of the same displays as his, but also served as the hub for the ship's various sensor feeds. As his first officer, she had more data at her fingertips that he did at any given time.

"You know, anything look weird down there?" He glanced at the main display. "Or up here?"

She consulted her sensor display. "No. Why?"

He shrugged. "I dunno. Sudden forms delaying our arrival. My gut got worried."

From the back of the bridge, Cynthia's raised voice said, "Well, we didn't know about the form!"

Wil and Zephyr both turned. From his station on the opposite side of the small bridge, Bennie said, "That sounds like it's going well."

They both nodded their agreement.

"Okay, fine. Yes. Yes, I understand! I said, I understand!" Cynthia slammed her palm down on her console. After taking a calming breath, she turned to the others. "They're sending a customs inspection team over."

Wil blinked a few times. "What? Over here?"

"Yes."

"To this ship? To board us?"

"Yes. With form 230."

"We went from not having the right form to being boarded for inspection?" Zephyr asked.

Wil moved back to his seat, turning the autopilot off. His flight computer was flashing a new set of coordinates, sent from Cynthia's station. Accepting them, he saw that they were being routed to a holding orbit.

"These people left the GC a month ago and already have delusions of bureaucratic grandeur," Cynthia growled.

Wil looked at the ceiling. "Gabe, Max. We're gonna be boarded soon. Gonna need ya to hide the goods."

"We just finished moving them to the front of the hold," Max complained from the ceiling speaker.

"Then you know exactly which crates to put back." He grunted. "Blame Cynthia."

"Excuse me?" she said. Wil spotted the claws she normally kept sheathed in her fingertips, sliding out. They weren't long but were incredibly sharp. Wil had found that out a few times, the hard way.

He held up both hands. "Kidding. Love you."

"You suck." She turned to her console. "They'll be here in twenty."

On the sensor display window inset on the primary display, Wil saw the yellow dot representing the Jdarum customs ship. He sighed. "Better tell Butterball's client that we're gonna be late."

Zephyr shook her head. "You know that name annoys him."

Wil grinned. "I do."

The team had been working with Botrobel Hjun for a few months. Wil didn't particularly like him, but he paid well and his jobs usually weren't that risky. The Rigellian broker approached them to act as smugglers delivering goods to worlds that were no longer part of the Galactic Commonwealth but still had a taste for GC goods. To keep up appearances, they also did the occasional above board shipping job as well.

It never ceased to amaze Wil how many worlds and sectors voted to leave the GC without factoring in where they'd get their next shipment of this or that luxury good.

He glanced at the sub-display. The yellow dot was drawing closer to the *Ghost*.

The bulbous customs corvette slid up alongside the *Ghost* and extended a docking tube. The ship was twice the size of the small Ankarran Raptor, the Arumii vessel looking like a snowman fallen on his side, covered in dark brown hull paneling.

Wil looked at Cynthia and Bennie standing with him at the starboard airlock. The light over the inner airlock door blinked red twice, then turned green signaling a good seal and that the other side held breathable atmosphere.

The doors slid open to reveal three beings that looked to Wil a lot like undecorated Mr. Potato Head toys. He waved. "Hello." Each of the three beings, standing nearly two and half meters tall, dipped forward on flexible limbs, in a type of bow. Their bodies didn't look like they bent in any way.

The lead potato head waddled out of the airlock on four rubbery boneless locomotive limbs. Each limb ended in a thick callous, making a soft thump on the deck as the being walked. Wil looked down. To him they looked like toes sans toenails. He put his hand to his mouth.

"Hello, Captain Holmes," the lead being said. Its voice came from a vocalizer strapped around the narrower upper portion of its body below a set of sensory organs that ringed the top portion.

Wil smiled and bowed. "Welcome aboard the *Do You Like Piña Coladas.*"

"Why are you bowing?" Bennie whispered. Wil slugged him.

Cynthia shoved the two of them aside. "Welcome aboard. I can show you to the hold."

One of the leader's six tentacles waved as it reached out to wrap around her offered arm.

"I am Senior Inspector Muplindo." Another of the tentacles waved toward the airlock and its occupants. "My underlings, Duulp and Siieve."

Cynthia nodded to the remarking Jdarum, then turned and headed aft. The trio of waddling potatoes fell in behind her. Muplindo could just be heard saying, "This is not a very clean ship."

Wil glared at the retreating inspection team, then at Bennie, who leaned back. "Why are you glaring at me?"

Wil shrugged. "I dunno. I need to glare at someone, and you're usually the one that makes the messes." He made his voice as robotic as he could. "This ship is dirty." He stormed off after Cynthia and their guests.

Bennie watched him go. "All this time, he hasn't gotten less weird. And now there's gonna be millions of them wandering the GC." He headed after Wil and the others.

By the time Bennie reached the landing of the stairwell to the cargo bay, Wil was in the hold with Gabe, Maxim, and the three inspectors. Cynthia had remained on the landing, watching. She turned to Bennie as he arrived. "Too crowded down there?" he asked.

"Watching Wil squirm is only fun in certain settings."

Bennie held up a little green three-fingered hand. "Don't need to know about that." He was thankful his quarters were on the opposite side of the corridor as Wil and Cynthia's.

Down below, Wil was showing the Senior Investigator and its colleagues one of the crates labeled for delivery on Jdarum. One of them, Siieve or Duulp, asked, "And how many of these crates are bound for our world?"

Maxim put a hand on the crate nearest him. "Nine."

The third inspector waddled over to another crate. All six

tentacles ran along two of the sides. "All sealed?" it asked in its synthesized voice. Wil realized that there were slight differences in all three voices. The Arumii must be able to adjust the vocalizer they wore to suit their preferences.

Watching the inspection team, Wil realized the sensory organs that ringed the top of their bodies must be eyes. They were solid black orbs that didn't blink or seem to move. Maybe they were something else, but he hoped they were nothing more advanced or sensitive than that. The smugglers' hold beneath their feet was shielded, but nothing was perfect. The other hiding spots scattered around the hold were even less well camouflaged from sensors.

Up on the staircase, Cynthia looked down at Bennie. "Why didn't you just hack into their systems before we arrived?"

The Brailack looked up at her. "I forgot until right before we left."

Her tail swished as she smirked. "You forgot?"

He shrugged. "I've been busy, you know. Rebuilding an order of guardians of peace that was almost completely extinct. Recruiting trainees, setting an example for them."

Cynthia held up a hand. "Isn't your droid friend doing most of that?"

Bennie scowled. "Some of it." He made a clucking noise. "Besides. I did try once we were on our way." His face scrunched up. "These burbloom fruit-looking goobers ripped all the GC standard gear out of their planetary network and hodge-podged their own system with off-the-shelf stuff, half of it old and out of date, the other half brand-spanking new." He shrugged. "The mix was too hard to crack on the fly."

Down in the hold, the Senior Investigator turned to face Wil, or at least turned its vocalizer toward Wil. "Very well. You are cleared." Two of the tentacles extended, holding out a tablet.

Wil took it and looked over the form displayed on it. He looked up. "This is form 230?"

Muplindo bobbed up and down, its rubbery locomotive limbs bending and straightening. "Yes."

Wil held the table out so that Max could see the screen. The big man blinked twice and looked at Wil, then the Senior Investigator. The effort to contain his laughter was herculean.

Wil pressed a thumb to the screen, then handed the tablet back.

As Wil escorted the inspection team to the airlock, Cynthia fell in next to him. "So, what's form 230?"

He turned to her, his face red. In a low voice, he said, "I promise I'm not smuggling contraband."

She pursed her lips and turned around, rushing back toward the lounge, her laughter echoing through what the crew called the ship's neck, the long corridor that connected the bridge and forward section to the larger crew space and cargo hold.

## CHAPTER 2

On the bridge's primary display, the Arumii ship pulled away from the *Ghost*.

Zephyr was staring at Wil and the others. "You can't be serious."

Wil nodded once. "As a heart attack." He grunted. "Literally one page. *I am not smuggling*."

Bennie clucked. "These people shouldn't have left the GC. They're doomed."

Wil shrugged. "As long as they keep buying...Do we know what we're delivering?" Everyone shook their heads. "Well, as long as these tentacled potatoes like whatever it is in our hold, we'll put up with their bureaucratic weirdness."

He powered up the sub-light engines, guiding the ship back toward the planet. Their parking orbit had taken them around the planet from their planned landing area, so they'd have to sit in orbit for an hour transferring lower and lower as they went.

The bridge hatch slid open.

"You sneaky, dirty old krebnack!" Nic burst in, tablet in one hand, the other balled into a small fist. "You no-good drennog!" Her ire was clearly aimed at her mentor, Bennie.

Bennie leaned out from his station and looked at his irate apprentice, his mouth forming a small O.

She stomped around past Cynthia's station toward Bennie's nest of monitors, keyboards, and who knew what else. He leaned back into his station as she reached him, swinging the tablet at his head.

"Are you out of your mind?" he screeched, barely avoiding the device.

"You've been hacking my tablet and online accounts!"

Everyone else turned their attention to the two Knights of Plentallus.

Bennie held out his hands. "Just to make sure you—" He yelped as her tablet connected with his forehead.

Wil leaned back in his seat. "Wrong answer."

Raining more blows on her mentor, Nic shouted, "You violated my privacy, you old creeper!"

"Will you—Ow! Stop—Ow!" Bennie was barely getting in a word between blows. His small furry apprentice was enraged.

Wil watched the theatrics for a bit longer before he leaned forward in his seat. "Okay! Okay! You two—" he started but was drowned out by screeching and the sounds of a tablet striking a Brailack skull.

"Enough!" Wil shouted. "If you two don't cut the crap, I will turn this spaceship around, and we'll go home."

Maxim turned to look at Zephyr, who shrugged.

Nic jabbed a finger at her mentor. "He accessed my online accounts, my search history, and scanned—"

Wil held up a hand. "Don't care."

Bennie opened his mouth but stopped when Wil leveled a finger at the little Brailack hacker. "Bennie. If you violate her privacy again, I'll space you." He wiggled the finger to silence the hacker's reply. Looking at Nic, he said, "And you. The bridge is a no-shouting—

and especially—no-shrieking zone. If you bust in here again, I'll find the most horrible orphanage I can and drop you off."

Folding her arms across her chest, Nic retorted, "I'm too old for —"

"Zip it!" Wil growled. She did. With a huff, she stormed back to the hatch and left the bridge.

Zephyr looked across the bridge. "What's wrong with you?"

Bennie was about to answer when Wil said, "Dude. You gotta get your shit in order. You can't be snooping on her. She's not a child." Again, he motioned for the hacker to remain silent. "And she can't be bursting in here causing a ruckus. What if we were entering the atmosphere and I needed to focus?"

The team hacker frowned. "We'd crash differently than your normal type of crashing?"

Wil made a rude gesture. "Just get this figured out."

Bennie waved a hand. "I already looked. She's too old to kill."

"What?" everyone else said as one.

Maxim was the first to speak. "That isn't what he meant. Why would you think it was?"

Wil sighed. "Dude, you find amazing ways to still be shockingly dark."

"Don't tell me you haven't thought about it. She can be annoying," Bennie fought back.

Zephyr shook her head. "Something is wrong with you."

The *Ghost* roared through the sky as she shed heat and reentry plasma. Zephyr pulled up a topographical map, insetting it on the primary display. A blue dot was blinking. "That's our LZ."

Wil nodded. "Cool. Touch down in fifteen."

"Doesn't look like we're heading for a spaceport," Maxim said. Their landing zone looked to be as remote a location as possible on this planet.

"Nothing sketchy about that," Cynthia said.

Maxim nodded. "Guess we better go get our party clothes on." He winked at Zephyr.

The Palorian couple left the bridge.

Bennie turned to look at Wil. "Want Nic and I to—"

"No," Wil growled. Bennie said nothing, turning back to whatever he was doing at his console. Wil had found that having as much visible muscle as possible often helped with some of these backwater deliveries. After the little show Bennie and Nic had put on, he was not in the mood for them right now.

On the primary display, the landscape changed from the small city they initially flew over, to a scrubby forest of bright pink trees, to what was now barren prairie and what passed for scrub grass on Jdarum.

In the distance, several three-meter-tall poles with blinking lights were visible. The lights formed two concentric circles: two kilometers and one, respectively, around the rural landing field. Wil guided the *Ghost* toward the rings of light, slowly easing power to the nacelle-mounted repulsorlifts.

On the screen, the crew could see another ship parked at the landing field. From what Cynthia could see, it was dark. Completely powered down. With the ship's first officer getting dressed down in the armory, she was sitting at the sensor station.

There wasn't much to the field they were approaching: space enough for three, maybe four, ships the size of the *Ghost*. A two-story building that likely served as field management office. A pair of the familiar potato-shaped beings were moving from the building toward a small service shed.

Down in the armory, Maxim was slipping his armored chest

plate over his head. "It's funny these old scout armors look intimidating."

Zephyr was snapping a gauntlet over her wristcomm. "I'm just glad we didn't get rid of them."

The pair had much more modern suits of armor in the small armory. They had bought these suits of scout armor shortly after meeting Wil and Bennie, when they decided to rob a space station full of criminal treasure. Despite being less powerful and carrying next to no armament, the old suits looked more menacing than their newer, more lethal armor did.

Maxim adjusted his own wristcomm before snapping a gauntlet around it. The gauntlet had a cutout that allowed most common wristcomms to fit inside, exposing their screen. This allowed the armor wearer to still use the common device. He held his arm out, turning it this way and that, looking it over. "We should get these repainted." A green icon flashed on his wristcomm's screen, signaling that integration with the armor was complete.

"Why?" Zephyr stepped into her boots. Each made a soft click as it locked into a greave.

Max snapped on his other gauntlet. "You know. To look more menacing."

She made a face.

"What?"

"Men," she sighed, engaging her armor's helmet.

"You know we'd look bad ass if our faceplates had a skull or flames." He clapped his hands. "Flaming skulls!"

She rolled her eyes, deploying her helmet.

Back on the bridge, Wil brought the *Ghost* around in a tight arc over the landing field. "Looks good?"

Cynthia nodded. "Nothing hunky."

Wil took his eyes off his console to glance over. "Hunky? You mean beside me?" He winked.

His wife looked up. "Not hunky?"

"Me, yes. The saying, no. Maybe hinky?" Wil offered.

She pursed her lips. "That's the one." She gestured to her console and the sensor data. "None of that."

He grinned. "No contact from the field office?"

She shook her head.

Wil shrugged. "Okay, then. Down we go." He guided the *Ghost* downward.

The *Ghost* slowed to a stop a handful of meters above the landing field. Power to the repulsorlifts gradually reduced, lowering the ship. Two loud thunks echoed through the ship as the landing gear unfolded, followed by two more as the gear locked into place.

The ship hit the gravel, sinking onto her articulated landing legs.

Wil put the *Ghost*'s systems into standby. "Green asshole, you go check in with whoever is in charge over in that field building."

"Why me?" Bennie asked, hopping from his chair.

Wil cocked his head. "Well, for one thing, I'm still annoyed with you. For another, would you rather help offload the cargo?"

Bennie drew himself up to his full one-meter height. "I'll go check in with whoever's in charge."

"You do that," Wil drawled. He looked to Cynthia, still at Zephyr's station. "Ready?" She nodded.

Bennie led the way off the bridge. He trotted ahead of Wil and Cynthia, shouting for Nic. The young Olop girl fell in next to him when they reached the main lounge space.

Cynthia looked at him. "This ship gets weirder and weirder."

Wil nodded his agreement.

Up ahead, the pair heard Bennie and Nic resume their shouting at each other.

"Maybe we make them fly in his Eagle 5-lookin' hunk of junk," Wil offered.

The shouting pair disappeared into the stairwell that connected the ship's decks.

Cynthia chuckled. "It does bear a weird resemblance to the ship from that movie." They reached the hatch to the same stairwell Bennie and Nic had just taken. She pulled the hatch open. "For the record, that movie wasn't funny."

Wil clucked. "You are dead to me."

"I'll remind you of that tonight," she quipped, pulling the hatch shut behind her. "Did Botrobel tell you anything about the buyer?"

Wil shook his head. "Afraid not. Butterball just said that these spuds have a serious love of drosh."

"Drosh? That's what in all those crates?"

They reached the cargo hold and crossed to the control pedestal. Wil tapped the icon to lower the ramp, then tapped the one next to it, cycling open the thick cargo doors at the ramp's top.

Wil put his hand atop the crate next to him. "Yup. Cases of twelve, flash frozen."

Cynthia shook her head. "I know I said smuggling was preferable to getting shot at all the time, but this feels..." She shrugged. "...Beneath us. Frozen hand snacks?"

"Hidden underneath harvester parts." Wil grinned.

Gabe stepped out of the starboard storage area where the ship's missile inventory was kept. "I am also in favor of not being shot at."

Wil smiled at his mechanical friend. "Hey, pal." He knocked on the container. "I mean, they are tasty. Like a burrito but with super spicy samosa filling." He wiped his other hand across his mouth. "With just the hint of thyme."

She shook her head. "Frozen hand snacks."

The hatch up at the top of the stairs opened; Max, Zephyr, Bennie, and Nic stepped through. The latter pair made their way down the cargo ramp with nothing more than a rude gesture from Bennie on his way past. He and Nic marched down the cargo ramp toward the lone administrative building.

Wil looked at Gabe. "Mind helping me with these?"

The droid inclined his head and moved to the crate nearest him, activating the built-in gravlift. With a hum, the one-meter cube rose a few centimeters off the deck.

The two armored Palorians clomped down the ramp to take up position on either side of it.

Bennie and Nic were almost to the landing field office. "So, what's in the office?" she asked.

He turned. "Ghosts, probably." When he saw the look on her face, somewhere between shock and disgust, he said, "How should I know?"

The young Olop girl gave off an elongated sigh. "Why do you have to be like that?"

Bennie shrugged. "It's fun." He jumped to the side in time to avoid her open-handed swipe.

She didn't slow down but glanced at him from the corner of her eye. "I was serious. Back on the ship. Don't snoop in my stuff."

Bennie came to a stop. "You know it can't happen. Right?"

She stopped a step or two after he did but didn't turn to face her mentor. "You won't tell him, will you?"

Bennie shook his head. "No." He looked to the admin building still a hundred yards or more away. Pointing to it, he said, "In theory, there should be a manager or some other staffer that any ship that lands can check in with. Since they didn't comm us, we're knocking on the door."

"Knights of Plentallus, knocking on doors and asking if we can park our ship," the young woman quipped.

Bennie lowered his voice. "Knights of Plentallus help how we can. Where we can."

She rolled her eyes.

CHAPTER 3

Max and Zephyr watched Wil and Gabe move the crates down the ramp to a spot just west of the ship. Over a private channel, Max asked, "Think any of the Tier 1 worlds will bail on the GC?"

Zephyr was scanning to the area east of the ship, her armor's sensors set to maximum range. She didn't look at him. "I'd be surprised if they did. These backwaters, they don't have much to lose, really. With the Peacekeeper fleet in shambles and stretched thin, they aren't getting much protection. Add to that, the Governing Council has raised taxes. Taxes these systems aren't seeing the fruits of..." She shrugged. "Not much in it for the Arumii."

"Not much in for anyone," Maxim replied. "Especially our people."

She turned her mirrored faceplate toward him. "What makes you say that?'

"First it was the Janus monster, and then the Farsight monsters." He shook his head. "Palor is being taxed the same as every other member world, all while being expected to churn out more Peacekeepers, faster." Before Zephyr could say anything, he continued, "Our people hang everything on being Peacekeepers. But the GC only sees us as a bottomless well of muscle. Now they're demanding more tax money, and more of our children, just so they can rebuild their army and police force."

"Our people keep the GC safe," Zephyr whispered.

"Who keeps us safe?" Max asked. "Who looks out for our people?"

Before she could say anything, her armor flashed two red icons on the heads-up display. She knew Maxim's armor was showing him the same thing. He turned to look in the direction the two dots were approaching from.

Switching over to external audio, Zephyr said, "Incoming. Two contacts."

Wil and Gabe looked up from the crate they were guiding. Turning to Gabe, Wil asked, "Mind getting those last two?" He nodded back up the cargo ramp. The droid nodded and headed up the ramp, passing Cynthia on her way down.

Zephyr turned to Wil and Cynthia. "Cargo vehicle and what looks like a limo."

Wil turned to his wife. "I wonder how they reach the pedals." He made a flapping motion with his arms. "Stubby little bendy limbs of theirs." He pantomimed driving a car, mimicking not being able to reach pedals.

She looked at him. "You don't think their vehicles would be designed around their physiology?" He opened his mouth, but she put a finger across his lips. "I doubt either vehicle is shaped like your Mr. Tuber Man." He frowned.

In the distance, the two vehicles had become visible. The lack of dust being kicked up behind them told Wil that both were modern gravlift-enabled vehicles. Made sense. This planet was fairly modern, despite their current surroundings.

Gabe came down with one of the crates, sliding it next to

the assemblage of other crates. "Be right back," he said, turning to head back up the ramp.

The limo pulled ahead of the cargo vehicle, coming to a stop just under the *Ghost*'s forward section. Wil watched as it came to a halt. He turned to Cynthia. "I didn't have time to form a mental image of a potato limo, but you know, that's not what I would have pictured."

Cynthia gave him a slow head shake. "I don't even want to know what you would have pictured."

The limo was twelve meters long and almost four tall. It was sleek, glossy black with neon blue trim outlining the windows, doors, and gravlift motors. A gull-wing door in the center rose.

An Arumii eased out of the vehicle, its rubbery locomotive limbs flexing as it slid out as if it had been on its back. *I wonder what the inside looks like*, Wil thought, watching the being straighten itself out. Two more Arumii slid out of the vehicle, taking up positions on either side of the first.

Behind the limo, the cargo vehicle came to a stop, turned in place, then backed toward the *Ghost*.

"Captain Calder. A pleasure," the leader said in a voice that, to Wil, sounded freakishly like the talking car from that show his granddad liked—the first one, not the spin-offs and reboots. The guy with the hair and the cool watch.

The lead Arumii extended two tentacles, intertwining them to form a thicker, more substantive limb.

Wil did his best to stifle the grimace on his face and extended his arm. He grasped the pseudo-limb as the two ends wrapped around his forearm. The tentacles weren't slimy like he expected.

"I'm Adfogn," the Arumii said in its computerized voice. "You have my goods?"

It was impossible to tell where it was looking. The black

marbles that were the being's eyes didn't move or blink. The sensor stalks above them waved in random directions.

Wil nodded to the cases off to the side. Gabe was maneuvering the last crate into place next to the others. "Sure do. Several hundred cases of flash frozen drosh."

A mouth that Wil hadn't noticed split open to reveal multiple rows of needlelike teeth. A pale blue tongue snaked out to run around the edge of the opening before withdrawing.

Wil leaned back. At least he knew where the front was now. "You all really love drosh, huh?"

The mouth closed and the computer voice said, "Oh, yes. My people have developed a distinct fondness for drosh. It was actually part of the public debate around withdrawing our membership in the Galactic Commonwealth."

Wil nodded slowly. "I get it. I'd struggle if Flamin' Hot Cheetos were at risk."

"I do not know what that is. Are they good?"

"No," Cynthia cut in. She smiled. "You have the payment?"

Adfogn bobbed on his rubbery legs. "I do." A trio of tentacles waved to his two companions, who headed for the cargo vehicle.

As the rear of the cargo truck opened, Bennie and Nic returned. Wil looked at them. "All good?"

Bennie shrugged. "No one home."

"What's that mean?" Cynthia asked.

Bennie made a face. "The place is empty. No one there." He nudged his apprentice, who was staring at Wil.

"Yeah, no one was there," she said.

"Looked like they didn't come in today," Bennie added.

"We searched the whole place," Nic said.

Adfogn shuffled. "That is correct. This field is rarely used. Which makes it perfect for receiving goods."

Wil cocked his head. "Your party."

Bennie looked up at the massive potato looming over him and Nic. "So, how much do you get for this stuff?"

Adfogn made another bobbing motion, all of its tentacles waving excitedly. "Nearly thirty credits."

"A case?" the Brailack hacker asked, rubbing his palms together.

Adfogn made an electronic noise, then said, "A unit."

Bennie, Wil, and Cynthia turned to the Arumii smuggler. As one they said, "A unit?"

It bobbed up and down.

Bennie rubbed his hands together, making a cackling sound deep in his throat.

"Like a tiny green Ferengi," Wil said.

Bennie spun. "You take that back!" His voice was reedy.

"You don't even know what that means," Wil said.

Bennie squinted at Wil. "You made us watch that show! Big ears, all goofy cackling."

"If the shoe fits."

Bennie growled.

The alien potato shuffled toward Wil, a tentacle reaching up to the vocalizer hung around it. A few taps, and Wil's wrist-comm beeped. "Payment," it said in the voice of a mid-1980s Trans Am. "You know, Captain Calder, there is much money to be made in bringing in more goods...directly. My people voted to leave the GC, but many have developed a taste for an assortment of goods from GC worlds."

Bennie poked Wil in the side, making him flinch. The little hacker looked up at the much more massive being, rubbing his hands together again. "We're listening."

Wil and Cynthia exchanged a look. The former palmed the

Brailack's head, shoving him away, and looked at Adfogn. "You mean outside our arrangement with Butterball?"

The Arumii made a noise like radio static. "Indeed. If we could come to an arrangement, we could split Botrobel Hjun's usual cut. We would of course have to still do some business through him, to keep up appearances."

Wil nodded as Bennie slapped at his hand. "Sixty-forty split of Butterball's cut," the Brailack said.

"I do not know who you are," the alien potato said, his forward locomotive bending to allow him to loom over the small hacker.

Bennie frowned. "Ben-Ari Vulvo, Knight of Plentallus."

"I do not what that is."

Cynthia side-stepped in front of Bennie before he could erupt. The Arumii straightened.

Adfogn was silent a moment. The only sounds on the empty landing field were the grunts and gurgles of Adfogn's two lackeys loading the crates onto the cargo vehicle. Finally, the smuggler said, "Fifty-five, forty-five."

"Deal," Bennie said from behind Cynthia.

Wil looked at Bennie, then Cynthia. He rubbed his finger and thumb together and grinned. She sighed, shaking her head. "I'm going to check on the kid."

To her back, Bennie said, "Make sure she's not—" He stopped when she raised a hand, making a rude gesture.

Up in the *Ghost*'s cargo hold, Cynthia found Nic on the practice mat working through her forms, lunging into a sweeping move with her practice bokken whistling through the air.

"Nice," Cynthia said. "You're really improving."

Nic stopped and turned. "Thanks." The fine fur around her face and rounded teddy-bear ears—according to Wil—flattened. Cynthia recognized it as embarrassment. Nic had been aboard the *Ghost* or otherwise with Rogue Enterprises for about six standard months now. She still hadn't gotten a firm handle on the kid's emotions.

After her adventure with Bennie, when he agreed to let her apprentice, they'd spent a month on Nexum doing a crash course to get her up to speed before returning to Fury to rejoin the team. Since then, she had come a long way in her training.

Cynthia took a seat on the bench next to the mat. "So."

"So," the young Olop girl said. She absently picked at her wooden practice sword with a claw.

"How's things been? You know, since you two got back?" Cynthia leaned back against the bulkhead.

"It's been fine," Nic told the ground. She looked up. "You guys have been great."

Cynthia sat forward. "That was so enthusiastic. I could feel the energy over here."

The younger woman made a face. "Can I ask you something?"

Cynthia tilted her head to the empty spot on the bench next to her. "Sure."

"How did you and Wil meet? Did you, you know...know? When you first met him?"

Cynthia was silent a moment. "I tried to kill him the first time I met him." She smiled thinking back to that day on Fury in Lorath's shipping company office. "I guess it was the second. The first time, he flirted, badly, and brought the PKs down on my boss."

"Not the story I expected," the younger woman said.

Cynthia shrugged. "Life is weird. After trying to kill him, I was assigned to watch him and the team—kill them, if necessary —during a job."

"What happened?"

"I decided not to."

"And you knew you loved him?"

Cynthia barked a short laugh. "No. He was a capable lay—" She looked at Nic. "Anyway. He grows on you." She cocked her head. "Why?"

The Olop girl's facial fur rippled, then flattened.

Cynthia smiled. "You like someone?"

Nic found the floor deeply interesting.

"I take it he doesn't know?"

Nic shook her head.

"You should tell him."

Another head shake. Cynthia smiled. One minute this young woman was screaming her lungs out at Bennie, the next she was an embarrassed kid with a crush.

"Max... Maxim...MAXIM!"

Max jolted awake. "What? Where?" He scanned the area ahead of him.

"You were asleep," Zephyr said.

"No. I wasn't."

"You jumped when I said your name. When I shouted it, for the third time."

Maxim turned to her. "I was resting my eyes." He was happy her mirrored visor hid her expression.

"Quite the imposing bodyguard," she replied, shaking her head.

"You woke me for a reason?" Maxim looked over to the cargo vehicle. The two Arumii were loading the last cargo module onto the gravtruck.

She turned. "You were snoring."

"I was no—" An alert popped up on his heads-up display, cutting him off. "You see that?"

She nodded. "Three contacts. Moving fast," she said, toggling her armor's comm system to external audio. "Wil, we've got company."

Wil, Bennie, and Adfogn turned to look at the two armored Palorians. Zephyr pointed to the west.

"Friends of yours?" Wil asked Adfogn.

The walking potato made a rocking motion, all six tentacles waving in unison. "Unlikely."

In the distance, three specks were quickly growing in size. The sound of repulsorlifts was just faintly audible. Adfogn turned to the two bodyguards. "Prepare to move the cargo." Turning back to Wil, he said, "I would like your assistance in defending my purchase."

Wil looked to the two Palorians. "Time to earn your keep."

Two visored helmets turned to the side. "Excuse us?"

Wil held up both hands. "Kidding. Kidding." Lowering his hands, he reached for his pistol. He turned to Bennie and nodded.

The three specks had resolved into three assault shuttles. Three mismatched, likely hundred-cycle-old assault shuttles. The lead ship roared over the *Ghost,* swinging out in a wide circle over the landing field. The other two ships, having slowed down, raked blaster fire across the *Ghost* and the surrounding field, sending gravel geysering with each impact.

Wil and Adfogn jumped out of the way, the latter moving surprisingly quickly for his size. Bennie watched the two shuttles roar overhead, then ignited his beam saber. Maxim and Zephyr stepped out from under the *Ghost,* their pulse rifles barking in unison. A burst of smoke erupted from one of the shuttles.

Adfogn looked at Wil. "You have a capable team, Captain."

Wil smiled. "We try." He ducked as the lead shuttle came around firing at the *Ghost* and the parked limo next to it, sending gravel flying as it lowed itself to the ground.

"They are going for my cargo," Adfogn intoned in his mechanical voice, three tentacles entwined into a single three-fingered limb to point at the shuttle that just touched down a hundred meters from the cargo vehicle. A sliding door opened to allow four armored Arumii to jump out. Their tentacles entwined into two limbs each, rifles held in both.

Wil nodded. "Okay, I get it now. That's pretty handy." He chuckled.

Bennie looked up at him, his green face tinted brown by the glow of his magenta beam saber blade. "Really?"

Wil shrugged. "What?"

"The other two are coming around to land!" Maxim shouted over the din of repulsorlifts. One of the attacking Arumii fell, several smoking holes in its lower body.

The moment the other two shuttles touched down, more Arumii jumped out, blasters and pulse rifles firing.

Maxim and Zephyr moved to the limo, using it for cover. "These guys are serious!" Max shouted, a blaster pulse striking the limo near him.

The sound of another beam saber activating drew everyone's attention to the top of the *Ghost*'s cargo ramp. Nic and Cynthia were standing there looking—if anyone asked Wil—

badass. His wife had her pistol up at the ready. She turned and fired four shots into an Arumii that was creeping, as well as a two-and-a-half-meter tall potato could creep, around the side of the limo.

"You have two of them on your team?" Adfogn asked, pointing to Nic's pink-hued beam saber. "Is there a store or something?"

From the top of the ramp, Cynthia shouted, "Ten shooters!"

She dove off the side of the ramp as multiple blast bolts struck the side of the ship. Nic deflected one shot and then ducked into a roll that took her all the way down the ramp.

While Cynthia and Nic were drawing fire, Maxim and Zephyr moved around the side of the limo, dashing to the cargo vehicle. One of Adfogn's guards pulled the other closer to the cargo vehicle. Zephyr's heads-up display showed that the downed guard was still alive.

Two armored Arumii charged around the far side of the cargo vehicle, each with a rifle.

"Down!" Zephyr shoved Maxim aside, swinging her own rifle up to take a snapshot. Her shot grazed one of their attacker's rubbery limbs, causing it to topple. The other didn't waste a second, firing on her. Blaster bolts struck her armor, sending her tumbling backwards.

From his place on the ground, Maxim rolled onto his side and fired two shots. Both struck their attacker in what he assumed was the head. The being dropped. He adjusted his aim, taking out the first Arumii.

One of the shuttles powered up and rose into the air, forward turrets moving to take aim at Wil and the others.

"Apprentice! On me!" Bennie shouted as Nic finished her roll down the ramp. She got to her feet and dashed toward Wil and Bennie.

She was almost to her two crewmates and their client when two pirates came around the limo, each with a plasma rifle. One turned its weapon on Wil, taking aim.

"No!" Nic shouted. She took three quick steps and leaped toward the attacking Arumii, her crimson blade slashing up at an angle. She hit the ground dropping into a roll, coming to her feet before the two halves of the Arumii pirate fell to the ground with a wet splat. The other Arumii made a low-speed turn toward the small attacker, its wide, many-toothed mouth open, emitting a rage-filled gurgle.

Nic looked up at the towering being moving toward her. Her beam saber was off and at her side. Something Bennie had drilled her on endlessly: turning your blade off when rolling or jumping around so that you don't cut your own leg off. Seemed like a dumb rule right at this moment as she wouldn't be able to raise her weapon in time.

A moment before the rifle's barrel lined up on her, the Arumii spasmed, then tipped forward to crash on top of Nic. She let out a startled yelp as the dead alien leaked neon green ichor all over her. "Gross!" she screamed.

Before Wil or Bennie could move to free the youngest member of the team from her potato-shaped prison, the ground between them erupted in superheated geysers. One of the two remaining assault shuttles had zeroed in on them, settling into a hover to fire on the quartet.

Bennie ducked back against the limo, peeking around the edge to look at the hovering attacker. He looked over to Wil. "Not good."

Cynthia reached Wil, helping him up as he nodded to Bennie. The pair raised their weapons and opened fire on the hovering assault shuttle.

The blaster bolts struck the shuttle's hull, doing nothing but adding to the preexisting scorch marks. The vehicle slowly rotated to bring its turret to bear on the pair.

Before the shuttle opened fire on Wil and Cynthia, a small metal cylinder with a magenta energy blade arced into the sky. The blade sliced up into the side of the shuttle into one of the engine cowlings. Something exploded, belching thick black smoke from the side of the craft. The beam saber hilt appeared, now deactivated, tumbling to the ground.

The assault shuttle fell into a slow spin, losing altitude. Bennie shrieked as his beam saber hilt struck the dirt directly under the rapidly crashing shuttle. He broke from cover, moving as fast as his small legs would carry him.

Wil watched the Brailack, then turned to Cynthia. "Guess we're gonna need a new Brailack."

She gave him a look, then leaned out to fire at one of the pirates that might have been thinking of firing on their little green friend.

Bennie reached the hilt, snatching it up as he ran past, not slowing down. The area around him was dark, shaded by the crashing shuttle. He leaped at the last minute, clearing the impact zone with next-to-no-room to spare. The shuttle hit the ground, sending a plume of dust in every direction. The blast of air caught Bennie before he landed, sending him cartwheeling through the air before landing with a screech.

The remaining Arumii pirates all broke for the remaining shuttle as it set down well out of weapons' range.

Wil and Cynthia were about to charge after them when a pair of tentacles landed on their shoulders. "Let them go," Adfogn said.

Cynthia looked at the smuggler. "Why?"

"This landing field is out of the way, but not invisible. Planetary security will be on their way. They learned their lesson. We should depart." All six tentacles waved erratically. "Plus, if we destroyed this crew, another would take its place. Like smuggling, piracy on Jdarum is experiencing a renaissance. Better to have a weakened enemy than a fresh new one."

Bennie joined them, covered in dirt head to toe, his beam saber hilt clutched in one hand. "Our price just went up fifteen percent. Hazard fee."

Adfogn rattled out a sigh from its vocalizer, his mouth open slightly. "Agreed." It leaned closer to Wil. "If you should come across any other laser sword wielders, know that I would pay a premium."

Wil smiled and nodded. "We'll be in touch."

The team watched Adfogn's limo and cargo vehicle depart the dusty landing field from the top of the cargo ramp. Wil turned and slapped the control pedestal.

Everyone stepped back as the thick cargo bay doors ground closed, the cargo ramp rising up to its closed position.

Wil looked over to Zephyr. "You look like shit." During the fight, he had lost track of the two Palorians.

She had her helmet under one arm. Her armored chest plate, several scorch marks dotting it, was in her other hand. She held the armor piece up. "Did its job."

Maxim wrapped a protective arm around her shoulder as he met Wil's gaze. "Time to upgrade." He knocked his free hand on his chest. "These are great for looking scary, but if we're gonna be dealing with this kind of thing, we're gonna need to use our better gear or find something else."

They reached the stairs and Wil extended an arm to the others. "Yeah. You're right. That old scout gear was past its prime when we picked it up. From now on, use your new gear, or if you want something else, I bet the place I got Jarvis from can hook you two up." He grinned. "Jarvis can have cousins." Though he hadn't used it in more than a year, Wil got a kick out of his combat armor having an AI that he'd named Jarvis.

From the speakers in the ceiling, Gabe said, "Captain. Two air cars are inbound."

Wil looked up. "Mr. Potato Head wasn't kidding."

Everyone dashed up the stairs.

On his way to the bridge, Wil tried to remember if he'd ever seen any Arumii in his travels. He was pretty sure he'd remember them. He would have to ask Bennie how long they'd been a part of the GC.

Wil nodded at Gabe, who was standing next to the pilot/command chair in the center of the bridge. "How far out are they?"

Gabe stepped aside, allowing Wil to drop into his seat. "The two air cars are still several hundred kilometers out. They have attempted to hail us twice and have been pinging our ident nonstop." The droid waited a beat. "To no avail."

Cynthia powered up her station as Maxim and Zephyr were dropping into their respective seats. Bennie was still in the crew area with Nic. The young Olop had not been happy when the others finally heaved the dead Arumii off of her. She was soaked through in the neon green lifeblood of the potato-shaped pirate that fell on her, contrasting Bennie's head-to-toe covering of dirt.

Gabe moved to stand near the hacker's station.

Zephyr looked up from consulting her displays. "Other than the two air cars, I'm not seeing anything out of sorts. I can't see every-thing up above, but looks clear. Nothing to worry about in orbit."

Maxim turned. "Weapons?"

Wil shook his head. "Not if we can avoid it. Might as well not burn an ident if we don't have to." The big Palorian nodded, loosening his armor's torso connections.

"I will be in engineering," Gabe said.

Wil nodded, eyes on the flight dynamics display on his console. He fed power to the repulsorlifts mounted in the forward section of each FTL engine nacelle. The *Ghost* tilted forward a moment before finding her balance on the twin repulsorlifts. Two loud clangs signified the retracting of the landing gear.

Over his shoulder, Wil said, "Babe, if anyone from local space control calls, I'm not home."

The *Ghost*'s atmospheric engines flared to life with a throaty boom, forcing everyone into their seat backs.

By the time the *Ghost* left orbit, the space control authorities were issuing a planetary alert for an unknown ship that left several bodies at an out-of-the-way landing field.

Cynthia looked up from her station. "I guess they put all their effort into bureaucracy, not investigative skills."

Zephyr clucked. "Yeah. That inspection ship isn't even in sensor range."

"Not that it had the weaponry to even try to slow us down," Maxim said.

The bridge hatch opened, and Bennie walked in. "What'd I miss?"

Wil pushed the FTL control forward. The stars on the primary display stretched into rainbow streaks.

Wil turned. "We decided on a movie. That new Brailack flick your sister's in?"

Bennie's face contorted. "Ew. No."

Zephyr stood. "She sent us an early copy, and you know she's going to ask if we watched it."

Bennie shrugged. "We'll lie."

"What if she asked you your favorite part?" Maxim tilted his head.

Bennie wiggled a hand. "I'll tell her I liked the part where she did the thing."

Wil shook his head. "She's not dumb."

"Meh. She believes it every time. I've never watched one of her vids."

"What about that one that won the award? The one set in the past—she was a warrior princess," Zephyr asked.

Bennie shook his head.

Zephyr made a face. "Quite the brother."

Bennie opened the hatch. "I didn't eat her when we were in the brood. That's something."

Wil paled. "I told you, man. No talking about Brailack child rearing."

Bennie waved Wil off and left the bridge.

Maxim slid an arm around Zephyr's waist. "Are we really watching her vid?"

Wil smiled. "Sure. According the blurb she included, it's Brailack *Star Wars*." He chuckled to himself.

"How would they even know what *Star Wars* is?" Zephyr asked.

Cynthia, tail swishing as she followed Wil out of the bridge, said, "I'm pretty sure he copied it from Wil's archive and sold the rights to someone in the studio."

From the back of the group, Zephyr said, "That tracks."

CHAPTER 4

Four days later, everyone was on the bridge watching the rainbow streaks of FTL flash by on the main display.

"Here we go." Wil pulled the FTL throttle back. The streaks shifted into pinpricks.

Directly ahead, the pale brown ball of Fury hung in space. No one was particularly thrilled that their home base was the fringe trading outpost that was more dirt and dust than civilization, but all agreed the lack of government or military oversight was nice, and the property prices were right. Their new warehouse home was quite nice.

"Is there a Peacekeeper convention going on that we didn't know about?" Wil asked. In addition to the planet's four moons, a dozen Peacekeeper ships—command carriers, cruisers, and corvettes—were parked in orbit.

Maxim leaned forward. "That is...a lot of ships." In fact, it was a larger Peacekeeper presence than any of them had ever seen over Fury. Normally, the fringe trading outpost barely warranted a garrison.

"I knew they'd find me," Bennie hissed.

Everyone turned to look at him. After an awkward silence, Wil said, "Care to explain?"

"Not really."

Cynthia shushed them all. "They're just here on a public relations tour." She tapped a control on her console.

The overhead speaker crackled before a voice came through. "... Planets are valued members of the Galactic Commonwealth. Task Force Epsilon will be in this sector for your protection..."

Cynthia toggled the channel closed. "It's a recording. According to a notice on the space control channel, they arrived three days ago. The task force commander said they'd be gone in another two or three days." She looked at Bennie, her expression flat. "We're cleared through to home."

"Something tells me our taxes are about to go up," Maxim complained.

Zephyr nodded. "Yeah. I heard from some friends on Kobona Four, they mentioned that a PK goodwill fleet arrived there a month before a tax hike. Must be the GC's newest tactic."

Wil smiled. "See, good thing I keep taking these smuggling runs." He turned his attention forward. "Okay, here we go." He guided the ship toward the swarm of Peacekeepers. "Everyone be cool." He glared at Bennie. "Everyone."

Bennie gasped. "What do you mean? I'm cool, like a codmember."

"Cucumber," Wil said, groaning at Bennie's butchering of the expression.

"Are you sure?"

"Very."

"You're a weird little criminal who has some explaining to do," Zephyr said. "You're supposed to be a champion of justice."

"Technically, we're all criminals," the Brailack hacker retorted.

Wil held a finger up. "Not now, Satan."

The *Ghost* fell in behind a Burzzad freighter. Cynthia looked past Wil. "Even their freighters are elegant." A few years ago, the team had tangled with a Burzzad cruiser. The massive craft resembled a swan in flight—a lethal swan, to be sure. The forward section housed a powerful energy weapon that had nearly destroyed the *Ghost,* if not for some quick thinking on Gabe's part.

"They're not boarding ships, are they?" Bennie asked.

Wil turned. "Okay. Spill it, Area 51."

Bennie gasped. "I don't like that you all assume the worst."

Cynthia quirked an eyebrow. "You freaked out when you saw the PK task force."

"You told on yourself, my little friend," Maxim agreed.

Bennie scrunched up his face. "Fine. I might have taken on a..." He raised both hands, making an air quotes gesture. "...'Side project' doing some..." He looked at the ceiling.

"Out with it," Wil growled.

He exhaled. "Fine. I hacked the main taxation database on Tarsis to erase a few overdue tax bills for some people."

Zephyr leaned forward. "You did what?"

"Some people?" Maxim repeated.

The Brailack hacker licked his lips. "Well...they called themselves the Three-Fold Path."

Wil frowned. "Is that like a religious organization?"

Cynthia ran a hand down her face, sighing. "The Three-Fold Path is a Guldranii crime syndicate. A pretty violent one, I might add. Xarrix kept them at arm's length."

Maxim turned in his chair. "Don't they stick mostly to their sector?"

Cynthia nodded.

"Thankfully," Zephyr said.

Wil shook his head. "Dude..."

Bennie's face scrunched up. "I didn't know they were syndicate goons until I was done." He spread his arms. "Then it was too late." His face contorted as his grimace turned to a smile. "The money was really good, too."

"We're not broke, and you scam most of your meals by waving your laser sword around and lowering your voice," Wil said.

Bennie flinched. "You can never have too much money."

Wil turned back to the primary display. The Burzzad freighter was de-orbiting toward one of the more remote settlements on Fury. "And you think the PKs caught on?"

Bennie shook his head. "It was a risk. The servers were firewalled with some PK personnel management databases. I didn't know that until I was in, either." He shrugged. "I'll give it to the Tarsi: their infosec is top notch."

"Dude..." Wil sighed. He didn't have time to berate Bennie for being Bennie, so he turned his full attention to guiding the *Ghost* toward Lwath, the town that Rogue Enterprises had called home for the last several years, first living out of the *Ghost* while she was parked in the spaceport, then buying their own warehouse in the spaceport district. A warehouse large enough to park the *Ghost* inside of.

The *Ghost* plowed through the atmosphere, plasma streamers obscuring the view on the display momentarily. After a moment, the pale brown terrain of Fury came fully into view. Lwath was a midsized town on the verge of being considered a city. The main spaceport ring was several kilometers in diameter, and the spaceport district beyond the ring stretched several more kilometers.

Their warehouse was bracketed in green on the primary

display along with their approved flight path around the spaceport and into the cavernous first floor of their home.

The *Ghost* roared over Lwath, her atmospheric engines glowing. Wil guided the nimble Ankarran Raptor Model 89 south past the spaceport and toward the Rogue Enterprises warehouse. It still sported its slightly crappy pale blue paint job from the previous owner of the building. Wil kept promising to hire someone.

From what the team had put together from the real estate broker, the previous owners ran a slaving operation from the building. An incredibly illegal and why-the-building-was-on-the-market slaving operation.

Zephyr leaned forward, rising from her seat to look over her console and Maxim's. "Are those cargo crates?" Next to the large rear door of the building, almost blocking it, were several dozen large cargo modules.

Maxim looked up, then turned to Wil. "Really?"

Wil had a pained expression on his face. "Not supposed to be here for another day." He checked the sensor display on his console to be sure he could still ease the ship into the hangar. It'd be a tight fit.

Cynthia groaned. "Babe, you have to stop. We're not a delivery service."

"I know, I know." He turned to Bennie, who was staring at him.

"Say it," the Brailack said, a grin splitting his face.

"No." Wil shook his head.

"Do it."

Wil's ears were turning read. "Fine! The money was good."

The *Ghost* angled around the warehouse before lowering to a hover a few meters above the ground at the building's rear. The heavy hangar doors slid apart to reveal the cavernous internal space that made up most of the first floor.

"Home, sweet home," Wil said, guiding the ship past the cargo modules into the building. Once the ship was fully inside the hangar, Wil reduced power to the repulsorlifts, easing the ship onto its landing gear.

The ship tilted and groaned as she settled. Wil put his station into standby and stood up.

He looked at the others. "I think you'd all look pretty good dressed as space UPS drivers." He pointed to Maxim. "He's got the calves for it."

Zephyr planted her hands on her hips. "I already told you, we're not doing uniforms."

He shrugged. "Worth a shot. I always thought I'd look pretty cool in an OG *Enterprise* jumpsuit." He nodded to the bridge hatch.

Cynthia shook her head. "No."

Gabe met them in the cargo hold. "I would like to run a diagnostic on the autodoc."

Wil looked at Zephyr. "You okay?"

She nodded. "Yeah, the chest plate did its job."

He raised an eyebrow.

She shrugged. "It tried to give me stitches."

Maxim turned to look at her. "Were you cut?"

She shook her head.

Both men nodded. Wil said, "Yeah, that's a problem."

Gabe inclined his head. "Indeed. I noticed several error codes in the autodoc's logs during our trip home."

Wil put a hand on Gabe's shoulder. "Enjoy."

"Enjoy moving those crates into the building," the droid

replied as Wil reached the control pedestal for the cargo doors and ramp.

Bennie clucked. "Got you."

Wil looked at his little friend. "Don't you have some sort of training to do with your..." He looked around. "Where's Nic?"

Everyone looked around. Gabe said, "In her bunk."

Zephyr nodded to the others. "I'll go check on her."

"You just don't want to help with the crates," Cynthia accused her friend, who waved a hand over her head, her ear-to-ear grin unseen by the others.

Zephyr pushed open the hatch on A deck, the topmost deck of the *Ghost*. With the ship powered down, the normal thrum of the engines was absent. During normal operations it filled A deck with the perfect amount of white noise. Now, all she could hear was the random pings and pops of the ship cooling and settling.

Nic had taken up residence on one of the guest berths, much to Wil's chagrin, as it reduced their already-not-great passenger capacity. Not that the *Ghost* did a lot of passenger business, but it was still something to gripe about whenever Bennie annoyed him.

She reached the hatch to Nic's room. The hand-drawn beam sabers crossed over her name in Galactic Standard stuck to the hatch with an adhesive strip. She smiled and knocked. When nothing happened, she knocked again, a bit more forcefully.

As the ship's executive officer, she could say three words and the ship's computer would unlock the hatch, but she knew that

Nic wouldn't appreciate that. She remembered when she was roughly the same age as the young Olop girl and how outraged she'd been when her parents entered her room uninvited.

She inhaled. "I'm not leaving until you open the hatch," she said loud enough to be heard on the other side. All of the hatches had the ability to seal, protecting the room's occupants, should the ship experience decompression, or the reverse, sealing off a decompressed berth. That said, they weren't sound-proof, as she and Maxim had learned when Wil and Cynthia got together.

The hatch opened inward. The lights were out. "What?"

Zephyr smiled to herself. Kids. "We're home."

"I know."

"You've been pretty scarce since we left Jdarum."

"So."

Zephyr sighed and pushed the hatch all the way open. "Okay, get dressed or whatever. We're going out."

The light flicked on, revealing the teenage Olop's room. It was exactly as Zephyr expected. Apparently, even apprentice Knights of Plentallus still liked popular musicians and vid stars.

"Out where?" the younger woman asked, walking back to her bed. The top bunk was pushed up into its stowed position.

Zephyr affected the most parental tone she could muster. "Just, out. I'll meet you at the cargo ramp. You have five micro-tocks." She turned on her heel and headed for the hatch to the stairwell.

Four microtocks later, a sullen Nic stepped off the ramp, dressed in her standard apprentice garb: dark tunic and trousers with lighter-colored undershirt. Her beam saber hung from her belt.

Maxim was a few meters away grumbling about Bennie's ridiculously complicated inventory management software. Wil and Cynthia's voices were coming from the back of the warehouse near the big doors. There was no sign of Bennie.

Zephyr made a show of checking the time on her wrist-comm. She smiled. "Good. Come on." She turned and made for the front of the building where a small conference room and reception area were the only other things on the ground floor. "We're going out!" she shouted. "Message if you need anything!"

From somewhere unseen, Bennie shouted, "Grab dinner!"

Nic fell in alongside the much taller and longer-of-leg Palorian woman. "Where are you...Where are we going?"

Zephyr ignored her. She exited the front door of the building and promptly turned toward what passed for downtown Lwath. Fury wasn't known for its sprawling metropolises. Most buildings were pale or dark brown, and only a scant few reached over ten stories.

After a few minutes, Nic tugged on Zephyr's arm. "Where are we going?"

Zephyr looked down, smiling. "Nowhere in particular."

"What?" Nic stopped walking. "Then why am I here?"

Zephyr turned, hands on hips. "Because laser sword or no, I can still kick your ass." She hitched a thumb over her shoulder to the edge of the commercial and retail district they were approaching. "Let's get a dwiffokl."

"Dwiffokl?" Nic scowled. "I'm not a child."

Zephyr smiled. "One, yes, you are. Two, you can sit and watch me eat mine." She turned and headed for the snack shop a half block up the street.

The snack shop was empty when the two women walked in. An older Kilden woman was behind the counter, her stubby head quills as wrinkly as the rest of her. Several appeared to have withered completely, leaving just a wrinkled nub.

"Hello, ladies," the shopkeeper greeted.

Zephyr smiled. "Hi, Ilpol."

"Two?" the woman asked.

Zephyr looked down. Nic shuffled a foot, then looked up at the shopkeeper and nodded.

Zephyr pointed to a small table on the side patio of the shop.

After the shopkeeper dropped off their bowls of whipped frozen bwenduun milk, the Palorian woman said, "So. How's your training going?"

"I'm still an apprentice." She took a bite of her dwiffokl. It was citrus flavored, just tart enough to make her tongue tingle, but still delicious. She licked her lips.

Zephyr smiled. "You've been an apprentice for less than a cycle." She took a bite of her own dwiffokl. Ilpol knew that she liked hers more sweet than tart and had brought her a bowl that was pale blue, flavored from zwoodlium berries. Hers was much sweeter than Nic's. "Things take time."

"He's a bad teacher!" she snapped. She composed herself, then said, "I feel like I'm being treated like a kid."

Zephyr cocked her head. "You are a kid."

Nic's face scrunched up, her muzzle drawing back to bear her incisors. "I'm almost an adult. And soon I'll be a Knight of Plentallus." She sighed, taking another bite of her snack. "I just feel like you all know what you're doing, and I don't. I'm like an extra grav-emitter. Useless."

Zephyr smiled. She wanted kids one day. She and Maxim had talked about it off and on since joining Wil, agreeing the time was just never right. Now she was across the table from a teenager, trying to figure out how to relate to her.

"You'll learn. That's what takes time. Learning. You're not useless, though. Far from it. You're a capable fighter. You're good with computers. Street smart, which, other than Cynthia, is a bit lacking on our team." Zephyr smiled. "We don't expect you to know what you're doing right now. Or be an expert."

The two ate their frozen snack in silence for a bit. Finally, Zephyr said, "By the way, you did excellent on Jdarum."

The fur on the younger woman's face flattened, a blush.

"What?" Zephyr asked. Nic shoveled more dwiffokl into her mouth. Zephyr leaned forward, putting a hand on the young Olop's arm. "What?"

"He was in danger."

"Who? Wil? He does that a lot, gets into dangerous situations." Nic looked down at her bowl and mumbled something Zephyr couldn't make out. "What's that?"

Nic was quiet a moment, then said, "How do you work with him?"

"He has his moments."

Nic shook her head. "No. I mean..." She took a deep breath. "He's just so cute. It's distracting."

Zephyr set her spoon down. "I'm sorry. What?"

"Those tight pants. That soft pale skin." Nic's facial fur rippled in a way that Zephyr wasn't familiar with. "That smile."

None of those things were things Zephyr found particularly appealing about Wil. She held up both hands. "Woah. No, thank you. I cannot and will not think about him like that." She shook her head. "Now I'm going to have nightmares. This is what Bennie went through."

"Bennie?" Nic quirked an eyebrow.

Zephyr waved a hand. "Saw Wil naked a few cycles ago. Said he had nightmares for months."

"Did he?" Nic leaned forward, eyes wide.

Zephyr shook her head. "No. No." She leveled a finger at the younger woman. "No. You have to get this out of your system now." Under her breath, she added, "What is it with women of the GC falling for him?"

She met Nic's gaze. "Squash it." She held up a hand, ticking a finger. "He's married." She ticked another finger. "To Cynthia. Who's an assassin." The ticked her third finger. "He's more than twice your age." She moved to tick off her outer thumb, then stopped. "That's about it."

Nic sighed. "So cute," she whispered.

"You have until you finish your dwiffokl to get it out of your system." Zephyr shook her head. "What brought this on, anyway?"

Nic wasted no time in launching into her thoughts on Wil, his anatomy, what she wanted to do to it, with it, and how often. It was astonishingly graphic for such a young mind.

Inside her head, Zephyr was screaming.

As they left the sweet shop, the older woman looked down at her younger friend. "Maybe next time we're out, I can train you on the *Ghost*'s systems?"

Nic looked up. "I'd like that."

"On the condition that the other thing dies out here and is never mentioned, or thought of, again."

Nic silent a moment. "I'll try..." She made squeezing motions with both hands held out in front of her. "Just so—"

"No." Zephyr cut her off.

## CHAPTER 5

Wil looked up from the tablet in his hands. "Why is this so complicated?"

Bennie, sitting on the opposite side of the table, clucked. "You just don't appreciate the power of BinvMan."

"BinvMan?" Wil repeated. "Really?"

The Brailack beamed. "You know...Bennie Inventory Man—"

Wil stared at him. "Yeah, no. I get it."

"I'm going to release it to the public."

"Like as a weapon of mass destruction?"

Bennie made a rude gesture. Wil looked back down at his tablet. The animated Bennie was helpfully pointing to a line on the ledger, his little green animated head bobbing up and down. Wil held out the device so Bennie could see the screen.

"What? You need to confirm the number of cargo modules in house before you can attribute a customer. Gotta do that before you can move to the next lot."

Wil turned the device around to look at it. "You got that from little you's head bobbing?"

Bennie shrugged. "Yeah."

"I think it might need more work." Wil looked at the tablet again. He tapped an icon causing animated Bennie to waggle a finger at him. Scowling, he tapped another icon. Animated Bennie nodded, bowed, and vanished. Wil sighed.

Bennie was watching him, grinning. "See."

Wil's eyes narrowed. He looked at the device, scrutinizing it. He pulled up the full inventory. After he and Cynthia brought in the crates from the back door, he and Bennie had retired to the conference room to go over the inventory and schedule deliveries. He was very much regretting that decision.

Sighing, he offered the tablet to Bennie. "This look right?"

The team hacker took the device and examined it. He shook his head, exhaling.

"You're an engineer?" Wil scowled.

Bennie turned his attention back to the device, humming as he tapped the screen here and there, paging through screens. He looked up again. "Yeah, you got a problem."

Wil nodded. He was hoping that he had just misunderstood Bennie's incomprehensible inventory app. The team hacker's expression killed that hope.

Bennie set the tablet down. "We're gonna be making deliveries until you're dead." He tilted his head. "I wonder who Cynthia will take as a mate after you?" He licked his lips.

Wil made a *tsk* sound as he snatched the tablet out of Bennie's hand. He ran a hand through his hair. He knew Bennie was just being Bennie, but human lifespans were nothing compared to most GC species. Including Tygrans. The genetic modifications he had been subjecting himself to over the last eight years would lengthen his life tremendously, to be sure. He had no idea if it'd be enough to keep up with Cynthia or not. If he could, he'd live two lifetimes to be with her. He shook his head. "Two."

Bennie looked up from his wristcomm. It sounded like he was playing a game. "What?"

"We have two ships." Wil smiled.

"Who's we? You got a turd in your pocket?" Bennie quirked an eyebrow ridge, leaning back in his chair.

"That ugly family truckster rust bucket of yours could help us do this in half the time. Her hold isn't that big, but you and Nic could do the smaller runs. While the rest of us take the larger ones."

"We're Knights of Plentallus. Not delivery people."

Wil winked. "You can do both. I have faith in you."

"I hate you."

Wil leaned back in the chair. "How's it going, by the way?"

Bennie looked at him. "How's what going?"

Wil cocked his head. "Your routine for *Dancing with the Stars*. What do you think? The whole Knight of Plentallus thing."

Bennie made a choking noise. "It's annoying and not nearly as profitable as I'd expected."

Wil smirks. "I'm pretty sure some of my *Star Wars* movies warned you about that."

Bennie waved a hand. "Blah blah. If it's not Nic searching the internex for human breeding methods, it's C7K2 being nitpicky about how I spend my time or which group I'm offending, or it's Nexuu politicians asking for favors."

Wil held up a finger. "I'm sorry. Human breeding methods?"

Bennie wasn't listening. He continued, "I thought it'd be all free booze and gifts. Maybe saving a planet here or there. It's so much more than that. C7K2 has been on me lately to recruit four more people into the program."

"Wouldn't more Knights solve your problems?" As Wil understood it, in their heyday, the Knights of Plentallus numbered in the hundreds, wandering the galaxy dispensing justice.

Bennie dropped his head into his hands. "Sure, but I'd have to screen so many weirdos to find four that didn't annoy me or seem like they'll cut their hand off. Then spend a few months, at least, on Nexum getting them to a point where they don't kill each other." He leaned back, sighing. "I can barely tolerate the apprentice I have."

A slight smile played across Wil's lips. The teenage Olop girl was certainly a handful. He still grinned at the memory of meeting the young woman on a doomed cruise ship infested with pirates. Despite being told it was dangerous, the young Olop fiercely wanted to help. He shook his head. "She's not so bad." Holding up a finger, he added, "Though I feel like I need to know more about her search history, though."

Bennie was lost in thought.

Wil watched him a moment longer, then grinned. "Realistically. This is all your fault. No one told you to get smitten by a drunk and dying space wizard."

Bennie blinked several times, then pulled a face. "True, but he had a laser sword." His already large pupil-less black eyes grew even larger.

Wil couldn't contain the chuckle. "I'm still a little jealous of that. I can't tell you how many years I colored a wrapping paper tube to look like a light saber."

Bennie smirked. "You should be. They're cool."

Wil raised an eyebrow. "You could...you know..."

Bennie leaned back. "Nope. You'll cut your arm off."

"No, I wo—"

"Yes, you will. At the Tower, there's a whole archive file of apprentices who cut off a limb. Or worse."

Wil's eyes widened. "Worse?"

Bennie waved his hand making a buzzing noise. "Anyway. What I'm sayin' is that I miss my old life. Sometimes." He made a face at Wil. "Not you, of course."

Wil smirked. "How? You're still running scams and hacking government computers. You're with us more than you're not."

Bennie shrugged.

Wil stood up. "Okay, that's enough of that." He pointed to the tablet. "Pick the loads you and Nic will take on Rust Bucket One."

"*Rocky. Nontee.*"

At the door to the conference room, Wil stopped. "That's not...Nope, never mind." He left the room. Maybe he'd have the team watch *The Expanse* again. See if Bennie picked up on his error.

Bennie watched Wil leave, then looked at the tablet. "I don't know why he can't figure this out." He quickly navigated the various menus of the application, shifting inventory around, creating a ship profile for the *Rocky Nontee* and assigning cargo to it. "Easy," he said.

An alert popped up on the screen, and a small animated Bennie wagged a finger.

Bennie clucked. "What?" He tapped the screen, but the other Bennie wouldn't go away. "Why you..." He tapped again and animated Bennie dodged his finger. "Oh no, you didn't." He scowled, about to dig into the application's code when the front door opened to allow Zephyr and Nic into the building.

He tossed the tablet on the table. "I could eat." He joined them in the lobby helping with the bags the two women were carrying. He took the one with dinner in it.

Wil put a plate on the table with a soft clink, careful to not disturb the pile of crisp meat carefully arranged on it.

"Bacon?" Maxim asked, a glint in his eyes.

Wil shook his head. "Afraid not. We've been so busy with all these Butter Ball jobs that I haven't had time to get home to do any shopping." He moved to sit next to Cynthia at the dining table. "Plus, with the whole associate membership thing, James said I should lay low to not...screw things up."

"He knows you well," Zephyr quipped, reaching for a pancake.

Cynthia was squinting at the plate of not-bacon. "So...What is that?" She reached out to poke one of the pieces with her fork.

Bennie snatched a piece and popped it into his mouth. "Tastes good. A bit saltier than bacon." He grabbed another piece. Around chewing, he said, "Yeah. I like it."

Nic leaned away from him. "It smells funny, and now so do you."

The Brailack hacker shrugged.

Cynthia looked over at Wil and nodded her agreement.

He frowned and grabbed a piece, holding it under his nose. "Huh. Yeah, not that yummy bacon scent." He took a bite then turned to Bennie, his face pale. He reached over to the plate and slid it to Bennie. "All yours."

Maxim reached for a piece only to withdraw his hand after Bennie slapped it. "Mine. You heard him." Maxim scowled but let the matter go when Wil shook his head, sticking out his tongue.

Cynthia poured Wil a cup of chlormax. "You didn't answer the question."

"Oh." He looked across the open expanse of the third floor,

the living space of the Rogue Enterprises building, to the kitchen space. "I don't actually know. I picked it up at the night market in Respili."

"What were you doing in that dren heap?" Zephyr asked.

Respili was about fifty kilometers from Lwath near what passed for an ocean on Fury. It was not known for anything in particular other than a salt crystal that Wil had discovered he loved on bread. He kept a jar in the back of the cupboard where Bennie couldn't possibly see it, let alone reach it. He glanced at the Brailack across from him. Bennie was happily shoving another piece of not-bacon in his mouth. "Nothing."

Sensing the lie, Bennie squinted at Wil, and his chewing slowed.

Cynthia watched this all play out, then got bored and said, "So, little green, you and Nic ready to schlep cargo?"

"Yay," Nic said, drawling. "Can't wait to deliver those, whatever they are."

"Shellfish livers," Bennie offered around a mouthful of not-bacon, his eyes still on Wil, sensing a secret. The nosy Brailack hated not knowing things.

She shuddered. "Yeah, that. It'll be great." She raised a hand, twirling one finger. "Exciting."

Wil smiled, looking around the table. "Cool. We'll get underway after breakfast." He looked at Bennie, still happily munching on piece after piece of not-bacon. "Or now."

"Good evening. I'm Klor'Tillen, and this is GNO News Break," the pale green Brailack journalist said. He consulted the tablet on the desk before him. "I'm filling in for Gulbar' Te, and tonight I have breaking news that two more systems have voted to withdraw from the Galactic Commonwealth, and a third is holding a referendum on the topic this week."

He turned to another camera pickup. "While the two systems that have just voted to leave are smaller Tier 4-member societies who would be missed but as yet weren't major contributors to the GC, the third, Tlanb is a Tier 1-member system. Maldo, the capital planet of the system, is the sole source for Maldoonian sherry." His large eyes blinked several times. "The GC has sent an ambassadorial mission to Maldo to see if they can't convince the Maldoonians to remain GC members."

He tapped the screen of his tablet, adding, "In a twist that could have repercussions GC wide, a separatist movement has been making waves, engaging GC representatives at rallies across the Commonwealth in systems that are considering leaving. It's not yet known who is funding these separatist representatives, but they are indeed well funded and seem to come from a variety of worlds, both in and outside of the Commonwealth."

The Brailack journalist cocked his head. "In other news, the GC's newest associate member, Earth, has ratified its first planetary constitution." He smiled. "Congratulations, Earthians, and welcome to the larger galactic community."

Klor'Tillen consulted his tablet and then said, "I'm happy to report that the Corporate Congress has wrapped up, and we have received reports of zero casualties or assassinations." He grinned. "That's a refreshing change."

PART 2

Once underway and on course for Maldo, Wil left the others in the lounge watching a Tygran action flick. He loved Cynthia and had nothing against her people and hated stereotyping an entire race, but Tygrans were terrible actors. Every single movie and play she had forced the team to watch—or worse, had taken Wil to see on a date—was like watching an eighth-grade production of *Persephone*.

He dropped into the chair at the small workstation and tapped a control on the desk. Leaning back, he waited for the call to connect. His eyes were drifting shut when his friend James' voice boomed. "Hey, loser!"

Wil jerked, falling backwards. His friend's laughter filled the berth. Standing, he looked at the display mounted to the bulkhead. "Asshole."

James Hawthorne's smile seemed wider than humanly possible. "How you doing, pal?" He shook his head, letting one last chuckle escape as Wil sat back down at the desk.

Wil smiled at his friend. "Same old, same old."

"Smuggling something, somewhere?"

Wil nodded. "Maldo." He waved a dismissive hand. "Sorry it's taken so long, but congrats."

James inclined his head. "Still a ways to go, but yeah, we're getting there."

"Getting there?" Wil laughed. "Man, Earth is an associate member of the GC!"

"Okay, sure there's that." James' grin faltered. "It wasn't easy though."

Wil leaned forward. "Not unanimous?"

"Far from it." Hawthorne shook his head. "The Indians and South Americans both held out." He clucked. "The Russians and Eastern European block came through in a pinch to get us over the line."

Wil shook his head. "Wonders never cease." James nodded his agreement. "So, what's next? What did the rest of the... What's it called? The Earth Government Alliance?"

"Not anymore. They renamed it right after the vote. The Earth Alliance."

"Easier to remember," Wil said.

James nodded. "Headquartered in Cairo."

Wil whistled. "To keep it from being a western-dominated organization." His friend nodded. "Good for the Egyptians," Wil continued. "This will be a big win for their economy."

"Already is. Beside the actual government building—which, based on the drawings I've seen, will make the UN complex look like a shanty town—they're also building a launch complex for diplomatic and military use," James said.

Wil quirked an eyebrow. "Fully unified?"

"Yup." James reached for something offscreen then produced a dark blue ball cap and held it so that Wil could see the logo embroidered on the front: a stylized Earth in gold thread with two rings encircling it. SPACE FORCE across the top and COMMAND curving along the bottom of the globe.

"Spiffy. Think I can get one?"

"See what I can do." James smiled. "You coming home sometime soon?"

"Can I?"

James sat the hat aside. "The votes are over. You're still not too popular, scorched ruin crossing most of the U.S. and all, but yeah, I don't think anyone wants your head anymore."

"Small favors." Wil shook his head. "No immediate plans, though, so all good. Just hold on to my cap." He looked at the hatch. "I better get back. Tygran adventure flick."

"Good?"

"Not even a little. Love—what're ya gonna do?"

Wil's oldest friend shook his head. "Don't be a stranger."

The screen went dark. Wil stood and left his quarters.

After seeing the *Rocky Nontee* off, the *Ghost* jumped to FTL bound for their next destination.

As the swift little warship neared its destination, Maxim said, "I vacationed here once."

Zephyr looked up. "Maldo? Really?"

The big man nodded. "My academy class. A group of us came during lokan break."

Wil grinned. "Young Palorians on spring break. I can just imagine."

"It was fun. We ended up in jail only once."

Zephyr quirked an eyebrow. "Only once?"

Wil turned to his first officer, his own eyebrow raised at her apparent multiple times in jail.

She smiled. "On my lokan break, we went to Gulveig."

"The Hulgian homeworld?" Cynthia interrupted. Hulgians

were large beings with three horns on their heads and stubby tails, massively strong due to the planet's higher-than-standard gravity. The team had worked for a Hulgian once, a business man who had designs on taking over the GC one corporate takeover at a time.

Zephyr nodded. "Yup. Lovely place, actually. We visited the capitol, Gandre. What they lack in height, their buildings make up for in architecture: all durasteel and glass. Arches everywhere." She smiled to herself, remembering the place.

"And the jail time?" Wil pressed.

Her smile widened. "Well, the first time...we found an underground fight club. One of my classmates, Rensin," she looked over to Maxim, "big as you, maybe bigger. He had won his round, then I won mine."

Cynthia leaned forward in her seat. "You beat a Hulgian street fighter?"

Wil's console beeped at him, the auto flight system letting him know that they'd be dropping out of FTL in thirty seconds. He pressed the icon to silence the alert and turned back to Zephyr.

Zephyr shrugged. "It was by weight class, so my opponent was a younger man, just getting started, but yeah, kicked his butt." She made a rolling gesture with her hands. "Anyway, the local crime boss for the area didn't like seeing a bunch of offworlders cleaning up the mat with her goons. She brought in the local security force, and a riot broke out—"

The *Ghost*'s sensors pinged, interrupting Zephyr's story. Then they pinged again. Everyone turned to their consoles as the star lines on the main display rippled and returned to pinpricks of light with a blue-green world directly ahead.

"Woah," Zephyr said. She did not look up. "Seeing this?"

Maxim grunted. "Didn't we just leave this party?" He looked up, nodding to the main display.

Wil followed his gaze as the large screen flipped to a tactical view of the planetary system, putting the forward view onto one of the smaller displays mounted along the lower edge of the screen. Several orange dots orbited the large blue dot that represented Maldo. As the sensors gathered data, more orange dots appeared. One by one, they flipped to green as the computer identified them as Peacekeeper vessels. The gathering over Maldo was at least twice the size of the one over Fury.

"I think Butterball might be getting ahead of himself," Wil said. He consulted his flight display. The Peacekeeper fleet was holding position in orbit. It didn't appear to be hassling anyone coming or going. Must be another friendly show of force.

Zephyr nodded her agreement. Botrobel Hjun, their Rigellian client had, until now, only been operating among systems and sectors that had already voted to leave the Galactic Commonwealth. Places that once cut off from free trade realized they missed certain things that would now cost much more to acquire.

"Maybe he thought they'd take their vote quicker?" Cynthia said. She added, "The PKs are transmitting the same message as the group over Fury."

"We're here to spread peace, love, and happiness. And only marginally higher taxes," Wil mocked. He made a course correction. "We good to keep to the schedule?"

Zephyr scanned her console, then looked up. "I can't see why not. Plus, if we bail, we'll need to get ahold of Bennie and Nic. Remember, they're meeting us here tomorrow."

Wil nodded. "That's right. Babe, can you reach out to Butterball's contact?"

Cynthia nodded, turning back to her console. Botrobel provided an encrypted contact list when the team agreed to work for him, ensuring they could reach him and any of his buyers directly and as quickly as possible.

Watching the planet grow increasingly larger on the primary display, Wil tried to remember if he'd ever been to Maldo. He knew Xarrix had an operation there, a big one, if memory served. Did Rhys Duch take it over? He shrugged. They were flying under an altered transponder, so there was no way Duch, or whoever was running the criminal underworld on Maldo, would know it was the *Ghost*.

"Apprentice. We're here." Bennie was in the small bridge of the *Rocky Nontee*, the light transport ship he purchased to escape the Bol Naar Syndicate on Multon a few months back. The ship had just dropped out of FTL and was burning hard toward a small crimson dot directly ahead.

A minute later, Nic walked in, taking a seat at the only other station on the cramped flight deck. All of the chairs on the *Nontee*'s bridge were modified to lower to the deck to allow small-statured crew members to sit without clambering or hopping. As the seat rose, putting her in position to wake up the console, she said, "There's no one else here. You could just use my name." Despite numerous upgrades and repairs since rejoining the team on Fury, the ship still smelled. "I thought you fixed the smell."

Bennie clucked. "Not as fun. Plus, once you're a Knight, I won't have a name to call you. I gotta use while I can."

To his back, she said, "Think that'll be any time soon?"

"Probably not. Buckle up and signal Botrobel's contact." He made a show of inhaling through his two small nostrils. "I don't smell anything."

She growled but said nothing. The *Rocky Nontee* was

approaching Sluip Nuv Two. The uniformly red planet was growing in size quickly. "We seem to be coming pretty fast."

"Shut up." Bennie had his eyes glued to the flight controls before him. Since adding the *Nontee* to the Rogue Enterprises fleet, Wil had given the Brailack hacker and Knight of Plentallus a few flying lessons. It was only a few because after two, Wil refused to continue, saying Bennie could crash into an asteroid for all he cared.

Nic's console updated. "Contact sent the all-clear signal." She tapped a few controls, studying the displays. "Space control has cleared us through to Platform 9."

Bennie didn't look up. "Okay." He gripped the manual flight control with one hand while rapidly slapping icons on the console. "Stupid mothergrolacker! Gabe said he fixed that."

"Please don't kill us," Nic said with zero sincerity. She was watching the burnt cinder of a world grow to fill the entirety of the forward window. "At least if we crash, we'll burn to a crisp immediately. No suffering."

"I'll show you suffering," Bennie growled. Something down in the hold rattled. "Go make sure the cargo is secured. We'll enter atmosphere in two microtocks."

Not waiting for the seat to lower, Nic hopped down and trotted out of the bridge.

Bennie had to admit their personalities were way too similar. Maybe that was why she infuriated him so often? If he had to find new recruits, he'd make sure they weren't like Nic. He shook the idle thought away and looked up and out the forward window. He'd gotten their inbound trajectory under control, but their speed was higher than he liked. It was higher than the ship liked, too. The warning light was flashing.

The speaker in the ceiling chirped. "Cargo's secure. I'll be down here praying if you need me." The speaker chirped again.

Pushing the reverse thruster throttle into the emergency

zone brought their speed down enough that Bennie slid forward in his chair, the restraints biting into his shoulders.

Five microtocks later, the *Nontee* was shedding reentry heat, albeit slowly, since the atmosphere of Sluip Nuv Two was nearly as hot.

Bennie tapped the intercom icon. "Okay, get back up here. I need your help."

When Nic arrived, he pointed through the window toward their destination. She cocked a furry eyebrow. "Is that it? Platform 9?"

Bennie nodded. "Yeah."

"It's moving."

"Yeah." His attention was split between his console and the heads-up display data on the window. Ghostly green, sometimes yellow, lines were floating between the ship and their slowly crawling destination. "Butterwhatever's data didn't mention that the platforms were mobile resource extractors."

Nic rode her chair back into position and looked at her sensor data. "Looks like it's moving about four kilometers an hour," she said. "Not very fast."

He gestured toward the window. It was dark out. "Only has to be fast enough to stay ahead of the day side terminator." The flight path indicator flashed yellow. Bennie swore, making enough of an adjustment to bring the ghostly arrow back to green.

Platform 9 looked like a multi-limbed insect with an armored shell. At nearly a kilometer long and half a kilometer high at the middle where the landing platforms were, it was a sight. Thick metal limbs churned up dust as the behemoth construct shambled along the dusty surface, pulling every rare and semi-rare element it could from the planet.

"What do they mine here?" Nic asked.

Bennie shook his head. "I don't know. Must be rare minerals." He pointed again. Trailing behind the slowly crawling complex was a trench thirty or forty meters wide and ten deep. Just barely visible in the twilight, work crews were scrambling along in the gap between the complex and the day side terminator.

"We're going to have to talk to Butterball about vetting his buyers more...aggressively," Wil said.

"Or at all," Cynthia mumbled.

Despite confirming that they would meet the *Ghost* when she landed, the buyer had changed the offloading schedule to be the next day. They were crammed into a cab heading downtown from the spaceport. It had taken a while to find a hover cab big enough for all of them.

"At least we get to see some sights." Cynthia slid her hand under his, intertwining their fingers. Outside the cab, the outskirts of Nosiium slid by, gradually moving from low buildings and warehouses to taller and taller buildings with more and more glass.

Zephyr smiled. "And they're paying for a hotel." The client —they still didn't know their name—had agreed to pay for a hotel for the night as well as to cover the docking fees for the *Ghost*.

Maxim grinned. "And we had to be here anyway to catch up with Nic and Bennie." Everyone made shushing noises.

Wil smiled and looked at the driver. Maldoonians were distant cousins to Trenbals, reptilian but sans tail. Maldo was more tropical than Baal, so at some point after colonization, the Maldoonians evolved to be more herbivore than carnivore. The driver's scales were a dull pink, offset by her gray sweater.

"We'll be downtown in a few more microtocks," she said, turning to look over her shoulder at the group. "Where you folks in from?"

"Effrolg Three," Cynthia said before the others could open their mouths. The rest of the team looked at her. She gave a minute shrug.

"Really? I've never met anyone from there. Nice place?" The driver turned her attention back to the road, guiding the cab. The vehicle could drive itself, but Maldoonian society didn't fully trust rudimentary intelligences.

Cynthia looked at the others, her face stern. She turned to the driver. "Yes. Quite nice. We love it. We're from Hozon Sera."

"Never heard of it." The driver looked back at them. "Bet it's nice." She turned her attention back to the road. "This might be as far as I can take you folks." Several vehicles were stopped up ahead at what looked like a road block. The sound of vehicle horns and shouting was just becoming audible.

Maxim leaned over to look past the driver. "What's going on?"

"Book signing?" Wil offered, craning his neck.

Everyone in the cab turned to look at him. Zephyr squinted. "Is that something you think would warrant a road closure?"

Wil's cheeks burned. "Maybe...for a good book?" He looked down, adding, "One they maybe made into a movie," in a low voice.

The others continued looking at him, slowly shaking their heads. After a beat, they turned toward the road block up ahead.

The driver watched all that, then said, "There's a rally in Ferluc Park tomorrow morning. The GC sent an ambassador to try and win people over. It's a forum or debate or something. The separatist representative is here, pleading their case. Has been for a ten day."

Zephyr leaned forward. "Who's making a better case?"

The Maldoonian woman turned, bearing her large flat teeth. "Not the GC." The scales along the top of her head lightened as they shifted. She guided the vehicle to the side of the road.

Wil pushed the cab's door open. "We've got time to kill. Let's grab a snack and watch the setup."

Everyone sighed and piled out behind him. Zephyr leaned in, swiping her wristcomm to pay the driver. "Thanks," she said.

The cab slowly backed up to turn around as the team walked off.

The park was surrounded on all sides by a mix of business and residential buildings. Tall trees with purple and pale blue leaves rustled in the breeze along the park's perimeter.

At the near end of the park was a permanent amphitheater surrounded by at least two dozen Peacekeepers patrolling the perimeter while a few dozen civilian technicians busied themselves setting up the stage and matching pair of lecterns.

Wil looked around. "I bet we can enjoy the view from there." He pointed. Across the street they were on was a hotel that had a large patio on the second floor. It was open to the air and there were plenty of seats and tables facing the park.

"And there's grum." Zephyr smiled.

Wil looked at his first officer. "It's like..." He glanced at his wristcomm. "Still morning."

"What's that saying you like? It's happy time somewhere."

"Happy hour." Wil grinned.

The *Rocky Nontee* eased to a rest on her four squat landing gear. The hiss of hydraulics and gasses venting from the engines to cool them off drowned out the squeal of the port side cargo doors sliding open. The ship featured two side doors and a smaller forward door with a cargo ramp.

Nic's ears flattened against her head. "I thought you fixed that." She shook her head and jumped down to the landing platform.

Bennie shrugged. "I put it on the list for Gabe." He leaped down to land next to her.

"That's not the same," she replied.

His expression made it clear the topic was now closed.

Platform 9 rocked like a ship at sea. Bennie stumbled a few paces. Nic dropped into a crouch, bracing herself.

Bennie smirked. "How long you been practicing that?" He righted himself and gestured to the airlock.

She stood, returning the expression. "A few weeks."

They turned as one when the airlock hatch a dozen or so meters from them swung open.

A stocky Mephistian emerged. "You Botrobel's people?"

Bennie stepped forward. "We're not *his* people. But we've got his cargo. You the buyer?"

The black and white furred man nodded. As Bennie closed the gap, he remembered an important thing about Mephistians. He stopped short but was still too close. His gag reflex flared. They smelled bad. Really bad. He shut off his sense of smell and continued forward.

"So, what do you all mine here?" Nic asked from where she was still standing.

Bennie waved a hand. "Ignore my apprentice. We're here to make a delivery and get gone." He made a show of looking behind the foul smelling being. "You got people to help unload?"

The man's beady eyes narrowed. "You don't?"

Bennie pointed to Nic. "Look like she can move crates?"

The buyer grumbled and raised his wristcomm. "Barry?

Bring Buffo and Swuik up to Landing Platform Bravo 1." He looked at Bennie. "Be just a microtock."

Bennie nodded. "In the meantime..." He raised his eyebrow ridges. When the buyer didn't react, he said, "Payment?"

The man made his own show of looking past Bennie into the *Nontee's* hold. "Crates look a little banged up."

"They do not," Nic said.

Bennie clucked. "They could be dented into dodecahedrons, as long as the contents are secure and viable. That's what matters." He cocked his head. "And in this case, the contents are in fine shape." He stepped aside, gesturing to the ship and open cargo door.

"For shellfish livers," Nic quipped.

"I'll be the judge of that." The buyer pushed past Bennie to climb up into the ship.

Bennie watched him go, then followed. Nic stayed on the landing pad. "Great, now the smell is gonna be in the ship."

Inside the *Rocky Nontee*, the buyer was tapping the control panel on one of the crates. He grunted and moved to the next after reading the display.

"His pals are here," Nic called from outside.

Bennie nodded. "Send 'em up."

"Yes, sir. Anything else, sir? Would you like tea?"

Bennie scowled, ignoring her. He looked at the buyer. "Happy?"

The man pointed to the crate next to him. "No. This one has a problem with the temperature regulator." He rapped a furry knuckle on the display. "Internal temp looks to have fluctuated significantly."

Bennie joined him, looking at the display. "So, eat these first."

The Mephistian frowned, crossing his arms. His pale blue

jumpsuit bunched in unexpected places. "No. We won't be taking this one."

A trio of workers climbed into the cargo hold. Two were Guldranii, and the third was a rail thin Sylban. The buyer gestured to his people. "Grab them, all but this one."

Bennie waved both hands. "No. No. They come as a set. Not for individual sale." He glared at the buyer. "You got problems, take 'em up with Butterball."

The other man shook his head. "No way. These are already spoiled. I can't move them, and I don't want them."

Bennie moved a hand to his beam saber hilt. "I don't care if you dump them overboard. We were paid to deliver all these crates. I don't want spoiled shellfish livers, either."

The buyer shook his head again. "I can't dump them. The foreman and company goons would notice." He inhaled and released an exaggerated sigh. "I'll deal with Botrobel. You just take these. Dump 'em in orbit or whatever." He put a hand on the crate.

"You'll pay in full?" Bennie pressed. The other man glared at the Brailack hacker but finally nodded. Bennie shrugged. "Okay, cool."

## CHAPTER 7

Returning to the table, Wil looked up from his wristcomm. "Bennie and Nic are on their way. Should be here around the time Butterball's buyer is ready to offload tomorrow. Gabe says he'll stay with the ship."

"I didn't know that piece of dren of his could move that fast," Maxim said, sitting his empty glass on the table. They had found a nice table right at the edge of the patio that Wil saw from the street. For a hotel bar, it was nicer than Wil had expected, which meant that it was not the hotel that Butterball put them up in.

Cynthia, watching the park, said, "I know Gabe has been playing with the engines off and on. Guess he made some improvements." She kept her attention focused on the park below.

"What's so interesting over there?" Wil asked, following her gaze as he sat down.

She glanced over her shoulder. "I'm just people watching." She turned around to face the others. "The GC is collapsing. This world, any day now—"

"The vote is in two weeks," Maxim interrupted. When

Cynthia turned her glare on him, he cleared his throat. "I, uh, asked the hostess when I went to the restroom earlier."

Cynthia rolled her eyes. "Anyway. These people are on the verge of something..." She shook her head. "...Something that could be big." She shrugged and pointed into the park. "It's also never a bad idea to keep tabs on any PKs in your area, just in case."

"Meanwhile, we're making sure they still have access to—what're we hauling? Candy or makeup or whatever," Maxim quipped.

Zephyr grinned as she slapped his chest. "She's right. That forum tomorrow, it's a big deal. A public debate with a GC representative." She nodded toward the amphitheater. "If they stay, nothing much changes. If they leave, a lot changes. For them and the GC."

"Their taxes go up...if they stay," Wil said.

The two women glared at him. Maxim leaned back, shaking his head slowly. Wil realized his mistake and closed his mouth. Ignoring him, Zephyr added, "When do you think was the last time a GC rep came to Maldo?"

Maxim, trying to save his friend, said, "At the end of the day, whichever way the Maldoonians end up going, it'll be their call, which is how it should be." He looked over the railing toward the park. "The separatist movement has some pretty solid names on the roster. I wonder who's here to make the case."

Zephyr turned. "You follow the separatists?"

Maxim shrugged. "I mean, I like to stay informed." He looked around the table at his friends and their expressions.

Zephyr's eyes narrowed. "My love..."

Maxim's eyes flitted between Zephyr and the exit into the building. He sighed. "I'm just saying. The idea isn't completely without merit. The separatists aren't trying to create a new GC or anything. They're just pointing out that the GC has been taxing member societies without providing much, and that members are free to leave the Commonwealth."

Cynthia crossed her arms over her chest. "I can't believe I'm taking this position, but it's not like members get nothing. Our repeated run-ins with your ex-coworkers are proof of that."

Maxim frowned. "Let's be honest. As much as we sneak around the PKs, they're not the force we thought they were when we served."

"Still," Cynthia pressed. "Most systems don't have a standing military. Without PKs, they've got nothing to keep neighbors from invading."

The big Palorian nodded. "I don't disagree, but is the level of taxation, which is increasing, worth hypothetical protection?" He held up a finger. "Not to mention recent history has sadly shown that the Navy isn't always going to be there when people them. Look at Borolo: every system Janus monster and his nightmares attacked. Wurrin, look at Farsight's recent transgressions. The Peacekeepers, as much as it pains me to say it, have been on the back foot for five or six cycles now."

"He has a—" Wil started, but stopped when the claws extended in the hand resting on his knee. Cynthia looked at him with a look that went with the claws. "Let's go check in and relax until dinner. Yeah?"

"There's the *Ghost*." Nic pointed. She and Bennie had landed the *Rocky Nontee* six berths down from the *Ghost*. It had taken a lot of arguing with the space control operator to get clearance in the same area of the port.

Bennie guided them toward the team's ship. Noticing Gabe under the starboard wing, he waved. "Hey, Gabe."

Parked next to the *Ghost* on stubby landing skids was a cargo vehicle. Gabe was speaking with a large, pale, blue-scaled Maldoonian and a Quilant woman.

Nic titled her head. "Wasn't the offloading supposed to be done already?"

Bennie shrugged. "Wil probably screwed something up."

As they reached the *Ghost,* Gabe turned. "Actually, the buyer rescheduled." He turned to the pair next to him. "But they are here now."

The Maldoonian turned to Bennie and Nic. "Like we told your bot friend, we were tied up. Now we're not." He turned to the cargo truck near the lowered cargo ramp. "Almost done."

Gabe made a metallic sighing noise before turning back to the telescoping work platform he had previously been on before the clients arrived. A panel in the ship's wing overhead was open, several pieces of equipment visible.

Bennie knew that noise all too well. He grinned. "We'll watch them if you want to continue whatever you were doing."

"We will?" Nic turned to look at him. "I'm hungry."

"There's food on the *Nontee.* Why didn't you eat?"

Gabe looked at his two friends, then the smugglers. He activated the lift, rising several meters to the opening in the wing.

Nic had her hands on her hips. "Because that stuff is gross, and calling it food is generous." She looked at the two smugglers. "What?"

The Maldoonians backed up, hands out.

Bennie scowled, then turned to the Quilant woman. "Well?"

"Well, what?" she replied.

Bennie made a show of pointing to the cargo ramp and crates visible at the top. She growled and said, "Hurry up, up there!"

"Yes, ma'am." A reply came from deeper inside the *Ghost's*

hold. Two younger Maldoonians appeared, guiding one of the cargo modules down the ramp on its internal grav lift.

"You said you were busy until now. With what?" Nic asked, not looking at the woman but watching the two younger beings as they wrestled the cargo module into their vehicle.

The woman rubbed the back of her head with a webbed hand, her thick catfish-like whiskers twitching. "None of your business, Olop."

Nic turned to Bennie. The two Knights of Plentallus exchanged a look.

The two younger Maldoonians got another crate off the ramp and to the cargo vehicle. The Quilant moved off to help the pair load the crate. The blue-scaled Maldoonian looked down. "She's high strung and thinks the boss's every move is a state secret. We were laying low. The PKs arrived day before yesterday and were searching the warehouse district we operate out of." He watched his colleague scold one of the two crate movers.

Twenty microtocks later, Bennie stood at the base of the work lift Gabe was on. He looked up. "Yo, Gabe! The criminals are gone! Ready to join the others?"

The self-redesigned engineering droid looked over the lift's railing. "Why? Are they not returning to the ship?"

"Wil said they found," he held up both hands, making air quotes, "a 'really good' Mexican joint to watch the show from."

"I do not know what that means." Gabe closed the hatch overhead. He pressed a control, sending the work lift platform down.

Bennie shrugged. "Join the club."

"Can we go now?" Nic complained. She rubbed her stomach.

Wil wasn't sure how an honest-to-God Mexican restaurant found its way to Maldo, but there it was, Taco Steve's! Not an analog. He'd found plenty of Earthlike things all over the GC. This place had actual cheese from cows. Chicken and steak, you name it. He'd tried to interrogate the staff, but to a one, they had all shrugged and asked if he needed more salsa.

Bennie slid his plate toward the center of the table as a belch that sounded like it should come from a much larger body escaped his lips. "You should've never brought us here. I'm never eating your Mexican food again. This is incredible!"

Across the table, Maxim reared back. "That's not okay." He waved a hand in front of his face.

Cynthia waved a hand, shushing them. "Looks like the forum is about to start."

Over the course of the previous day, the park had filled with thousands of spectators. Half of the Peacekeepers Wil and the others saw the day before were moving through the crowd, while the others maintained a perimeter near the stage.

The restaurant was situated on the opposite side of the park from the hotel bar they'd camped out at yesterday. The patio was almost as nice but had bottomless chips and salsa.

The GC sent a Tarsi to represent them. The three-legged man was flanked by a pair of Peacekeepers in power armor.

"Wow. They sent a Tarsi," Zephyr said.

Nic stood on her chair. "I've never seen a Tarsi in real life."

"Imagine an asshole, then give him a third leg," Wil said, not taking his eyes off his remaining taco.

The separatist representative stepped out on to the stage. A middle-aged Harrith man.

Cynthia looked down at the stage. "That tracks." She turned to Zephyr. "They've been mad since your thing, right?"

Zephyr looked out toward the opposite side of the stage. She tilted her head. "I mean, the Peacekeepers did try to completely destabilize their sector and pitted them against their neighbors."

Maxim smiled. "Not something one tends to forget."

Everyone nodded.

"Still, seems a bit in-your-face that they'd be leading the separatist charge. They're not even members," Bennie said.

Zephyr gestured to the park. "I'm not sure if it's impressive or sad how many are out there."

Maxim took a bite of his meal. Around chews, he said, "I think it's good. They're engaged. This isn't something they should take lightly. I looked, and there are forums like this scheduled all around the planet."

Sitting back down, Nic watched the adults as she scooped up the spicy concoction in the bowl before her with a chip. Wil said it was called silsa or balsa, or something. "So?" Everyone turned to look at her. She suddenly found her empty plate interesting.

Wil cocked his head. "What's on your mind?"

She looked up, her facial fur rippling as it flattened against her face. "I don't understand what the big deal is. The GC is huge. Who cares if a few systems vote to leave?"

Cynthia nodded. "You're right. The GC is huge: thousands of planets, hundreds of different races. Each contributes with taxes. Each enjoys open trade and the protection of the Peace-keepers."

"In theory," Maxim quipped.

Cynthia shot him a look. He found a chip that needed to be eaten. She continued, "The problem comes up when too many people start withdrawing. The taxes stop coming in, things get harder to fund. Trade routes collapse. The military, social programs, everything suffers. The suffering drives other systems and sectors to withdraw, which further reduces funding." She made a rolling motion with her hand. "You see where this goes."

The youngest member of the team sat silent for a moment, then nodded. "That makes sense. I guess." She screwed up her face. "Why doesn't the GC just ask what everyone wants and do that? Or at least try."

"From the mouths of babes," Wil muttered.

Cynthia nodded. "You might as well learn this now. Adults rarely know what we're doing."

Nic shrugged. "Oh, so it's not just him?" She pointed at Bennie.

Zephyr and Maxim chuckled as one.

Bennie clucked. "Whatever. Let's go. This has moved into boring territory."

Wil flagged the server and paid the bill. "Okay, let's go. We can walk along the park, see if three-legs can make a coherent point."

"Doubt it," Maxim said, standing up.

Before anyone could answer, the amphitheater exploded.

The first explosion was backstage, sending shrapnel and a few Maldoonians flying into the air. Before the crowd could even react, several more explosions ripped the park apart.

"What the actual fuck?" Wil shouted, picking himself up off the street. The first blast knocked all of them, and hundreds of others on the street below, to the ground.

Maxim sat up, knocking the salsa cup from its place on top of his head. "Grolack." He wiped a chunk of tomato off his cheek.

Zephyr looked around. "Where are Bennie and Nic?"

Cynthia got to her feet. "Damn. They're fast." She pointed down to the street. Bennie and Nic were darting across the street into the smoke-filled park.

The others joined Cynthia at the patio's railing as the two Knights of Plentallus vanished into the cloud of smoke hanging over the park. Down below, people were picking themselves up, looking around in stunned silence. The silence was short lived. Screams started filtering in from the park and rose in volume as more and more victims came to their senses and realized their pain.

Wil looked at the others. "I guess we're helping." He jogged toward the stairs down to street level.

Acrid gray smoke clung to the ground. Pieces of amphitheater and people littered the ground.

Maxim took in the scene. "These weren't large charges."

Zephyr nodded her agreement. "Small anti-personnel charges, at most."

"They certainly weren't stingy with them," Wil said.

Cynthia turned a slow circle. "I think chaos and terror were the goals."

Bennie approached them, appearing like a ghost out of the smoke. "There's a group over there that needs basic triage." He pointed then moved off before the others even acknowledged, vanishing back into the park. Of Nic, there was no sign.

Wil nodded in the direction Bennie pointed. "One minute, he's stealing our food and rigging elections. The next, he's helping the innocent and triaging catastrophe victims."

"Little green's got layers," Cynthia agreed.

"Like an onion," Wil replied. "But, yeah."

"Little krebnack's complex, I'll give him that."

They reached the group of Maldoonians that were in need of help. Two of them had dozens of lacerations each, likely from high velocity shrapnel. Their scales were nowhere near sturdy enough to deflect the dangerous debris.

Wil smiled. "Never tell him that." He knelt down next to a woman, her pale green scales tinged red by blood from several deep cuts. "How can I help?"

"I am detecting no life-threatening injuries," Gabe said. He added, "However, she," he pointed to a Maldoonian with dark blue scales at the edge of the group, "has a broken leg that should be set." Cynthia nodded, joining him as he moved to the injured woman. Wil patted the woman's arm and stood to join Cynthia and Gabe.

While the others helped that group, Maxim and Zephyr moved off in search of others that needed assistance.

Bennie and Nic reached the remains of the amphitheater's stage as two armored Peacekeepers stepped in front of them. "Stop right there," the one on the right said, their voice augmented by internal speakers.

The pair stopped and Bennie held out his hands. "We're Knights of Plentallus. We're here to help." He glanced at Nic. "Well, I am. She's—" He saw the look on his apprentice's face and waved a hand. "Doesn't matter."

The trooper on the left looked at their companion, then said, "The ambassador is dead, and the separatist's body hasn't been recovered." They nodded to where the Tarsi man had been standing earlier. One of the pillars that lined the back of the stage had fallen, crushing the man and the lectern. They nodded to the hilt on Bennie's hip. "Can you help clear debris with that?"

Nic nodded. "Felgercarb right, we can."

The trooper nodded to their companion, who motioned for them to follow. "This way, please." Nic and Bennie fell in behind the armored individual.

The amphitheater stage itself was littered with debris. The

bombs had toppled most of the pillars that ringed the back of the stage, sending them onto the stage as raining stone chips and multiton boulders.

Nic pointed at the pillars. "Whatever this was, they didn't plant the explosives on the stage, just near it."

Bennie nodded. "I noticed that. Probably too hard to rig the stage itself." He looked at the debris. "Easier to send the pillars down on everyone on the stage."

The trooper reached a half-toppled pillar. Barely visible amid the debris were two sets of armored boots.

The two Knights wasted no time. A pair of *snap-hisses* followed the glow of their beam saber blades igniting. Bennie looked at Nic and nodded to one side of the boots. He moved a meter to the other side.

"Be careful not to—" he started.

"I know," she interrupted.

"I know you do. I'm just say—"

"Well, don't."

He sighed and slowly drove the tip of his blade into the stone.

## CHAPTER 8

Four hours later, after the last victim was transported to one of the local medical centers and the last body had been counted, if not identified, the Rogue Enterprises team stumbled out of the park at the opposite side from where they entered.

The explosives the attackers used made up for their limited power by being numerous. Every trash bin, amphitheater pillar, and other structure in the park appeared to have been rigged to explode, and they all did. From what Wil could see, the Maldoonians would be rebuilding the park for months, if not years.

"I'm parched," Wil said. All of them were filthy: covered head to toe in a mix of smoke, blood, and dust. Wil glanced at Zephyr. She was limping. He had no idea why.

They'd worked until the local authorities finally got themselves sorted and thanked the civilians and outsiders, sending them on their way.

Everyone nodded. Bennie pointed ahead of them. "There's a bar two blocks up, next to the shuttle stop for the local transport back to the spaceport."

Maxim, his arm around Zephyr, offering support, looked down at the grime-covered Brailack, his Knight's outfit of earth tone trousers and top covered in mud. "How do you have a bar scoped out already? We just left the park. The park that's a smoldering ruin full of dead bodies."

Bennie looked up, tapping his temple with one finger. "Always be prepared. Knights of Plentallus motto."

"That's the Boy Scouts' motto," Wil said without looking down.

Zephyr looked over. "I thought the motto of the Knights of Plentallus was—"

Bennie waved a hand at her, then turned to Wil. "I don't know what a Boy Scout is, but whatever."

Cynthia looked from Wil to Bennie, then to Nic, her tail swishing. She shrugged.

The bar was emptier than not. Between the civic emergency and it being between lunch and dinner time, few locals were drinking. The lights were low. A tuneless Trollack song was playing loud enough to be heard but not so loud as to block conversation. The team took seats around a large table in the middle of the space.

The Maldoonian bartender came over with a tray loaded with glasses of water. "You all look like dren."

Cynthia shook her head while she absently plucked caked-on dirt from her tail. "We went into the park to help with the wounded."

The man's pupil-less eyes widened. "Wow. First round's on me." He stalked off, reaching for something on the top shelf when he got behind the bar. Over his shoulder, he said, "Only the best for heroes."

"So many bodies," Nic said.

Wil looked over at her, realizing she'd been silent since the team left the park. He glanced at Cynthia, giving a tiny shrug. "You okay, kid?"

She drew her legs up and wrapped her arms around herself.

"There was just so much destruction and death. Who would do that?"

The others exchanged glances, not knowing what to say. The local authorities had no idea who set the explosives. As yet, no one had claimed responsibility.

Zephyr reached out, patting Nic's shoulder. "Sometimes there's no explanation."

Cynthia shook her head. "I can't imagine what the desired outcome was."

Maxim nodded along. "Yeah, not sure who gets a bump in support from something this heinous."

Wil looked up from his wristcomm screen. "They still haven't found the separatist spokesman's body. That might tip public opinion." He shook his head. "I can't imagine who thought doing something like this would sway people away from the GC." He shrugged.

The bartender's arrival stopped the conversation. "Here you are, folks. Enjoy." The small, short-necked brontosaurus deposited seven frosty glasses of grum on the table.

Zephyr looked up, frowning. She pointed to Nic. "She's underage. A tonic, please." The shiny scaled man smiled at Nic. "My apologies, young miss. Be right back."

Gabe watched everyone, then said, "This may have simply been an act of chaos."

Everyone took sips of their drink. Zephyr slid the extra out of Nic's reach just as her slow-moving hand neared the frosty mug. Nic scowled at the older woman.

Maxim said, "You're right. It could have been anything. Local malcontents, someone upset at the GC or the separatists, or just generally angry." He shook his head. "Sometimes there's no logical reason."

The table was silent. Then Bennie belched.

In light of their collective exhaustion, the team agreed to keep it to two drinks. The bartender tried to comp their second round. Everyone but Bennie agreed they should pay for it. After a lengthy argument, the Brailack hacker begrudgingly paid for his drink.

Approaching the *Ghost*, Gabe said, "Captain. There is a cargo module at the foot of the *Ghost*'s cargo ramp."

Everyone turned to Wil, who blushed. "I don't remember accepting any cargo." He scratched his head. "Am I doing it unconsciously now?" He stifled a yawn and ran a hand through his hair, dislodging yet more dust.

Bennie groaned. "I like money as much as the next guy—probably more—but you have a problem." He shook his head, continuing on.

Wil nodded. "I think I do. I don't..." He trailed off, looking at his wristcomm. "Am I just accepting jobs without thinking about it? Is that a thing? A condition?"

Cynthia shoved him forward with a sigh.

They reached the ship at the same time the heavy doors at the top of the ramp split apart. Wil slowed to look at the crate next to the foot of the ramp. He scanned the crate's manifest display with this wristcomm. The crate was assigned to the *Ghost*. Destination to be disclosed. That was weird. He'd have to reach out to Butterball.

Wil held up a hand. "Gabe, wanna help me get this up into the hold?"

The lanky droid did not slow down. "No. I have to configure the *Rocky Nontee* for remote flight back to Fury." He continued past the *Ghost* to the parked *Rocky Nontee* a few slips away.

Bennie, behind the droid, pressed his lips into a thin line

and shook his head, barely containing his laughter. He turned to Gabe. "Thanks, big bot."

Gabe nodded.

Bennie went up the ramp.

He turned to Cynthia and the two Palorians, who also ignored his pleas, heading up the ramp behind Bennie.

Wil sighed. "I'll help."

He jumped. Looking down, he said, "You're stealthy."

Nic rocked on her heels, her facial fur flat. Looking at the duracrete, she said, "Makes it easier to sneak around the tower on Nexum. C7K2 has freakishly sensitive audio receptors."

Sighing, Wil woke up the manifest display again, activating the built-in gravlift. He looked up from the console to see Nic sitting on the crate's top. Damn, she really was stealthy. She pointed toward the ship. "That way." He frowned and pushed against the crate.

The last time they were on Doshi, the client had only older model cargo modules, pre-built-in gravlifts. Wil couldn't remember sweating as much as he did on Doshi. Stupid Doshi.

"You're drifting to the right," Nic warned.

"Thanks," Wil growled.

"No problem. If you get hot, you know, I can hold your shirt."

Wil looked up and around the crate. He was barely halfway up the ramp. "I'm okay, thanks. I think."

"Any idea what's in this?" the Olop girl asked, patting the top of the crate.

They reached the top of the ramp. Wil gave the module a shove, sending it gliding deeper into the hold. "No clue."

Nic hopped off. "Hope it's not shellfish livers."

Wil caught up with the cargo module and powered down the gravlift. The crate eased to the deck with a thud. "You and me both." He moved to the control pedestal and slapped the icon to close the doors and raise the cargo ramp.

"Thanks for the help," Wil said.

Nic looked at the deck. "Sure." She turned to wander off.

"You doing okay?" Wil asked.

She stopped, not turning. "Yeah. Why?"

Wil wiped his brow, unsure if he was taking grime away or adding it. "I dunno. You seem...weird."

She spun. "Weird? Weird how? I'm not weird! You're weird!" She spun back toward the back of the hold, darting for the stairwell up to the common deck.

Wil watched the retreating Olop. He threw both hands up. "Well, that—that right there was weird." He headed for the stairs, making sure to go slowly enough that Nic would be clear by the time he reached the common deck.

The assassination of the GC spokesbeing threw the Peacekeeper flotilla into disarray. Like a shaken beehive, the corvettes and smaller ships were flitting around the lone command carrier, seemingly unsure what they should be doing.

Wil tried everything he could to sweet-talk his way past the Peacekeepers in orbit, to no avail. Every ship leaving the planet was subject to a slightly more thorough than normal inspection. Apparently, no exceptions were being granted.

The fact that they were flying with an unoccupied light freighter tagging along under remote control didn't make the Peacekeepers any more inclined to wave them through the rapidly thrown together checkpoint.

Thirty minutes after docking with the *Rocky Nontee*, the Peacekeeper corvette slid away, wishing the crew good journeys.

Wil plotted the course back to Fury. Tapping the control that sent the flight path to the *Nontee*, he looked around the bridge. "All set?"

Zephyr looked up from her console. "We're clear to jump to FTL."

Wil glanced over to her station. "You're good with the telemetry?" She nodded. "Okay, then. Off she goes, we'll follow." Zephyr nodded and turned her attention back to her console. On the primary display, the boxy *Rocky Nontee* surged ahead of them, and with a flash of light from her three main thrusters, she leapt to light speed.

"Our turn," Wil said, pushing the light speed control lever forward. The stars on the display screen stretched into rainbow streaks.

Maxim turned to Wil. "Ready?"

"Sorry, what?" Wil turned to face his tactical officer.

The other man raised a jet-black eyebrow. "You agreed."

Wil looked at the ceiling, expelling a loud breath. "I know." Under his breath, he added, "But I was hoping you forgot."

Bennie turned. "Sucks to be you." He tapped the small hole that was his ear in the side of his head. "Everyone has better hearing than humans."

Wil made a face.

The big Palorian man stood up. "See you in the hold."

Cynthia and Zephyr exchanged a knowing look and stifled their laughter. A month back, during what had seemed like a simple security gig, the client's ex-girlfriend got past Maxim and Zephyr and almost got to the client. Her taking the time to beat up Wil provided enough time for Bennie and Nic to get the client to safety. Wil had not heard the end of the ridicule for weeks.

After that, Wil agreed to let Maxim train him in hand-to-hand combat. He'd dabbled over the years with Peacekeeper techniques as well as later letting Cynthia train him. In all instances, a few days into training and Wil tapped out.

Cynthia got up, putting her station into standby. "Well, have fun." She looked at Max. "Don't bang him up too much. I need him mostly functional after you're done." She winked at Wil and left the bridge. One by one, the rest of the crew left the bridge to retire for the night. Wil sat alone for a few minutes, hoping that Maxim might find something to distract him. A ping on his wristcomm disabused him of that hope. Sighing, he put the bridge into standby and left.

After changing into clothes more suitable to sparring, Wil and Maxim reconvened in the cargo hold. Wil stepped onto the padded mat. "Try not to leave bruises anywhere anyone will see."

Maxim shrugged, giving his friend a menacing grin. "No promises." He stepped onto the mat. "Fighting stance."

Wil followed his lead, setting his feet and rolling his shoulders. He shook both arms out.

Maxim cocked his head, then launched into a fury of blows aimed at Wil's upper body and head.

Wil yelped, taking a step back, and both hands flew into defensive positions in front of his face. The moment Maxim's attack slowed, Wil ducked low and let fly his own attack: several jabs that his opponent absorbed on his arms, leaning into the attacks.

Forty sweaty, bruise-filled minutes later, Wil was lying on his back panting. "I think my spleen hurts."

"What's a spleen?" Maxim asked from the bench next to the mat. The two had worked through numerous close combat moves taught to first year cadets in the Peacekeeper academy on Palor. Wil couldn't recall a single name for any of the moves. He knew he hated them all, though.

"I don't know, but humans have them, and mine hurts. I think you broke it." Wil looked over to where Maxim was sitting. "You and Zee figure out your ceremony yet?"

"Odd conversational pivot, but yes, we've narrowed it down to three...sorry, no, seven. Seven locations."

"Venues?"

"Planets."

"Dude, Nic will be old enough to drink before you two get this figured out." He cocked an eyebrow. "And by you two, I mean you. I know it's you."

Maxim's cheeks flushed a deep blue. "Stop complaining. We're almost there. This is important." He stood. Wil whimpered. "Man, cut it out." Max offered his hand. Wil took it, groaning as he got to his feet.

The two squared off. Maxim said, "Guiji-Klo-Wan stance."

Wil cocked his head. "Which one is that?" He moved his feet.

"No."

He shuffled to another foot placement.

"Still no. Look." Maxim struck the appropriate stance.

"Oh, yeah. That one. Crouching tiger." Wil adjusted his stance. Maxim nodded, then attacked. Wil blocked several attacks and parried one with both forearms before Maxim landed a lick to his right thigh. Wil's knee hit the ground. He tilted forward, feigning a fall. Before he hit the ground, he tilted, grappling Maxim's leg, bringing his own up and around the bigger man's waist, forcing him backwards onto the mat.

Maxim grunted as he hit the mat. Wil rolled away, getting back to his feet, slowly. "That's definitely going to bruise."

Rolling over to get to his feet, Maxim was about to reply

when something near the forward section of the hold made a thud.

Both men spun. Wil looked at his friend. "You heard that, right?" Max nodded. "Good. Go take a look."

Maxim glared. "We both go." The two crept forward. "Do you see anything?"

Wil shook his head. He pointed toward the hold, which was mostly empty save for a few crates that were always aboard, plus the mysterious crate they picked up on their way off Maldo.

Maxim noticed the direction of Wil's gaze. "If you brought a monster on board…"

Wil leaned back. "Come on, son." He pointed at the crate. "What kind of monster could fit in a crate that size?"

"Juvenile Qwaptar. Wokkalo of any age." He inhaled. "Ridblomin. Gods, those are scary. The claws and teeth and that spine…" He shuddered. "Oh, and a crate that size could hold a dozen or two globular cell-rippers."

Whatever was in the crate thudded against the side.

"Dude, you're freaking me out. Also, what's a rutabaga?"

"Ridblomin. Vicious things. They look kinda like those things on your planet…Drop bears?"

"Koala bears?"

Maxim pointed at him, nodding. "Those. Except they have really long claws on their seven digits, and their spine is a ridge of poisonous quills." He shook off the image.

They reached the cargo crate. Wil looked at it. "How many space koalas can fit in there?"

Maxim took a step back.

Wil glared. "Man." He turned to the crate as it thudded again. He reached for the control panel. "Please don't be flesh eating space koalas." He tapped the lid release and stepped back, fists up in a defensive posture.

When nothing happened, Wil crept closer to the crate. He

looked at Maxim, wiping his forehead as he did. The other man made a *go on* motion. He looked at the crate, reaching for the lid.

Wil was thinking about the ways he'd defend himself if two dozen space koalas leaped out of the crate at him, when the lid popped up.

Wil screamed.

"Hello. This is GNO Morning Briefing, and I'm Gulbar' Te." The Burzzad newscaster was staring right into the camera pickup, his face somber. "We're received word of an attack on Maldo." He shifted in his seat. "A rally that was scheduled to take place, allowing a GC representative to discuss and debate the current political situation, was bombed."

Turning to another camera, shuffling his tablet from one place on the desk in front of him to another, he said, "The GC representative was killed along with his aides and three Peace-keepers. The separatist movement representative is also believed dead, though his body has yet to be found." His long neck swayed uneasily, each of his three rounded eyes blinking at random. "We'll keep you updated as we uncover more details."

## CHAPTER 9

Wil backpedaled, one foot catching the other. He tipped backward, falling to the deck.

Maxim looked down at him. "That was the most masculine scream I've ever heard." He offered his hand.

Wil slapped it away. "I was startled, and that wasn't a scream. It was an excited utterance." He got to his feet as two faces peered over the top of the open cargo module. "Who the wurrin are you two?" At least not space koalas.

From the mid-level bend in the access staircase, Bennie shouted, "What's going on?" Cynthia and Zephyr were several steps behind and above him.

Wil looked at over. "We're o—What's going on," he waved a hand at Bennie, "with this?"

Bennie made it to the deck, his beam saber illuminating several feet around him.

"Are you..." Wil squinted. The cargo hold was dimly lit, being in night mode. "...In a thong?"

Bennie shrugged. "I don't know what that means."

Max nodded toward the mostly naked Brailack. "I think he means, what the wurrin are you wearing?"

Zephyr and Cynthia reached the deck, each giving the team hacker a wide berth, keeping their eyes fixed ahead. The latter said, "There's even less of it in the back."

Wil and Maxim both made faces.

Cynthia looked past them to the two beings still looking out over the top of the cargo crate. "Who're they?"

The two fully-clothed men turned back to the crate. Maxim squinted. "Good question."

Wil waved a hand. "So? Who the hell are you two?"

Behind them, Zephyr and Cynthia stepped around Bennie as he powered down his beam saber. "Those two are why Wil screamed?" the Knight of Plentallus asked.

Wil looked over his shoulder. "It was a shout of surprise. An excited ut—"

Maxim waved both hands in front of him. "It was a scream. Move on."

"Sounded like a scream to me," Zephyr agreed.

"It was an incredibly masculine shout of surprise," Wil countered.

Bennie clucked. "You probably peed."

Wil started toward Bennie. "You naked little—"

"Boys!" Cynthia shouted. She looked at their uninvited guests. "Again. Who are..." She cocked her head. "Wait a micro-tock, I know you."

One of the crate's occupants stood up, a man.

"Oh, hey." Wil snapped his fingers. "We do know you." He frowned, running a hand through his hair. "You're that dude that was trying to convince the Maldoonians to break with the GC."

The Harrith man shook his head. "I was simply presenting information and alternatives." He shrugged. "The Maldoonians, like all people, are free to decide for themselves."

Zephyr crossed her arms. "Space 'em."

Bennie nodded his agreement, turning back to the staircase. Everyone, now behind him, winced. Every hand in the hold flew up, shielding eyes.

"What's going on?" Nic said from the top of the stairs. She looked around the assorted adults. Her eyes settled on Bennie, and she sighed. "That's not right. We've talked about this."

Bennie clucked. "You're all haters." He struck a pose. "The Brailack body is a thing of beauty." He looked at Wil, one eyebrow ridge arched.

Wil reared back. "Why are you looking at me?"

Bennie winked.

Wil pulled a face. "Don't do that." He turned to the separatist spokesman, then looked up at Nic, still near the hatch to the common deck above. "Stowaways."

"Do we space 'em?" the young Knight of Plentallus asked.

"Yes," Zephyr said at the same time Maxim said, "No."

Wil shook his head. He pointed to the Harrith man and the young woman that was with him. "You two. Out of the crate." He looked at Bennie. "Please go make yourself presentable."

After helping the two Harrith stowaways out of their crate, Wil ushered everyone upstairs. Once everyone was comfortably on the common deck sitting and standing around the dining table, he said, "Okay. First, who the hell are you, and how'd you get aboard my ship?"

The man shrugged. "One of you brought us aboard, I assume." He winked at Nic, who growled at him. "My name is Blu'T'Ohm. Blu'T'Ohm Ka-tan."

"Separatist spokesman," Zephyr added.

The Harrith man nodded. He gestured to the young woman next to him. "This is my aide, Gul'P'Ulo."

The younger Harrith woman ran a hand through her close-cropped brown hair, revealing several earrings on her right ear. "Hello."

"What's the second thing?" Nic asked.

"What?" Wil turned to her.

She shrugged. "The second thing? You said—"

Wil waved hand. "Adults are speaking." She frowned. He turned back to their stowaways. "Nice to meet you, Bluetooth and Big Gulp. How'd you get aboard my ship?"

"It's Blu'T'Ohm." The other man enunciated each syllable.

"Wasting your time," Cynthia said, sighing.

Blu'T'Ohm sighed. "Money makes a lot of things possible. We saw your ship, saw that it was listed as having made a cargo delivery." He shrugged. "I bribed a few port dock workers to smuggle us into the crate and mark it as being assigned to your ship."

"That is rather disconcerting," Gabe said from the side of the room.

Maxim nodded.

Zephyr cocked her head. "Why us, though? Why this ship? There were plenty of others in the spaceport."

"Nicer ones, too," Bennie added, ducking out of Wil's reach.

Blu'T'Ohm smiled. "Easy. I knew your ship when I saw it. No matter what ident it was under."

That got everyone's attention. They all knew that Ankarran Raptors weren't overly common starships in the GC. The Peacekeepers kept the Ankarran shipwrights tightly under their control.

Seeing the looks on everyone's faces, the Harrith man held his hands out in front of him. "Nothing nefarious. I wasn't always a separatist, after all."

Wil frowned, unsure of the relevance. The team hadn't been to Harrith before. Well, outside that one time, before they were really a team. His eyes widened. "Wait a minute." He looked at the others. "You were at the battle? The Harrith Incident?"

Blu'T'Ohm cocked his head. "We don't call it that, but yes. I was a sub-officer aboard the *Valiant Flame*. We were slugging it out with two Quilant cruisers when you all did..." he shrugged. "Well, you know."

The man's assistant chimed in. "Everyone knows the *Ghost*."

Her boss nodded.

Bennie sighed. Loud. Louder than necessary. "This is all incredibly boring. How'd you get out of the park?"

Zephyr looked at him. "That's the thing you're most interested in?"

The Brailack hacker shrugged. "I'm interested in a bunch of things, but right now, yeah. Look at him." He gestured to the Harrith man. "Things were exploding and he," hand wave to Gul'P'Ulo, "*they* don't look like the escape-from-an-exploding-park type."

Wil sighed. "Crass, but not wrong."

Blu'T'Ohm smiled at Bennie. "Luck." He turned to his aide. "The event was about to start. Gul pulled me back to tell me something moments before the first explosion. Before we knew what was happening, it was all chaos and explosions." He spread his arms. "I thought I was the target. We fled."

"And came to the spaceport?" Gabe asked.

The elder Harrith nodded. "Seemed reasonable. If someone is trying to kill you, don't be where they can find you."

"Now what?" Maxim asked.

Blu'T'Ohm tipped his head. "I wish to hire you."

"Excuse me," Cynthia said.

Zephyr nodded and pointed to her friend. "What she said."

Wil stifled a yawn. "Why us?" He shook his head, trying to clear the grogginess. He was so tired.

Blu'T'Ohm inclined his head. "Well, you're you, all of you, for one thing." He gestured at them all, stopping at Cynthia, then Nic. "Not you two. I don't know you two."

The two women rolled their eyes. Wil put his arm around Cynthia. "My wife." He nodded to Nic. "Some kid we found." Nic opened her mouth, but Wil waved. "Kidding." He turned to Blu'T'Ohm. "It's late. I'm about to fall asleep standing up. Why. Us?"

The other man nodded. "I obviously need security." Everyone nodded. "And transport. From what I know of you all, that's your thing."

Cynthia looked around the table and raised her hand. "Yeah, but we don't like you."

"Or your politics," Zephyr added.

Blu'T'Ohm shrugged. "That matters?"

"Yes," Cynthia and Zephyr said at the same time as Wil, Maxim, and Bennie said, "No."

Everyone looked at each other. The two Harrith looked at each other. Nic shook her head and looked at Gabe, who gave his best mechanical shrug.

Wil knew this silence well. The team rarely fought, beyond the typical squabbles of people in small starships. But when everyone went silent at the same time, that was never a good sign.

He clapped his hands. "Okay. I think this is a time and place to table this discussion." He looked at Zephyr. "Let's show them to the brig."

Everyone's but Bennie's mouth fell open. Zephyr said, "We do have an empty berth."

"Those are for paying customers. Not stowaways."

Blu'T'Ohm frowned. "That seems a rather exaggerated reaction."

Wil smiled. "Next time, buy a ticket." He stood and offered his hand to Cynthia. "'Night, all."

Zephyr looked at the two Harrith. "Sorry." She gestured toward the hatch Wil and Cynthia were heading for. "This way."

The younger of the two Harrith shook her head. "I'm not sleeping in a jail."

Maxim fell in behind the pair. "Afraid you are." He knew Wil was just being petty, but it was his ship. "Honestly, as brigs go, it's not too bad."

The younger woman looked up at him. "You sleep there."

He chuckled. "I'm not the stowaway."

After making sure that their stowaways were as comfortable as possible in the ship's small brig at the forward end of the corridor, Maxim closed the door to the berth he and Zephyr shared.

"They are not happy." He pulled his shirt up over his head. "I can't believe you made *me* lock them up," he complained, chucking his sweat-soaked shirt into the small cleaning unit in the corner of the room.

From the small refresher in the opposite corner, Zephyr said, "Seemed fitting."

Frowning, he squeezed in behind her, having shed the rest

of his sweaty shipboard clothes. Over the years, the two Palorians had adopted basic coveralls of Peacekeeper design as their everyday uniform aboard the *Ghost*. "You know it's not that cut and dry." He reached for the faucet control of the small showerhead.

She looked at him. "He's advocating the slow dismantling of the Galactic Commonwealth, my love. What's not to understand?"

After almost an hour of mopping the training mat with Wil, then skipping post-workout stretches thanks to the two Harrith in the brig, the hot water felt wonderful on his aching body. He remained silent a moment, savoring the feeling before saying, "The GC is just a construct. He's not advocating murder, regicide, or anything else like that."

Zephyr turned. "A construct that has existed for thousands of years. A construct that gave our people a purpose beyond bludgeoning each other."

"Bludgeoning others on someone else's behalf isn't exactly a noble calling," Maxim replied.

Zephyr's glare spoke volumes, but she added, "So many people are going to suffer if he's successful. Sure, he's not advocating war and killing, but that's what's going to happen. You know it." She ran her hands through her hair, wringing water out as she did. "I'll grant you that there are a lot of problems with the GC and even the Peacekeepers, but they're better than galaxy-spanning anarchy." She cocked her head, hands on hips. "No?"

Maxim nodded, reaching past her to shut off the shower. He had served aboard ships most of his career, but the idea of bathing in recycled water that he might later be drinking, still weirded him out. Not that he didn't like having actual water showers, but still. Gross. He did his best not to think about it.

He sighed. "You're not wrong. But if nothing changes, how's

that help anyone? I don't want the galaxy to fall to chaos, but this separatist movement could be just the kick in the butt that the GC needs to fix things."

The pair dried off in silence, lost in their own thoughts about what a galaxy without the GC or Peacekeepers might look like.

He crawled into bed next to her. "Tabled until tomorrow?"

She smiled and rolled over, turning her back to him. "Computer, lights."

"That was pretty cruel, putting them in the brig," Cynthia said, getting into bed. She couldn't see inside the refresher but could hear the water of the shower running. She had a strict rule that Wil did not get into bed without a shower. It turned out, human sweat did a number on her olfactory sense, giving her headaches. Making him bathe more often helped.

"Hey. I didn't make them smuggle themselves onto the ship." There was a pause, then, "It's the principle of the thing. You know, gotta set an example."

"For whom?" She watched his face, trying to not laugh, seeing him think about it.

"Well, anyone else who might try to sneak aboard."

She chuckled. "Because there's a network they all communicate over." She sighed. "Hurry up."

Wil's head appeared in the opening to the small refresher compartment. "Have plans?"

She grinned, baring her teeth. "Only if you hurry up."

His head vanished back inside the refresher. "Be right there."

She picked up a tablet from the small shelf set in the bulkhead that served as a nightstand. "Are you really okay with what he's all about?"

"Who?"

She lowered the tablet. "Who do you think?"

"Oh. Will my answer impact the next half hour?"

She clucked. "Awfully optimistic there."

He leaned out. "You're cruel."

"No, it won't affect cross cultural relations." She hated Wil's euphemism but had given up.

"In that case...Sorta." He came out of the refresher in a towel that was quickly shed as he slid under the covers next to her.

Wil leaned over for a kiss and she pressed a finger to his lips. "Explain."

He groaned. "The GC has been pretty much the same for, what? A few thousand years?" She nodded. "That's a long time. Look how hard Gabe and the droids had to fight. Look at how little has changed for the Palorians in all that time. They're still pretty much stuck being Peacekeepers or outcasts."

She nodded. "No argument. Things could for sure be better." He leaned in. She leaned back. "But burning it all down to make change?"

He shrugged. "Humans do it all the time."

She sighed. "Nothing about that surprises me." He leaned in, and this time, she didn't lean back. "To be continued."

Wil smiled and clapped his hands twice. The lights went out.

"You busy?" Nic asked, poking her head inside the *Ghost*'s small computer room.

Gabe didn't turn around. "Bennie is not here."

She walked in, looking around. The space was barely big enough for two. The ship's computer core and accessory systems took up two thirds of the room. "I know. He went to bed." Once, Bennie had told her about how he found the space when he first came aboard the *Ghost*. How it looked like a wild animal might have taken up residence. That Wil hadn't even known the first thing about the ship's computer systems.

Gabe turned from the terminal he was working on, thin data tendrils sliding back into his fingers. "I see. What is it I can do for you?"

She leaned to the side to peer behind Gabe. "What're you working on?"

Gabe stepped aside, allowing her to see the terminal's screen. "I am running an improvement algorithm against the weapons system. When it is complete, the targeting computer will be able to transition between targets 42 nanotocks faster."

She pursed her lips, rocking on her heels. "Neat." She stepped up to the fold-out terminal to get a better look.

"Did you come in here to check on my progress?" The tall, light gray droid inclined his head. In all his years with the crew of the *Ghost*, dealing with biologicals had not gotten any easier. This new one was especially difficult. A variable he had yet to quantify.

She looked up at the lanky droid. "What? Oh. No. I wanted to ask about the GC, and everyone else is..." Her facial fur rippled. "Asleep. Or busy?"

Gabe inclined his head. "Yes. I can hear them." Nic made a face. "What would you like to know?" he asked.

"Why does Blu'T'Ohm want to end the GC? The Harrith aren't even part of it."

Gabe was silent. His optical sensors whirred as they refocused. "A surprisingly astute question."

"No offense taken."

"You would have to ask Mr. Ka-Tan, but you are correct that the Harrith are not members of the Galactic Commonwealth. They have, in fact, resisted several overtures from the Commonwealth Council to join."

"Why?"

Gabe made a shrug-like motion. "I do not know. You would need to ask a representative from the Harrith government. If I were to guess, it would be due to their lack of trust in the Commonwealth's motives. Bringing the Harrith sector into the fold would go a long way to erasing the tarnish that the rogue Peacekeepers and Councilors caused."

"Guessing that adding a sector as big as the Harrith would be a big win for the GC financially?"

Gabe tilted his head, his optic sensors whirring. "You are quite intelligent."

The young Olop woman returned his head tilt. "Still not offended." She ran a hand along the bulkhead. No dust. She looked up at Gabe, who towered over her. "Why do they want to help that guy? If he wants to ruin the GC and all?"

He simply said, "You have met Bennie, so I will forego pointing out greed. Mr. Ka-tan will likely offer a sizable retainer." She nodded. He continued. "The others have more complex motivations. Maxim and Zephyr are disgraced, though eventually vindicated, Peacekeepers. The visible faces of the GC. Their people have a deep and complex relationship with the Commonwealth. For thousands of cycles, the Governing Council has dictated their society's growth and purpose. Their split on the topic is indeed interesting. As far as the whims of this crew go."

The young Olop girl nodded. She scratched one of her round teddy bear ears, then said, "What about Wil?"

Gabe was silent. Finally, he said, "Wil is chaos personified."

Nic nodded slowly. "Thanks, Gabe." She smiled up at him. "That helped." She patted his arm as she turned and left the computer room.

Gabe watched her go. He turned to the terminal, data tendrils snaking out of his fingertips, sliding under the keys. *I will outlive them all and likely still never understand them,* he thought to himself.

## CHAPTER 10

The next morning, Wil exited the stairwell onto the common deck. He looked around, spying the entire crew already assembled around the kitchen table. "Last night wasn't a dream, right?"

Zephyr shook her head. "Nope. They're up there."

Wil sighed. "Damn." He looked at Maxim next to the coffee-maker-turned-chlormax-machine. "Hit me."

The big man poured him a cup, then met Wil at the table, offering the steaming mug. "I'll go with."

Bennie looked from his plate of something Wil couldn't identify. "You were just up there. You could have poked your head in."

Wil made a rude gesture. "Come on, Max." He pulled open the hatch to the stairwell.

The *Ghost*'s small brig was on the same level as the crew and guest quarters. The hatch was right next to the staircase, the forwardmost compartment on A deck.

Wil pushed open the hatch, entering the brig. He looked into the even smaller cell. "Sleep well?" The brig only had one cell connected to the even smaller foyer.

Blu'T'Ohm looked up from the lower bunk. "No. Your brig smells like farts." His assistant, in the top bunk, nodded her agreement.

Behind Wil, Maxim nodded. "I'm pretty sure Bennie comes up here to do just that."

The Harrith man sat up. "Why in the gods' name..."

Wil turned. "He does? Why?" He waved a hand. "Never mind."

Maxim shook his head. "He was doing it on the bridge foyer. I think the beatings finally convinced him to find a new venue."

Wil shook his head. "There's literally a toilet a few steps from the bridge. Little green weirdo." He turned his attention to their guests.

"That's...incredibly off-putting," the young assistant said, swinging her legs over the side of her bunk. "Are we allowed to leave the cave of farts now?"

Wil and Maxim stepped back out into the corridor to make room, the latter pressing the release on the cell door before stepping out. The two Harrith joined them a moment later. Maxim held open the hatch to the stairs.

"Just in time for breakfast," Wil said, falling in behind the procession.

Reaching the common deck, Blu'T'Ohm turned to Maxim. "So, what brought you to Maldo?" His expression said he had an idea of the reason.

Maxim shrugged. "You know. Business."

The other man made a noncommittal *mmhmm* noise.

Exiting the staircase behind them all, Wil said, "Running cargo pays the bills."

Blu'T'Ohm made a show of looking around the common deck. "Hmm. Ship this size, not particularly made for cargo. At least not mainstream cargo. Not enough volume to haul the more lucrative jobs." He turned to Wil, a knowing look on his face. "However, things of a more sensitive nature that have a higher profit-to-square-plor-of-deck-space ratio...Seems like a ship this size, with its unique capabilities, would do well in that space."

Wil glared and pointed to the kitchenette.

"What's for...breakfast?" Gul'P'Ulo asked, taking a seat next to Bennie, eyeing his plate.

The Brailack hacker looked at her. "What do you want for breakfast?" His voice was a few octaves deeper than normal.

Wil clucked. "Will you stop." Bennie turned and made a similar noise back at Wil.

Zephyr cleared her throat. "This wasn't supposed to be a long run—"

"Or one with guests," Cynthia added.

The ship's first officer nodded. "So, it's oatmeal."

"Oat, meal?"

Maxim, dropping into the seat next to Zephyr, smiled. "Earth thing. Like protein mush, but with actual flavor."

The senior of the two Harrith nodded, knowing exactly what protein mush tasted like. Anyone who served in a military would be all too familiar with the staple of all space-borne navies.

Gul'P'Ulo looked again at Bennie's plate.

"I season mine," he said.

She made a face. "With what?"

Wil slid a plate in front of each Harrith.

Gul'P'Ulo took a bite. "This isn't bad."

Nic looked to the young woman, pushing a small jar toward her. "This makes it better." It was the same color as Bennie's meal.

Gul'P'Ulo took the jar and sprinkled the contents across the top of her bowl. After taking another bite, she smiled, her eyes closed. She turned to Nic, who nodded.

"It occurs to me, Captain. Should my assumptions be correct, my success improves your bottom line," Blu'T'Ohm said.

"Mercenary way to look at it," Cynthia replied with a level gaze.

He nodded once. "Yes, but so much in life can be boiled down to what seem like mercenary choices."

Once the pair of Harrith were seated and had plates before them, everyone ate their breakfast in companionable silence. Finally, Blu'T'Ohm said, "So. To circle back to last night, I'd like to hire you. All of you. Rogue Enterprises, I believe you call yourselves?"

"For what, exactly?" Wil asked.

"The other day. That wasn't the first attempt on my...*our* lives. The most devastating, to be sure. We clearly need security." He gestured around the common deck. "And transport. Our shuttle is still back on Maldo, possibly with explosives hidden somewhere inside it." His aide shuddered at that. He nodded his agreement. "Speaking of, Gul'P'Ulo, please arrange for the sale of the shuttle." She nodded, making a note on her wristcomm.

"I don't like it," Zephyr said. Her position hadn't changed overnight.

"Same." Neither had Cynthia's. She continued, "Helping him does nothing but potentially speed up the collapse of the GC. Is that really something we want to be associated with?"

"If I may?" Blu'T'Ohm raised a hand, cutting off any reply

to the question. "You're right, I'm opposed to the GC. But I'm not in favor of chaos. My people have done just fine for thousands of cycles without the GC's support or involvement." He steepled his fingers as he leaned on the table. "I'm merely proposing that each society evaluate what's truly in their best interests. For some, that might be to remain in the GC, but others may decide that being on their own, or part of smaller, more regional alliances, serves their interests more."

"He makes a good point," Maxim offered.

Zephyr and Cynthia turned their gazes to him. Wil and Bennie leaned back, happy to let the big Palorian be the one to take the verbal beating that was about to take place.

Cynthia beat her friend to the figurative punch. "Sure, on paper, it's all freedom to choose and everyone for themselves. In reality, it'll be larger societies preying on their smaller and weaker neighbors, forming empires."

Zephyr added, "Brushfire conflicts and border skirmishes will be everywhere. Everyone will be so busy either fighting their neighbor, preparing to fight their neighbor, or worrying about having to fight their neighbor that trade and everything else will come to a standstill."

"It hasn't on Harrith," Blu'T'Ohm replied.

When the two women turned their glares on him, he did not flinch. "Sure, our relationship with our neighbors has its ups and downs, but for the most part, things have been more peaceful than not. Until," he leveled a finger first at Zephyr, then Maxim, "rogue elements in the GC council and Peacekeeper command decided that our stability was a problem."

Zephyr pursed her lips.

"He's not wrong." Wil couldn't help himself. He knew he was in danger the moment the last syllable left his mouth.

"Except that he is," Cynthia replied. "Sure, Harrith and its neighbors enjoy a peaceful coexistence. Great. That's after, what, two or three wars that cost tens of millions of lives over the course of a few hundred cycles?"

Blu'T'Ohm inclined his head. "You make a fair point."

Wil shook his head. "Okay, we can go round and round on this. I say we vote on it." He looked around. "In favor." His hand went up along with Bennie and Maxim's.

"Opposed."

Cynthia and Zephyr each raised a hand.

Nic looked around. "Do I get a vote?"

Wil shook his head. "Not until you're old enough to drink."

She hissed. "Then why have I been sitting here this whole time?"

Bennie looked at her. "I forgot you were here."

She made a rude gesture and hopped off her chair and headed for the staircase hatch. "I'll be in the hold, training."

Wil turned to Gabe. "Gabe?"

The droid looked at each of his friends. "Had this issue arisen a cycle or two ago, I would have voted against. The droid nation fought for our sovereignty, and I suspect there is no shortage of those who would like to subjugate droids again. Additionally, as new members of the GC, we have a vested interest in its continued survival." His optic sensors shifted and focused on the Harrith man. "However, that is no longer a worry. Arcadia is far enough along to be fully self-sufficient. We can take care of ourselves as well as help any neighbor who needs us. So, I vote to take the job. The money is good and I have a computer core on order that will need to be paid for."

Wil smiled and pumped his fist, then turned back to Gabe. "Wait, what? How much is it?"

Gabe turned and left the common deck, heading down the short corridor to engineering, computer center, and medbay.

Wil watched him go, then turned to Blu'T'Ohm. "I guess it's time we discussed our fees."

After some back and forth over the team's rate and Bennie's rider for having official Knight of Plentallus support was ironed out, Wil stood up. "Okay. I'm going to go adjust our course. We're not provisioned to get to Qehirg, so we're gonna need to stop along the way."

"Will that interfere with my schedule?" Blu'T'Ohm asked, glancing at his wristcomm and the schedule displayed on it.

Wil shook his head. "No. In and out. We'll get stocked up for a longer mission and be on our way."

The other man nodded his approval, for all that it mattered to Wil. Their standard contract made it abundantly clear that aboard the *Ghost,* his word was final.

Bennie stood to follow Wil. He turned to look at the two Harrith still at the dining table. "To be clear, you're paying for the supplies."

Wil took the two steps from the common deck to the neck that connected the ship's forward and aft sections. Over his shoulder, he said, "Someone pick a movie." He vanished into the connecting corridor, Bennie behind him.

Gul'P'Ulo looked around the common deck. "What's a movie?"

Cynthia leaned over. "Never ask that in front of Wil. Also, if he mentions *Star Wars, Star Trek,* anything extended universe, or the word *serenity*—Walk. Away. Ask no questions."

"Ohh," the young woman said, unsure what to make of the exchange or what any of the words she just heard, meant.

Maxim dropped into the big sofa opposite the wall-mounted display. "I vote the *Minions* series."

Zephyr sat next to him, offering a water bottle. "The one with those yellow pill-shaped mutants that speak gibberish?"

Cynthia escorted the two Harrith across the common deck to the lounge space. "I'm afraid I don't know what's going on," the senior-most Harrith said.

Maxim nodded to the sofa. "Team tradition. Watch crappy vids from Earth during long transits."

"Why?" Gul'P'Ulo asked.

"What else ya gonna do?" Zephyr shrugged.

Blu'T'Ohm opened his mouth, then closed it, taking a seat next to his assistant. "So. What is a minion?"

## CHAPTER 11

"Why are you following me?" Wil finally asked as he reached the bridge hatch. He looked over his shoulder at Bennie. Most of the hatches on the *Ghost* were traditional hinge-mounted affairs, capable of sealing in an emergency and the like. The bridge hatch was a more modern double sliding affair. The seal wasn't as good but could keep the bridge airtight, if needed. At least for a while. The security door just aft of the bridge by the port and starboard airlocks worked the same way, adding an extra layer of protection.

Wil pressed the button next to the wide hatch, waiting a heartbeat for the two thick curved panels to slide apart before stepping onto the bridge.

Other than a ring of low ambient lights set in the ceiling, the space was dark. Everyone's consoles were in standby mode, their displays dark and keyboards unilluminated. The moment he stepped over the threshold, the lighting shifted, and displays came to life.

Bennie ignored him, moving around Wil to his station. Several displays popped to life when he approached.

Wil woke up the master flight controls. They were on

course for Fury, only another seven hours out. He looked over to Bennie. "So?"

The Brailack hacker looked up from whatever he was doing at his station. "I wanted to run an idea by you."

Wil grimaced. It was never good when Bennie wanted to run ideas by anyone, let alone privately. He looked up Qehrig on the navigation system, scrolling through stellar navigation charts. Four days travel from their current location. No way he was eating that much oatmeal.

Pulling the FTL control lever back toward him, he looked at Bennie again. "Spill it." On the primary display, the rainbow streaks shrunk back to pinpricks of light.

"So, the conversation earlier about what it might look like in a galaxy without the GC..."

"Chaos, war, and death? Yeah, I remember it." Wil nodded. He punched in a search for a commerce station between them and their destination. Finding one, he updated their course, bringing the *Ghost* around to the proper heading. The stars on the display swept sideways.

"So, we're already making some inroads with other smuggler types on these first worlds to leave the GC, thanks to Botrobel. What if we keep doing that, but add a new service?"

Without looking up, Wil said, "I'm listening." He double checked their course and pushed the FTL control lever forward. The stars stretched back into their rainbow streaks.

"Weapons," Bennie said.

That got Wil's attention. All of it. He looked up from his flight console. "What about them?"

"We sell them." He held up a thin green finger. "Think about it. With every sector that leaves, scrambling to either attack or defend against their neighbors, we could make a killing as arms dealers."

"You are a disgusting little psycho." Wil shook his head,

putting his console back into sleep mode. He stood. "Let's pretend you never suggested we become arms dealers, yeah?"

"But why—"

"No."

"Think of the—"

"Not today, Satan. Not. Today."

Wil left Bennie alone on the bridge.

The team's hacker looked around. "I think it's a great idea," he murmured. "Stupid Wil."

After three movies featuring jabbering yellow creatures, the team split off to their various tasks before dinner.

After showing their guests to the lone remaining guest berth, Maxim joined Zephyr in their quarters. "That was too much *Minions*."

She nodded her agreement. "You picked them. We should start a list. Like that series with those huge, lanky blue people... One a night is enough." She was sitting at the small desk built into the bulkhead, scrolling through what, to Maxim, looked like news feeds. Every time the *Ghost* dropped from FTL, the computer automatically connected to the nearest communications node and downloaded messages, newsfeeds, and anything else the crew flagged as a priority.

He shook his head. "Maybe we just don't watch that series anymore." He shook his head again. "So unrealistic, that weird hair organ thing."

"Maybe that series and the *Minions*?" She made a face. "I still can't believe we're doing this."

"Discussing some of Wil's more horrible vids?"

"This job, you dupus."

Max clucked. "I think it's *doofus*."

"You're sure?" He nodded. "Then you're that. A doofus." She waved a hand. "We're protecting the devil."

He made a face. "That's a bit melodramatic. Don't you think?"

"No." Her hands found homes on her hips.

"My love," he tried.

"Don't you 'my love' me," she scolded.

"It's just a job."

"So is assassination, and we don't do that."

"Has anyone ever asked?" The look Maxim got forced him to take a step back, running into the door. He held up both hands, palms out. "Sorry. I'm making light of your concerns." Her expression softened, so he continued, "I'm not blind to your worries or to some of the language Blu'T'Ohm and other separatists use."

She nodded slowly. "I know how you feel about the treatment of our people by the Tarsi and the greater GC, but you really think the GC splintering into warring nation-states is the answer?"

He gave her a shrug. "That's where we're different. I don't see that as the only outcome of all this."

Zephyr was silent for a moment. She loved Maxim. She disagreed with him, even though his outlook was rosier than hers. She did not see this situation ending well. With a sigh, she decided to table the discussion. "I'm thinking doorip mash and those crinkly things Wil brought back from Earth."

Maxim grinned. "French fifes. Yum."

"How did you break another one of these?" Wil asked, holding up a large display. He and Bennie were back on the bridge after dinner. The team hacker had remembered that one of his displays had started shorting out and asked for help replacing it before they reached the commerce station.

Bennie looked up from where he was sitting under the console. "You. You broke it. You threw your stupid Kel statue at me." He pointed at the small blue bearlike statuette on Wil's flight console. He got to his feet, a data cable in one hand. "If you'd stop trying to harm me, we wouldn't go through so many displays."

"No." Wil turned, lowering the damaged unit to the deck. "This isn't me. You get the statuette because you say and do horrible things."

Bennie inched up onto his toes to reach behind the console mounted to the bulkhead, fishing a bundle of cables out. He flinched, withdrawing his hand. Something was stuck to it. He didn't look at Wil. "Sounds like victim blaming." He wiped his hand on his trousers and reached in again. "Gimme the end of the cable. I'm gonna run it through here this time."

Wil turned and picked up the new display. He balanced it on his hip. "Is this one bigger?"

"That's what she—"

"Nope!"

Bennie looked over his shoulder, smirk plastered on his face. "Figured might as well upgrade." He held his hand out, little green fingers wiggling.

Keeping the monitor balanced, Wil grabbed the power cable and fed the end to Bennie. "So, these don't have a data cable?"

"For what?" Bennie finished and gestured to Wil to mount the display. "To talk to the computers?" He chuckled. "No. All of our displays are wirelessly addressable. That's why it's so easy to transfer station functions from place to place." He chuckled again. "Wires to connect displays. Cute."

Wil stepped back, watching the display power up and connect to the station's systems. Choosing to ignore the little green turd's jab, he said, "So, listen. I want you to dig up what you can."

"About selling arms? Excellent. I've already got a few ideas and some quiet inquiries queued up."

Wil shook his head. "I already said...No, just no."

Bennie cocked his head. "Okay, then what?"

"On whether the Rockies will win the championship. On Bluetooth, you little green goblin."

Bennie's mouth formed a little circle. "Oh. Sure. Like what?" He turned to his console, confirming the monitor was integrated with the rest of his systems.

Wil rolled his hand. "You know, who's paying him, who's he working with, or for. Whatever you can find. Dive deep."

"You think he's hiding something?

Wil shrugged. "I don't know. You saw that park. He lived, and the Tarsi that the GC sent didn't."

The Brailack nodded his agreement. "Not to mention a half dozen or so PKs. Okay, I'll get started tomorrow. I'm beat."

As the two of them exited the bridge again, Wil said, "That was a lot of *Minions*. Max loses movie privileges for a while."

Bennie smiled. "Yeah, he does."

"Good afternoon. This is your GNO Morning Briefing," the blue-skinned newscaster said, turning his compound eyes to the camera. "I'm Xyrzix."

"And I'm Klor'Tillen," his cohost said. "There's increasing

turmoil in the Humbaba Reach. According to unconfirmed reports, the Gulveig system has been acquiring warships. Lots of them." He turned to another camera pickup. "Much to the concern of their neighbors in the Qetesh system."

Xyrzix looked down at the tablet before him. "The Supreme Speaker of the Hulgian Hierarchy has assured his Sylban neighbors that the rapidly growing fleet was merely a precaution against aggression from any quarter and not directed at them."

Klor'Tillen smiled, his pale green skin accentuated by his light gray blazer. "The Sylban have officially asked for the GC to intercede."

His colleague shook his head. "As one might expect, the GC has so far declined, citing a long-standing policy not to get involved with non-member political or military issues."

The Brailack journalist chuckled. "The societies of Humbaba Reach are the first Tier 2 and 3 members to withdraw from the Commonwealth. It will be interesting to see how things shake out."

Xyrzix made a clicking noise deep in his throat. "Agreed. Though it does seem that this stance by the GC Council might be more punitive than we'd normally see."

Klor'Tillen nodded his agreement, then said, "We'll keep on the Humbaba Reach and keep you posted."

*PART 3*

## CHAPTER 12

"What the hell?" Wil said as the *Ghost* dropped out of FTL. The commerce station was another jizz stop, which, like last time, caused Wil to giggle. He still found it hilarious that some random company in the GC had picked *that* term. It was surrounded by hundreds of ships of all shapes, sizes, and classes. Not least of all, two Peacekeeper corvettes. "Used to be there was never a PK around when you needed them; now they're freakin' everywhere?"

Cynthia glanced at her console and the incoming call icon flashing. "One guess what this call is about." She reached up to snug the earpiece in her ear. Then she reached for the comm switch. Her finger covered over the control. "What ID are we flying?"

Bennie looked back from his station, grinning. "I'm trying something new." He inhaled. "*I Didn't Do It.*"

Everyone groaned.

"Bit of a mouthful," Maxim said.

Rolling her eyes, Cynthia turned back to her console, accepting the incoming call. Everyone waited in silence as she nodded and shook her head while murmuring to the comm pickup on her console.

When Wil was on the verge of exploding from the wait, she turned. "Yeah, they're doing spot inspections."

Wil swore at the same time Zephyr did. He said, "Do they even have jurisdiction?"

Maxim grunted. "You want to ask them?"

Wil groaned. "Better go let our guests know."

Maxim nodded. This close to Peacekeeper ships, and a commerce station, there was no need to man his station. The moment they powered up the *Ghost*'s weapons, they'd be reduced to atomic particles and vague memories by the PKs, and likely the hidden but legal defensive weapons all around the commerce station's hull.

Max found Blu'T'Ohm and Gul'P'Ulo in the lounge huddled over a pair of tablets on the kitchen table. "Sorry to interrupt." He couldn't see what was on the screens

The senior of the two Harrith looked up. "We're there? The commerce station?"

Maxim nodded. "We are, but there's a hiccup. Two PK ships are loitering and doing random inspections. Guess who got picked."

Blu'T'Ohm frowned. "I don't believe it is in any of our interests that the Peacekeepers discover us aboard your ship."

Max pursed his lips. He knew the man thought the GC was out to silence him and wasn't yet sure if he bought into that particular theory. He did find it odd that the news outlets weren't talking more about the missing and presumed dead separatist. He exhaled. "Okay. Come on." He pointed toward the hatch to the stairs.

"Where are we going?" Gul'P'Ulo asked.

"Cargo hold," Maxim said. He tapped his wristcomm

screen, opening the team channel. "I'll be in the hold showing our clients the off-tour space."

"Copy that," Wil replied from the device's speaker.

"Off-tour?" Blu'T'Ohm repeated.

They reached the cargo hold and headed for a spot near the starboard bulkhead halfway along the hold's side. Despite how often the crew smuggled things, they rarely used the smugglers' compartment in the floor of the hold. Wil still kept a few things in there, luckily nothing explosive like Trilorrium. For the first cycle and a half or so after they met Wil, the crew didn't even know it existed. Or that Wil was keeping several gembs of the highly volatile, highly illegal crystal in it.

Max tried to remember how to open the compartment. "I know there's a ..." He pressed a section of deck plating next to where he thought the seam was. Nothing. He scowled, pressing another section. That time something clicked. "There we go." With his bearings, he moved his hand to the side and pressed the other hidden panel and was rewarded with a second click. A section of the deck popped up.

Max slid the released deck plate away. "Won't be comfy, but it is shielded."

The two Harrith leaned to peer into the compartment. The younger might be able to sit comfortably once the cover was on, but Blu'T'Ohm most definitely would be forced to sit hunched over.

"It smells," Gul'P'Ulo complained, leaning back.

Max hopped in and pulled out a duffel bag. "How'd this get in here?" He held it up to his face, inhaling. "Ew." He tossed it into the center of the hold. "Okay, in you go." He held his arms out to help the smaller Harrith into the smugglers' hold. Once both were in, he hopped out.

From the speakers in the ceiling, Zephyr said, "They're

docking." A slight clang echoed through the ship to punctuate her announcement.

Maxim nodded to the two Harrith as he slid the deck plate over them, forcing both to crouch down. "See ya soon."

There was a low ding before the port airlock's inner doors parted. A Peacekeeper in a crisp commander's uniform stepped in, flanked by four black-armored troopers, each with a pulse rifle held firmly in front of them. The commander looked around. Spying Zephyr, he inclined his head. "You're the captain?"

She shook her head. "Executive Officer..." she sighed. "... Ferro. Colette Ferro." She extended her hand, indicating Wil. "Captain Dawp Hicks."

"Dwayne," Wil corrected. Zephyr shrugged.

The big Peacekeeper nodded to Wil. "Commander Parch."

Wil stepped forward. "Nice to meet you. So, you all just blockading commerce stations now?"

The awkward silence was broken by Maxim arriving. He spied Wil and the much larger Peacekeeper commander squaring off and cleared his throat.

Commander Parch turned to Maxim, then looked over his shoulder to his troopers.

The four armored troopers stomped past Maxim. The big Palorian turned to follow along with Cynthia. She looked over her shoulder at Wil but said nothing.

Wil extended a hand to the Commander. "This way."

By the time Wil and the others escorted the Commander to the lounge space, the stairway hatch down to the cargo hold was closed. Maxim, Zephyr, and their new friends were already in the cargo hold.

"Don't see many Ankarran Raptors this old out and about anymore," Parch said from the kitchen space. He moved to the corridor connecting the lounge to the spaces aft. "Engineering?"

Wil nodded. "And the medbay and computer core." Falling in behind the Commander, he said, "She's a classic alright. Still has it where it counts, though."

The other man nodded but said nothing, pushing open the hatch to engineering.

Down in the cargo hold, the four armored troopers were looking in every nook and cranny.

One of them opened the hatch to the missile storage room on the starboard side of the cargo door at the forward part of the hold. "Lotta missiles," the voice said. The armor still masked the voice so that no one Peacekeeper sounded any different from the others. The armor concealed the gender of the wearer as much as the voice.

Maxim tilted his head. "Can you ever have too many missiles?"

The trooper chuckled. It came out sounding similar to Gabe's metallic laugh.

One of the other troopers toed the duffel bag that Maxim now realized he had forgotten to stash after finding it in the smugglers' hold. "What's this?"

"Don't open—Ah, man," Maxim groaned. The trooper had the bag in one hand and unzipped it with the other. The smell leaped from the bag like a caged animal escaping.

"Oh, my gods. It's getting through my armor's filters." The trooper dropped the bag, stumbling backward. They turned to Maxim. "Why is that just lying there?"

Maxim shook his head. "Good question."

Up on the common deck, Bennie and Nic were sitting at the

kitchen table watching the Peacekeepers move through the space. Nic watched the Commander and Gabe exit the engineering space. "I can kinda see why Blue isn't a fan."

Bennie nodded. "Yeah, this sure feels like they're overcorrecting to the whole 'Where's the GC?' issue." His apprentice nodded. "The PKs took a beating against ol' monster face Janus, but this massive mobilization across the GC is just..." He waved a little green hand. "A lot."

Across the common deck, the Commander turned to Wil. "And what's your business at Jizz Stop 69?"

Wil coughed. "I'm sorry. This is Jizz Stop 69?"

"Yes."

"Sixty. Nine?"

Cynthia rolled her eyes. "Oh, gods."

"I don't understand." The Commander looked around the room. Zephyr shrugged when his gaze fell on her.

"Humans," was all she said.

Cynthia put a hand on Wil's shoulder. "Moving on." She looked at the Peacekeeper Commander. "We good?"

Whether the other man realized that his question had gone unanswered or not, he tapped his wristcomm. He said, "We good?"

A tinny voice said, "Yes, sir. Nothing out of the ordinary down here."

Commander Parch looked at Zephyr, then Cynthia, and finally Wil. "Everything seems to be in order."

Wil opened his mouth but flinched instead as a single sharp claw jabbed his backside.

A few minutes later the inner airlock doors slid closed, sealing with a faint hiss. The light over the door faded from green to red. A thud announced the retraction of the Peacekeeper corvette's docking umbilical.

Wil looked at the two women next to him. Bennie and Nic opted to stay in the lounge. "That was fun."

The *Ghost* settled on her landing gear at the outer edge of the cavernous docking bay. It turned out that negotiating docking clearance was easier after the entire space control deck watched your ship get pulled over and searched by a Peacekeeper patrol.

The commerce station's docking bay was the largest single open space on the station. The *Ghost* settled in next to a Brailack freighter twice the Ankarran Raptor's size. The perfect spot to not attract attention, being dwarfed by the larger vessel. Wil wasn't sure if it was pity or that the space control operators were sure that the *Ghost* wasn't a problem. He didn't care which it was. It got them a parking spot fast.

After putting the ship's systems into standby, Wil said, "Okay, I'll take the green asshole and go grocery shopping. He nodded to Max. "Someone needs to keep our guests safe. You and Zee mind—"

"I've got something to do on the station," Zephyr interrupted.

Bennie looked up at her, eyebrow ridges arched. Nic reached over and put a hand over his mouth. "I'll stay with Max and guard them."

As the crew funneled into the common deck from the ship's neck, Cynthia looked around. "Uh. Where are they?"

"Who?" Bennie asked.

Maxim swore and darted to the stairwell, flinging open the hatch and vanishing down the stairs toward the cargo hold below.

After exchanging looks, everyone ran after him.

Reaching the cargo deck, Cynthia looked at Wil, then at Maxim sprinting across the hold. "The compartment isn't airtight, is it?"

Wil shrugged. "Never tested it."

Maxim reached the hidden panel, pressing the two sections of deck plating one after another to release the panel. It slid up and out of the way.

The two Harrith looked up, shielding their eyes. "That was a long inspection." Blu'T'Ohm breathed. The compartment didn't smell as bad as the gym bag, but it wasn't fresh smelling either.

Maxim looked at the others, then down at the two Harrith, offering a hand to each.

"Yeah. They really looked everywhere," Wil said from the bottom of the stairs.

"Very thorough," Cynthia agreed.

"There were probes," Bennie said. Everyone turned to look at him. "What?"

Wil squinted at his Brailack friend. "I knew it was Brailack that visited Earth in our past. You little green probe loving..." He shook his head and turned to the two Harrith. "Never mind. I'm taking probe guy to get groceries." He looked at Cynthia. "Babe, you mind doing a supply run for anything they need? Take Gabe." She nodded. He looked around. "Okay. One hour. Let's get in and get out." He pointed to the two Harrith. "Let Cynthia know your clothing sizes and anything else you need; otherwise, stay out of sight. Max and Nic will be here if you need them."

He walked over to the pedestal that controlled the heavy cargo bay doors and cargo ramp. His wristcomm authenticated with the device, and he slapped the control that triggered the doors and the ramp.

He looked over his shoulder at Bennie. "Come on."

Bennie sighed and looked at his apprentice. "Don't do anything to embarrass me or the order."

The young woman scowled, scrunching up her muzzle. "You're embarrassing."

Wil pushed Bennie down the ramp, not at all interested in the retort the little hacker had on his lips. The pair took the lift up from the docking bays to the main shopping district. This station was far more modern than the last one of the same brand they visited. The commercial and retail district had high ceilings and lots of light. Two concentric circles connected by two wide walkways contained this level's shopping options. The directory said there were three such decks.

This one was the consumables section. Bennie insisted that they bypass the inner circle, closest to the bank of lift tubes that ran through the center of the station. "These are the high-rent stalls. We want people who are more cost-conscious. They'll be in the outer ring."

Wil sighed and followed his friend. The team had learned long ago that not only did Bennie fancy himself a master negotiator, but he was actually pretty good at it.

They entered a shop that featured several rows of fresh fruits and grains. Wil picked up a large qorrum, careful to avoid the pointy nubs that covered the outside. "Could have a burger night with fries..." He held on to the prickly-skinned tuber. He looked down at Bennie, who was examining a bag of grain that Wil didn't recognize. "Never seen that one before." The rice-sized granules seemed to shift color as they moved within the bag.

The Brailack looked up. "It's from Brai. Mostly used to make these delicious dumpling-like things. Called floomb." He made a soft purring noise. "So good."

Wil nodded. "You know how to make them?"

"I can message home and ask the house chef for a recipe." He hefted the bag onto one narrow shoulder.

Following Bennie to the next row of staples, Wil said, "So, you find anything yet?" He watched Bennie pick up a packet of crispy yipsee strips. "Not those. Get the spicy ones."

"I like this flavor." Bennie looked up, frowning. "And, yeah. No smoking blasters or anything, though."

"I don't care. The spicy ones are better and don't make your farts toxic." Wil pointed as authoritatively as he could at the package next to the one Bennie was holding. "Like what?"

Bennie exchanged bags of snacks. "As you might expect, the finances for an organization with the goal of encouraging systems to leave the GC are murky." He shrugged. "But nothing looks illegal. More like his supporters would rather not be tied to his mission, lots of shell corps and anonymous donations. There isn't any type of official movement or organization per se. From what I could see, he gets routine deposits in his account. Like a stipend. I dug around a few other known separatists as well just to cover the bases. About the same, finance-wise."

Nodding, Wil picked up a wheel of fyolpi. So many things from home had an analog, but cheddar cheese, so far, wasn't one of them. "Taco night." He looked down at Bennie again. "That's it?"

"What part of 'no smoking blaster' did you not understand?" Bennie said, walking toward the payment terminal.

After the two Harrith gave Cynthia a list of clothing sizes and needs, they followed Maxim and Nic back up to the common deck.

Nic sat to next to Gul'P'Ulo at the kitchen table. "So, you're like, his apprentice?" the young Olop asked.

The Harrith woman looked at her. She reached up to fidget with the earrings adorning her right ear. "More like, assistant, I guess. I manage his calendar. His travel arrangements." She shrugged. "That sort of thing."

Nic nodded. "Like it?"

The other woman opened her mouth, closed it, frowned. "Yes. It's quite rewarding. I get to see the wide variety of species that make up the Commonwealth and help encourage them to find their own path. To get out from under the Commonwealth's rules and taxes."

It sounded rehearsed to Nic.

Gul'P'Ulo ran a hand through her hair. She turned to look at Blu'T'Ohm. "Sir, where are the tablets?"

He screwed up his face as he rubbed his chin. "Good question." He slapped his knee. "I think I left them downstairs in that stinky pit." He locked his gaze on hers. "Be a dear."

She sighed and got up. Nic hopped off her chair and followed her off the common deck.

Max watched the two young women leave. "Chlormax?"

"That would be lovely," Blu'T'Ohm said, dropping into one of the chairs at the kitchen table.

Down in the cargo hold, Nic and Gul'P'Ulo were looking at the floor for the smugglers' compartment. The Harrith woman looked at Nic. "You know where it is?"

Nic chewed her lower lip. "I think so?" She stomped on the deck. Nothing happened. "Somewhere around here." She moved to another section, pressing it. When nothing happened, she moved a few steps to the side and repeated the process. "Hmm. I know Maxim was right around here."

"I think it was over here." The brown-haired Harrith woman moved to another section, stooping to push on the deck plate.

"No, that's too far." Nic turned around and pressed another section. It clicked. "Oh, here it is!" She moved her hand and pressed the other section.

While Nic held the panel up, the other woman slid into the smugglers' compartment and retrieved the two tablets. Crawling out, she spied Nic's beam saber hilt. "What's that?"

Nic let the deck panel fall in place. "This?" Her hand fell to the hilt. "My beam saber. I'm a Knight of Plentallus." Her facial fur rippled. "Well, an apprentice."

The young Harrith woman nodded. "I don't know what that is."

Nic scrunched up her face. She'd heard Bennie explain the order to others, though rarely did she pay attention to what he was saying. She had certainly read enough of the histories to know all about the order, but how to explain it to someone that's never heard of it? "You see, it's like the Peacekeepers but older. Before them."

"A military?"

Nic shook her head. "No. Not military or even police. They," she caught herself, "*we* were guardians of peace and justice. The Knights of Plentallus went where they were needed, helping all who needed it." She made a hand waving gesture. "Everyone respected their judgment even though they had no legal standing."

The pair made for the stairs back to the common deck. Gul'P'Ulo said, "And you and Ben-Ari the only ones?"

Nic nodded. "For now. The order was almost completely gone. The team met the last Knight and helped him finish his mission. Bennie took to him and before he died, he gave Bennie a few lessons and the information he'd need to access the Tower."

"The Tower?"

Nic shrugged. "Like a base of operations." She smiled.

"With a gift shop."

They reached the common deck. Maxim was engaged in a conversation with Blu'T'Ohm about the merits of smaller sector level alliances over a construct like the Commonwealth. They angled toward the lounge seating.

Dropping into the large overstuffed chair, Gul'P'Ulo nodded. "Like it?"

Nic shrugged. "Sometimes. It's kinda lonely right now. Just the two of us."

The Harrith woman gestured to the ship. "What about the rest of your team?"

Nic smiled. She liked everyone aboard the *Ghost*. "I met them all a little over a cycle ago, I think. On a cruise ship that had been taken over by pirates."

"Pirates?" She scrunched her face, trying to recall the news story she'd heard. "You mean the—"

Nic nodded. "Yup."

"Wow."

Nic smiled.

"Gul'P'Ulo, ready?" Blu'T'Ohm called from the table. His and Maxim's discussion had wound down. The Harrith woman nodded. Smiling to Nic, she got up from the chair and joined her boss at the table.

Letting them have space to work, Maxim moved to take her seat in the lounge. He had a tablet in hand, reading it.

Nic looked over at him. "What ya reading?" He turned the device to show her the screen. "Top caterers on Palor..." She looked up at him. "You two are unbelievable. Just take her some-where special and be done."

He pressed his lips together. "She deserves something special."

"In this life or the next?"

He made a face and went back to his reading.

## CHAPTER 13

Zephyr reached the public comm terminals three levels above the retail zones. This deck did not have high ceilings and bright natural light. If she were asked, she'd call it dingy. The public comm terminals were in a commercial suite next to the station's leasing office, which, despite being near midday station time, was closed.

She stopped at the kiosk in the front lobby, raising her wrist-comm to pay. The kiosk screen directed her to booth 14.

She looked up to see a light blinking over one of the closet-sized booths. Only about a third of them were occupied, judging by the number of heads she could see over the cubicle walls that separated the booths. The management software had spread the customers out so that each booth had an empty one next to it, which she appreciated. She sat down in booth 14 and flicked a contact to the terminal.

"This call will be charged at a rate of three credits per tenth a tock. Please acknowledge."

"Three credits?" Zephyr shook her head. This call would cost nothing from the *Ghost*. "Acknowledged."

The screen flickered the logo of the communication company.

She waited while the terminal negotiated with the station's communication system. The company logo was replaced by a happy little icon slowly working its way along a dotted line toward a satellite dish. Once that process was complete, she was treated to an ad for sexual performance enhancement pills while the signal made its way to the destination.

The screen flickered again. Zephyr was bracing for an ad featuring lunch meat or something else equally annoying when a familiar face appeared.

"Well, as I live and breathe," the Palorian woman on the screen said. She smiled. "How have you been?"

"Hello, Rush." Zephyr smiled. "I'm good—great, really. Yourself?"

Zephyr hadn't seen Rush since before she and Maxim were framed. The two women worked together in the Intelligence Bureau for several cycles before Maxim joined the unit. The other woman nodded. "Good to hear, and likewise, all things being equal."

Zephyr nodded. "That's why I'm calling. If I read you right."

"You always did." Her friend smiled. The two of them had worked together for so long that they knew each other's facial expressions. "What's on your mind?"

"A new client of ours..." She shook her head. "What's the temperature there? Around all this separatist stuff?"

"You mean, will Palor vote to leave the GC?" Rush shook her head. Her jet-black hair, cut in a tight bob, swayed. "No. At least not yet."

Zephyr was glad to hear that. Her friend continued, "Not for lack of interest, though. The nationalists are keeping a tight grip on power, but I'm not sure how long that'll last. Many in high command, as well as the congress, feel that Palor could thrive in an environment where we were more than just the galaxy's police force."

Zephyr was silent for a moment. That wasn't exactly the news she was hoping to hear. "Really? That's...a surprise."

"Is it?" her friend replied. "I know we haven't spoken in a while, but you don't exactly lead a low-key life. I have a pretty good idea of what you've been up to and what you and your man have seen. It surprises you that there's a segment of Palorians that would like more in life than patrolling systems and sectors that don't want them there?"

Zephyr sighed. "I guess not. I was just hoping this madness hadn't spread that far."

"That ship has left spacedock, I'm afraid." Her friend grinned. "There's hope yet. No vote's been called. It hasn't even come up. Palor's a GC member for a while still." Rush cocked her head. "Enough about that. How're things out there? Has Maxim got over whatever is keeping you two from having a damn joining ceremony?"

"You are well informed." Zephyr quirked a brow. She smiled. "I don't know what that man's problem is. He has run headlong into battle without armor. More than once. Once in his underwear, but that was Wil's fault. But locking down even a single detail about our joining seems to freeze him up completely." She shook her head.

"Intelligence never sleeps...Or something like that. He'll get there. Or he won't, and you'll lose patience. Either way, I'm certain of the outcome." They shared a laugh that caused Zephyr to look over the partitions around her booth to ensure she hadn't caught anyone's interest.

The two continued to talk a while longer, catching up on more mundane things like life, pets, the latest in Peacekeeper armor and arms upgrades, and things like that.

"I told you to just have everything delivered," Bennie complained. The shopping bags he was holding in each hand were dragging on the ground.

Wil, similarly encumbered, looked down. "Whatever, that adds another ten percent to the cost of everything." He curled one arm, then the other. "Think of it as chance to get free weight training. Your arms are too scrawny." He made a face. "Don't drag 'em."

Bennie scowled. "Brailack aren't known for our bulging muscles."

"Or any."

"Whatever. Suck it."

Wil clucked. "You suck it."

Without warning, Bennie changed the subject. "So, you think your people will still want to join the GC now that...you know."

It took Wil a second to process the subject change. He shrugged. He'd never admit it to Bennie, but he was rethinking foregoing the delivery option on their purchases. Somehow, he got stuck with the Brailack grain they'd bought.

He shook his head, remembering Bennie's question. "I dunno, man. They aren't consulting me. Timing sucks, to be sure." He shrugged. "Beyond that, I really don't know, but I hope so."

Bennie tried to shrug and winced. "Upside. If they join, it'll be cycles before things really go to dren. Could be a few great cycles for your backwards people."

"Fuck you. And, yeah."

"They'll get a few cycles of peace. They can learn to play

nice with others, and if they're like you, stock up on advanced weaponry for when things really fall apart."

Wil shook his head. "That's the part that worries me. The fending for ourselves. Last time I was there we had two, or maybe three, fighting ships."

Bennie looked up at him.

Wil continued, "And whether it's two, three, or twenty, they wouldn't last ten minutes against a Brailack corvette, let alone a PK command carrier."

Bennie clucked. "One. Brailack corvettes are nothing to scoff at." Wil rolled his eyes. Bennie ignored him and said, "Two. I've got it. The perfect idea. We can sell warships to Earth."

Wil looked down at him. "Where are we gonna get warships?"

"We'll just be the middlemen. If they're not now, someone will soon be building ships for sale."

Wil sighed. "We're not selling arms, or warships, to Earth."

"Earth's loss."

"Almost certainly." Wil shook his head to try and usher the idea of Bennie selling warships out of the *Ghost*'s cargo hold from his mind. "They'll just have to figure it out on their own. It sucks, and I'm annoyed, but such is life."

Bennie looked up. "We can get drunk later. That usually makes you feel better."

Wil huffed. "Yeah." When he looked down at Bennie's face, he added, "Still not selling arms to Earth."

"Looks like the GC found another spokesbeing," Bennie said as the team and their clients arrived at the sports arena where the forum was due to be held in a few hours.

The organizers had invited Blu'T'Ohm and a GC spokeswoman to hold a forum on the topic of separating from the GC. The entire arena was full, possibly because news of Blu'T'Ohm's survival had finally leaked to GNO. Wil guesstimated the attendance at upward of fifty thousand beings.

Qehirg was an independent colony, so the population was a slice of the GC as a whole. After all this time, there were still races that Wil had never seen before.

He looked at the two Palorians in their scout armor. Zephyr's was still sporting the damaged chest plate from their earlier adventure. Wil had put in an order from the same armorer he bought his current armor from, but the backlog was immense. She would have to make do for now.

His armor, sans helmet, was under his long brown duster. Jarvis, the sentient intelligence that resided in his armor, was tapped into the mesh network comm channel his wristcomm shared with the rest of the team. Every time he donned the sophisticated armor, he wished he had more reasons to wear it. The fit was perfect. Jarvis was an excellent copilot.

"Bennie, you and Nic stick with Blue," Wil said. He gave up on trying to make Bluetooth stick as the man's shipboard nickname and went for the shorter, less Earth-specific, Blue. Trying to explain Bluetooth to the others had given him a migraine anyway.

"Copy that," the Brailack hacker and Knight of Plentallus said. He was in his Knight *uniform*, as Wil called it: earth tone tunic and darker undershirt, with canvas trousers. When the Brailack wanted to be all business, he could be. It was just rare.

Nic, also in her uniform, nodded, and the pair moved off toward the stage.

Wil looked at the others. "Max and Zee, you stick out like sore thumbs, so hang back near the upper levels." He turned to Gabe. "You and Cyn and I will work the crowd." Everyone nodded, then dispersed.

Jarvis said, "Would you like me to begin active scanning, sir?"

Wil nodded. "Why not? Scan away."

The forum was set to start in half an hour, and the arena was already full. The organizers had told the team that the wait-list numbered in the thousands.

A short time later, as the team moved through the crowd, the forum's organizer, a middle-aged Rigellian woman, welcomed the audience to the forum and went over the rules for the afternoon. In no uncertain terms, she outlined what would be acceptable and what would not be acceptable behavior.

Then she welcomed Blu'T'Ohm, then the Tarsi woman representing the GC for the afternoon. For a second, Wil thought it might be their old friend Slivyrn Grythlorian. Then he realized he wasn't actually very good at telling one Tarsi from another.

"Anything hinky?" Wil asked on the team channel.

"Nothing up here," Zephyr reported.

In a low voice, Nic said, "There's a weird looking Ficu by the stage."

Wil chuckled. "Ficu are weird looking." He angled back toward the stage, whispering apologies as he pushed people aside. "I'll take a look."

Cynthia had moved to the second level and was walking down the stairs that split the two sections. "What's this place for, normally?"

Gabe, also on the second level, several sections away, said, "The Qehirg Rangers play Dwapnarball here every ten rotations."

"Who knew Dwapnarball brought in crowds this size?" Wil said.

"I did," Bennie retorted.

"As did I," Gabe said.

Wil made a face no one but the Hulgian woman next to him saw. "Whatever."

The sketchy Ficu ended up being nothing more than a regular Ficu being an exemplar of his species. The forum continued for nearly three hours without incident. The local authorities had been warned about what happened on Jdarum, so security was appreciably tight.

Two of the most boring hours later, Wil watched as the last few stragglers on the ground level filed to the arena's exits. He had moved to the second level toward the end of the forum, trading places with Cynthia.

The GC's spokeswoman had done an admirable job of presenting the value in continued Commonwealth membership. Cynthia hated to admit, but Blu'T'Ohm masterfully dismantled the GC representative's arguments.

From her place next to Bennie, Nic said, "Bummer nothing happened."

"For you, maybe," Blu'T'Ohm replied. "I'm perfectly happy not being attacked."

"Boring."

Cynthia watched the exchange, then said, "Okay, let's get back to the *Ghost*."

"Qehirg Space Control, this is the *Good Ship Lollypop* requesting departure clearance," Cynthia said. She looked up at Wil. "That better not be a weird Earth sex joke or something."

He chuckled. "It's not." Her look said she didn't believe him, but she let it drop.

The bridge hatch slid open, letting Zephyr enter. "Blu and Gulp are in their berth."

Cynthia watched her friend take her station, then said, "We're clear for departure and burn to the designated transfer orbit."

Wil fed power to the repulsorlifts in the ship's engine nacelles. As the *Ghost* rose into the air, he brought the atmospheric engines online. Once they were high enough above the spaceport, he fed power to the powerful thrusters, pushing the lithe Ankarran Raptor off into the clouds, followed by several sonic booms.

Zephyr shook her head. "That will endear the locals to us."

"They'll get over it. Maybe," Wil said, watching the clouds on the primary display gradually thin and recede, giving way to the black of space.

Qehirg was a well-established Tier 2 world. As such, orbit was a pretty crowded place. Space control was housed in two orbitals holding opposite orbits from each other on either side of the planet.

"Space control has cleared us out of orbit. Sending you the plot," Cynthia announced.

The primary display updated with a ghostly green arrow showing their path out of the gravity well.

Wil turned to look at Zephyr. "Did Blue tell you where his next stop is?"

She looked up from her console. "Oh, yeah. He's due on—"

The entire ship shuddered, and something over the primary display erupted in sparks when it overloaded, sending a cascade of static across the large screen. The static lasted a moment before the display's secondary circuits took over, returning it to normal.

"What the h—" Wil started.

The ship shook again, and the bridge lights dimmed.

"Shields are up," Maxim reported, gripping his station as the whole ship rocked.

Wil regained his composure and slammed the flight controls hard to port, sending the *Ghost* into a tight banking turn.

Zephyr shouted, "Contact. One of the ships in a parking orbit opened fire on us as we passed."

"Rude," Bennie said, gripping his station tightly.

"Why didn't our sensors detect their targeting sensors?" Wil said, pulling them out of the turn, only to pull the controls over to the other side and slightly back, driving the *Ghost* into an arcing starboard climb.

"Where is he?" Wil demanded.

"Getting a fix," Maxim said. "I don't think he targeted us. I think it was a snap shot. A good one," he added.

Zephyr nodded. "Damage to our short-range comms gear and starboard shield emitters."

"Weapons online," Maxim reported.

Wil glanced at the tactical display that lived on a smaller monitor below the main display. A bright red triangle was angling toward them from the right, burning hard from its place in orbit. He pushed the flight control forward and to the right, driving them right at their attacker.

"Two away!" Maxim shouted a second before two missiles streaked across the bottom of the primary display, arcing toward their attacker.

Now that they had sensors on the other ship, Wil could see that it was a modified gun boat: fast, lightly armored with guns and a few missiles. The first missile struck the small craft's shields, causing them to flare orange. The second missile rushed through the weakened shield to strike the gunship, ripping the hull near one of the stubby wings apart, sending the ship spiraling, trailing atmosphere and flames.

On the screen, the other ship went into a corkscrew spin, blaster bolts streaking from its top- and bottom-mounted turrets. Despite the damage, the gunship was still in the fight.

As the weapons' fire splashed against their shields, Wil changed course just as their own blasters opened fire.

"Careful letting him linger on the starboard side," Zephyr warned. "The shield emitters are still glitching. Shield strength is only fifty percent."

Wil looked up at the ceiling. "Gabe, anything you can do about the starboard shield emitters?"

"I am working on it," the terse reply came back from the ceiling speakers.

Wil smiled, turning his focus back to their mysterious attacker.

## CHAPTER 14

"I've got space control squawking in my ear, demanding to know what's going on," Cynthia said.

"Let 'em know we're being attacked. And that we didn't start it," Wil said. He brought the *Ghost* around again in another arc, trying to keep their weapons lined up on the smaller ship. The other pilot was good. The gunboat's double turrets meant it could fire no matter the angle of attack, and while the *Ghost* did have a blaster turret set above and behind the bridge, it had a limited firing arc. The rest of the Raptor's weapons were forward facing.

"Damn it, hold still!" Wil shouted.

"I've got two locals inbound," Zephyr announced. "Local security boats. Not much to look at."

"I've got a lock!" Maxim shouted as he slapped his console.

From deep inside the ship, two more loud clunks sounded as missiles were fed into the launch tubes by the auto loader in weapons magazine.

The screen flickered, but they could still see the two missiles streak from the bottom of the display.

The second the missiles were clear, Wil threw them into another maneuver.

"Missiles on him," Maxim announced. "Impact in...Dren!" He looked up from his console. "He jumped to FTL."

Wil pulled back on the throttle, letting the two local security ships catch up to them.

"Hey, Zee, can you scan for the debris from our missile strike?"

She hummed to herself. "Sure. Wait one." More humming as she consulted her console, adjusting the ship's sensors. "There it is." She sent the coordinates to Wil's flight console.

"Sending kill order to the missiles," Maxim said. "Both have powered down...detonating."

Wil guided the *Ghost* to the site of the still expanding cloud of ship parts. He looked up. "Hey, Gabe. I know you're busy, but you mind doing a quick spacewalk?"

Zephyr cleared her throat.

"What? That's what it's called."

"What is it you would like me to do?" the ceiling answered.

"There's a bunch of debris from the ship we just chased off. They were waiting for us, so I'd like to see if we can learn anything from the parts of their ship they left behind." He set the ship to keep station where they were. "I can go if not."

"It will be faster if I go," the droid replied. Despite his continued adjustments to his overall physical design, low powered thrusters were always a part of Gabe's overall design after first experiencing them during his first post-death body design. Flight was no longer an option, at least not in gravity.

On Wil's console, he saw that the cargo bay was depressurizing.

"You think we'll find any clues?" Bennie asked.

The bridge hatch opened, allowing Nic and their two guests to enter.

"What in the name of the old gods was that?" Blu'T'Ohm demanded.

Wil turned his chair to face the new arrivals. "Just a minor hiccup."

"Sounded like we were in a battle," Gul'P'Ulo said.

Bennie leaned out of his station. "Just one of your fans, trying to kill you. And us."

Cynthia hissed, interrupting any reply. "The locals would like to speak with us."

"Great," Wil sighed.

"Captain. I have collected several pieces of debris that I believe could yield answers," Gabe's voice said over the intercom.

Wil nodded. "Awesome. Thanks, pal. Bring it all aboard and tuck it somewhere out of the way. We're gonna have company in a few minutes."

"Acknowledged."

Blu'T'Ohm titled his head. "Debris?"

Wil nodded. "Figured we might get an idea of who your secret admirers are." He shrugged. "Until then, we have company coming."

"And you're saying you don't know who was aboard the ship?" the Trollack captain of the lead Qehirg system patrol boat said.

"For the third time, yes," Wil said.

The locals hadn't wanted to board the *Ghost* but seemed to have no problem spending an hour asking the same six questions over and over via the main display on the bridge.

"Yet, they knew you," the Trollack insisted. "They specifically targeted your ship."

"Unless they did an eeny-meeny kind of thing and picked us at random, yeah, I'm assuming they targeted us," Wil said for the tenth or maybe the fifteenth time.

"Please understand that this is deeply troubling," the walleyed security officer said as he plucked at the collar of his Qehirg civil defense uniform.

"I get it. It's really nothing. We get shot at a lot." Wil smiled, hoping that would put the other man at ease.

Stubby, catfish-like whiskers wobbled. "I, uh, that's a little disconcerting. It's just that the GC representative thought that having less of a Peacekeeper presence would lead to fewer, well, things like this happening."

Wil was enjoying watching the poor man squirm. He got it and felt bad for him. The Tarsi that had verbally sparred with Blue had insisted on traveling light, no Peacekeeper cruisers in orbit. No squad of troopers on the stage. Wil knew there was a squad or two somewhere, but they weren't in orbit.

Finally, waving a hand, Wil said, "Look, Lieutenant." He squinted. "It is Lieutenant, right?"

"Lieutenant Commander," the Trollack man corrected, bobbing his carp-like face.

Wil smiled. "We're pretty pressed for time, Lieutenant Commander. There's no hard feelings." He held up a finger to forestall a reply. "We'll send along any data we have, but otherwise we'd really like to get going."

"Of course, Captain. Again, please accept our apologies and please do send along any data. We'll bring these brigands to justice."

"Brigands?" Bennie whispered from his console.

Wil waved a hand to shush him, then to the screen, said, "Will do. Thank you." He turned slightly to look behind him to Cynthia. She closed the channel.

"Captain."

Wil jumped in his seat, then looked around. He glared at Maxim, then looked at the ceiling. "What's up, Gabe?"

"What are we looking at?" Maxim asked.

Once the *Ghost* jumped to FTL, everyone left the bridge to cram into the engineering space at the rear of the ship's common deck.

Bennie stood on his tiptoes to reach for a piece of the debris scattered across the work table. He held it up. "This is a power bus phase modulator." He turned it over. "Most of one, anyway."

Gabe inclined his head. "That is correct." He pointed to a larger piece of metal and wires. "This is a section of the lateral targeting array."

Wil took in the lateral array and the other dozen or so pieces of battle-damaged technology and gull plating the droid brought aboard. He was about to say something when Zephyr said, "That's a Peacekeeper design." She pointed to a piece of metal with wires sticking out of it.

"Indeed," Gabe said.

Maxim picked something up. "This, too. It's a data network repeater node." He looked at Wil, then Gabe. "That ship wasn't PK, though."

"Indeed," Gabe said.

Nic looked around the assembled adults and droid. "Okay... so?"

Standing just inside the door to the engineering space, Blu'T'Ohm said, "So. So it means the Peacekeepers, and by extension the GC Council, are trying to kill me. To silence me! To silence the separatist cause."

"Reading quite a bit into it, aren't you?" Cynthia asked.

"What other interpretation is there?"

"Actually." Gabe held up a finger.

The Harrith man continued, ignoring the droid. "It's not enough to hold public debates. Killing those who speak out ensures their continued control over civilization."

"This was a not a Peacekeeper vessel or operation," Gabe said loud enough to cut off any reply. He picked up a piece of something or other. Wil didn't know what it was. He held it out to the two Palorians. "This appears to be Peacekeeper technology, as well, does it not?" Both nodded. He turned to Blu'T'Ohm, then Wil, twisting the ruined device, separating a dented covering from more components, several of which weren't scorched. "However." He offered the device to their Harrith guest.

Blu'T'Ohm squinted, examining the thing Gabe handed him. Finally, he looked up. "It's Harrith?"

Gabe nodded. "Indeed."

Wil looked at the ceiling. "I need a drink."

"I don't understand," Nic said, looking from adult to adult.

Following the group out of engineering back into the lounge area, Bennie looked at his apprentice. "If he's right," he hitched a little green thumb toward Gabe, "someone on Harrith Prime is trying to make it look like the Peacekeepers are trying to off Blue."

"But, why?" the young Olop girl asked.

Bennie shrugged. "He's annoying. That might be enough reason."

The Harrith man looked down at Bennie. "You're not nice." He shook his head. "This makes no sense. Why? Who?"

Wil reached the kitchenette, heading straight for the refrigeration unit. He removed several bottles of grum and handed them out.

Cynthia took a sip of her drink. "Why? To make the GC look even worse. To look like they're weak and lashing out."

"They nearly killed me. Twice!" the Harrith man replied.

"You're still here, though," Nic offered.

He made a face. Gul'P'Ulo patted his arm. He looked at his assistant and smiled. To Cynthia, he asked, "And the who?"

She shrugged. "Good question. Why would your government want to kill you?"

Blu'T'Ohm rubbed the back of his neck. "They wouldn't. Why would they?"

"You're annoying," Zephyr offered, holding a fist up for Cynthia to bump.

"And encouraging people to leave the GC," Cynthia added.

Before the conversation could degrade, Wil held up a finger. "Seriously. Why would the Harrith want to kill him?"

Maxim took a long drink. "Who could want to point the finger at Harrith?"

Bennie made a face. "Did you just have a mild stroke? We just went over that."

Wil made a lunge for the Brailack hacker, making him flinch. He smirked. "That's right." He turned to the others, awaiting an answer.

Nic scratched her head. "So, someone on Harrith is trying to frame the Peacekeepers for trying to kill him?"

Nods all around.

"What if it's someone trying to frame the Harrith?"

Everyone exchanged a look. Bennie said, "That's dumb."

Wil sighed. "Okay, well this is a mystery for the Scooby gang to solve later. We've got damage that needs addressing."

Bennie spun to the two Harrith. "On your dime."

Blu'T'Ohm sighed. "How long will that take? What's wrong?"

Wil shrugged and turned to Gabe. The droid made a rattling sigh. "Several of our starboard shield emitters are in need of replacement. Three starboard power couplers were overloaded, two of them fused. Until we replace them, the next fight could be our last."

"Caldicoldicot," Zephyr said.

"Bless you," Wil said without turning.

Zephyr sighed. "You dummy."

Before she could continue, Wil snapped his fingers. "The zergling place."

Bennie made a growling noise as he rubbed his palms together. Fried zergling was one his favorite snacks of all time. They even beat out, by a slim margin, the spicy red crunch snack Wil picked up on Earth whenever he could, Cheebo's or something. Bennie stole a bag whenever he could.

Nic grimaced, leaning away from her master. She shook her head. "Gross."

Ignoring the two Knights of Plentallus, Zephyr said, "It's not very far. Few days at most."

"A few days?!" Blu'T'Ohm threw his arms up. "Of course! Who cares about our schedule?"

Gul'P'Ulo cleared her throat. "Actually, sir, our next scheduled forum is on Ashvini II, in a week."

He glared at his young aide. "Traitor."

Wil smiled. "We'll make repairs and lay low until your next appointment. Not a moment longer." He held up three fingers. "Scout's honor."

"What's a scout? Is that a military organization?" Gul'P'Ulo asked.

Wil nodded. "Child warriors. The best of us become Webelos. You don't want to mess with Webelos."

The Harrith woman nodded. "Incredible."

"Good evening. I'm Megan, and this is your GNO News Break." She tossed her blonde hair as she turned to another camera pickup. "Tonight, we have breaking news." She turned to Gulbar' Te.

The Burzzad journalist's three eyes blinked in sequence. He cleared this throat. "We're receiving reports from Cleblon that one of the lead voices in the separatist movement, Blu'T'Ohm Ka-tan has been attacked, possibly more than once." Again, he made a cough-like sound. "By Peacekeepers."

The Burzzad held up a hand. "Before our comm lines are flooded, please remember, right now this is unsubstantiated."

Megan picked up the thread. "We're working on confirming the reports now. We're also attempting to reach Mr. Ka-tan for comment. As far as we can tell, he's gone into hiding."

Her co-anchor nodded. "As you may know, what we all refer to as the separatist movement is more a loose affiliation of outspoken proponents of the dissolution of the Galactic Commonwealth." He cracked a smile. "As you can imagine, getting a comment from such a loose knit group is posing a challenge."

Megan bobbed her head. "We'll be back with more as we get it."

## CHAPTER 15

"You know." Bennie rubbed his chin. "The hold is mostly empty. I bet we could fit a lot of frozen zerglings in here. Bet they sell them in bulk." He turned to the others.

Zephyr looked across the bridge at him. "No."

"But—"

"No!"

Bennie harrumphed and turned back to his console.

On the primary display, Caldicoldicot was a blue-green marble. A couple dozen ships and orbitals were visible. For once, there wasn't a large Peacekeeper task force waiting for them in orbit.

Wil looked over his shoulder. "Cyn, can you get us landing clearance somewhere we can make repairs?"

"Sure thing." She turned her attention to her console.

Zephyr said. "I'll get a punch list from Gabe."

Wil nodded. On the primary display, Caldicoldicot was much closer. "Bennie, can you find us a place to stay? It's two days' travel from here to Ashvini II."

"So...three nights," Bennie said. "On it."

The bridge hatch slid open to admit Blu'T'Ohm. Over his

shoulder, Wil said, "Hey, Blue. We're almost there. Zergling central."

The other man sighed. "I hate zerglings. Fried or otherwise."

"Then don't pet or eat any while we're here," Wil snapped. "Caldicoldicot isn't planning to leave the GC anytime soon. That means no one should expect you here. We'll make repairs. Make plans and get you to Ashvini II in time for your next rally."

The Harrith man said nothing.

"We're clear down to the Leko Spaceport," Cynthia announced. "A couple of mechanics down there had pretty solid reviews and open availability."

Wil nodded as he accepted the nav plot she sent to his station. The all-too-familiar ghostly green arrows appeared on the primary display, guiding the ship toward the orbital track that would eventually bring them into the atmosphere to land at Leko Spaceport.

The Leko Spaceport looked exactly like ninety percent of the galaxy's spaceports: a duracrete ring five kilometers in diameter and nearly forty meters tall. The interior of the ring was a mixed bag of mechanic bays and other shipping-related service providers. The ring's center was a patchwork of landing spaces of various sizes arranged to maximize the interior parking space.

Some spaceport rings were nearly as wide as they were tall, allowing the engineering firms on the first level to bring smaller ships inside. Leko was not like that. The *Ghost* was backed aft section first into the Koni & Rinta Engineering bay. Most of her forward section was sticking out of the workshop's large doors.

"We're only going to be here two rotations," Zephyr repeated to the pair of Tleb in greasy aprons. Neither was actually looking at the Palorian looming over them. The *Ghost* held both mechanics' gaze. She reached out and tapped the nearest little canid alien on the head. "Hey."

"Sorry. Two rotations. No problem," said either Koni or Rinta, she wasn't sure which. They'd introduced themselves in a jumble when they ran out to meet the ship.

She looked both of them over and sighed. She looked to Maxim and shrugged. To Gabe, she said, "Good luck." The droid remained silent, inclining his head.

Wil arrived in a rental hover car. He leaned out the open window. "Ready?"

Zephyr looked at Wil, then the two Tleb. "If I come back in two rotations and the ship isn't repaired, I'll turn you two into decorative coin purses."

One of the small beings took a step back. "No worries. We're on it." They turned to their colleague. "Right?"

The other one nodded and the first turned back toward Zephyr. "See."

Zephyr turned to Maxim and Cynthia and shrugged.

"This?" Blu'T'Ohm looked around the room. "This is where you expect me stay for two days?"

Bennie leaned to the side. "Two beds. She's," he pointed to Gul'P'Ulo, "with you."

"What? No?" both Harrith said as one.

The team booked a series of rooms on the same floor of the Grota 8 Lodge. The room the two Harrith were going to stay in was in the center of the cluster of rooms.

Wil smiled. "Sorry. Easier to keep track of you two if you're in the same room."

"This is outrageous."

Nic clucked. "Better than dead."

Blu'T'Ohm's expression spoke volumes about his current opinion of the young Olop girl.

Wil put his hand on Maxim's shoulder. "Okay, we're gonna go find a weapons market. Probably back at the port. Everyone else, get comfy."

"I've got something to do," Bennie replied. Everyone turned to look at him. "What?" He headed off toward the bank of elevators. Their rooms were on the fifth of twelve floors.

Wil nudged Maxim. "Let's go."

Cynthia watched the two men follow Bennie, then turned to their client and his aide. "Come on. We'll order dinner and something on a pay channel."

"Because I'm paying for this?" Blu'T'Ohm quipped.

Cynthia cocked her head. "I wasn't going to put it that way, but..." She shrugged, extending an arm into the room.

Zephyr, Nic, and Cynthia followed Blu'T'Ohm into the room they'd been assigned.

Gul'P'Ulo looked around. "I need a new line of work." She followed everyone into the room, letting the door slide shut behind her.

Nic picked up the control tablet for the entertainment display. She looked over to Cynthia. "I could go for Privlip. Think they have it here?"

Cynthia raised her arm to check her wristcomm. "Only one way to be sure."

"And fried zerglings," Zephyr said. She caught Blu'T'Ohm's eye. "Sorry. They're good."

Nic nodded. "And you don't want to hear Bennie's complaining if we don't get them."

Cynthia nodded. "He gets screechy."

The man sighed. "Fine, just keep them downwind of me." He shuddered. "Disgusting."

Bennie walked out of the lodge and looked around. They were not in what he thought of as a good part of town. Granted, it was still orders of magnitude better than the neighborhood the Rogue Enterprises building was in back on Fury.

After consulting his wristcomm, he headed off toward an industrial area a few kilometers away. He started to hum.

He had only been walking ten minutes or so when a zergling darted onto the street ahead of him. It turned its long, bone-plate-covered head this way and that. Stubby vestigial wings fluttered as it sniffed the air.

Bennie froze, his hand slowly moving to the hilt of his beam saber. He knew that seeing zerglings in the wild wasn't unheard of but was surprised to see one so close to the city. He glanced to the right. What city was that? He couldn't recall the name and didn't want to risk raising his arm to consult his wristcomm.

The zergling's upper limbs swayed, and the two thick talons at the end of each limb clicked as they moved. The zergling snuffled around a little longer, then darted off, continuing what-ever errand the thing was on.

Bennie watched it move off, then whispered, "Glad they're tasty, because they're ugly as sin." He tapped a few icons on his wristcomm to summon a cab. A single zergling wasn't much of a worry, but they tended to flock, and he wasn't at all confident in his abilities to fend off a zergling swarm.

He reached an intersection and checked his wristcomm. Spotting another Brailack up the street, he said, "Hey. You know where the Guindock Wholesale office is? My map says it's right here," he motioned around the intersection, "but I don't see anything."

The other Brailack, a few shades darker green than Bennie,

came over. He nodded across the street. "Right there. What business do you have with Guindock?"

"My own," Bennie said, waving a hand in front of the other man's face.

The other Brailack clucked. "What're you doing?"

Bennie gave his own tongue click. "Never you mind." He crossed the street.

The inside of Guindock Wholesale was exactly what Bennie expected: dimly lit, shadows in every corner, and stinky. At the back of the room was a single desk with a decrepit Tleb woman sitting behind it. She looked up. "What?"

Bennie strode toward her. "I hear you have the best prices on," he looked around, "special seasonings."

The little woman on the other side of the desk stared at Bennie longer than he felt was comfortable before saying, "You a cop?"

"I look like a cop?"

"Yes."

Bennie clucked. "You look like a cop."

She cocked her head. One upright ear fell flat against her head. "That doesn't make sense."

"You got the stuff or not?"

She squinted at him a moment. "I do. What're you looking for? Spicier or something a little more subtle?"

He rubbed his chin. "I think some of both?"

She hopped off her chair, vanishing from sight, appearing a moment later at the edge of the desk. "Come with me. We have samples." She pushed a door open, leading further into the building.

As Bennie followed, he said, "You can do bulk, deliver to the port?"

"Of course."

"As far as moonlit strolls go, this isn't the worst I've taken," Zephyr said. She and Maxim were walking the perimeter of the lodge. To an outside observer, they looked like a couple enjoying a nighttime stroll. Despite appearances, both were on high alert, scanning their surroundings.

Maxim smiled. "I'm certainly not mad about it."

They reached the edge of the building and turned to follow it toward the small green space that abutted the rear of the lodge.

After a few a steps, Zephyr made a soft noise meant to get Maxim's attention. Without moving his head, he looked to the side, catching her eye. She made a fractional nod toward the green space.

He followed her gesture, spotting someone or something crouched near a shrub.

They continued walking. "I wish I had more than a stunner," Maxim whispered, barely loud enough for Zephyr to hear. "Not sure if it'll even work on a zergling."

Zephyr nodded her agreement. "Yeah, that was a delicious pan fried nuflonog."

"Still there?" he whispered.

She nodded. "Angling toward the rear entrance."

Max made a show of looking at Zephyr, then looking at their surroundings. "So beautiful out here."

They reached a spot where the building's lighting was out and darted away from the building toward the green space.

The moment they had the dark on their side, they slipped fully into their Peacekeeper training. They split up, in order to approach the target from opposing sides in a pincer move.

Using nothing but hand signals in the low light, they moved

as one. Their target had only moved a few steps from where they had seen it initially.

Nodding to his partner, Maxim bolted. From a few dozen meters away, Zephyr did the same. Both of them angled toward their target.

After years of working together both in the Peacekeepers and with Wil and the crew, they knew each other and each other's moves like the back of their respective hands. He went low, she went high.

"Grolack!" the mystery person shouted in surprise as they were tackled to the grass by the two Palorians.

Zephyr had her stunner trained on the person as she stood up. Maxim rolled off and stood. "So glad it was a wild zergling."

"Who the wurrin are you? Why are you assaulting me?!" the interloper demanded. It was a male D'nini. He spied the stunner and threw his arms, all four of them, into the air. "Please don't kill me!"

"Who are you?" Maxim demanded.

"Why are you skulking around out here?" Zephyr added.

The D'nini man looked at his attackers, crossing his lower set of arms. "I'm a reporter."

"Reporters don't skulk," Zephyr replied.

"The good ones do."

"I don't think that's how it works," Maxim said. He added, "You were being creepy." He offered a hand to help the man up. One of the upper arms reached out to grab his.

The man straightened. "That's rude."

Max shrugged.

Zephyr holstered her stunner under her jacket. "Why are you being not creepy outside our hotel?"

"Blu'T'Ohm is in there, right? The leading voice of the separatists?" The two Palorians exchanged a look. "I'll take that as a yes."

"We didn't—" Maxim started.

The man's upper left hand pointed at his chest. "Reporter, remember."

"How'd you know?"

The D'nini man beamed, his lower right hand moving to point at his chest. "Repor—"

"Yeah, yeah. Reporter, we remember," Zephyr growled.

The reporter's face fell. "He posted to GalShare that he was laying low to avoid those who are trying to kill him."

"And he said where he was?" Zephyr spluttered.

"Well, no, of course not!" The lower right arm moved, but Maxim trapped the wrist and stopped it. The reporter frowned. "I have a girl that knows how to hack GalShare posts and get location data out of them."

Maxim rubbed his face with his free hand. "Gods help us."

Zephyr looked at the reporter. "Scram. You're not getting anywhere near him, or a story."

"But—" He saw the look Maxim was giving him, behind Zephyr, and closed his mouth.

As the D'nini reporter headed for a parked air car on the far side of the green space, Zephyr turned to Maxim. "We better tell the others."

"Social media..." the big man sighed.

## CHAPTER 16

Wil sat his closest-thing-to-pizza-the-GC-had down. "Are you shitting me?" Maxim shook his head. Wil turned to Blu'T'Ohm. "Really, man? Social media?"

The team was relaxing on the top floor of the building in a bar and lounge space with an open-air patio taking up half of the space. Several other hotel guests of various races were scattered around the space engaged in their own conversations.

"I don't know what that is, but the movement has an audience, and it's important to keep them informed. That's the whole point. Transparency," the Harrith man's assistant defended.

Cynthia looked at her. "You posted the update?"

The younger woman nodded. "He can't be trusted to remember his password."

Bennie, back from his errand, shook his head. "We shoulda charged double."

"You're already robbing me!" Blu'T'Ohm protested. Bennie shrugged.

Wil sighed. "Think our mysterious friends are as clever as Clark Kent, down there?"

The lights inside the bar area snapped off, followed by the lights strung from poles around the patio area. Several guests gasped as the top floor was plunged into darkness.

"You walked right into that one," Maxim said, checking the charge on his stunner.

Wil nodded as he stood. Scanning the sky, he said, "Don't see any inbound."

Bennie consulted his wristcomm. "I'm in the network. Seeing if anything looks binky."

"Hinky," Wil corrected. He then said, "Let's head back to the rooms. Feeling a bit exposed up here..."

Everyone nodded. As they passed the bartender, a spherical droid with eight spindly limbs like a daddy long-legs, Maxim said, "Put it on 518." The droid chirped, not pausing its polishing of glassware.

The elevator doors slid apart to reveal a dimly lit corridor. "Shouldn't there be emergency lighting?" Nic asked a moment before her beam saber came to life with a *snap-hiss*. The blade bathed the elevator and hallway beyond in pulsing pale red light.

Bennie did the same, adding deep magenta light to the dark hallway. As a group, with one Knight leading and one bringing up the rear, they made their way to the rooms assigned to them.

"Let's hole up in Blue's room," Wil said.

They crept as quietly as possible down the hallway. The architect of the Grota 8 Lodge, for whatever reason, decided that the elevator bay would be at one end of the corridor of rooms, not in the center.

From the back of the group, Nic said, "If the lights are out on this floor—" Behind her, the elevator doors slid open.

"Then they know where we are," Cynthia said, pushing the two Harrith to move faster.

"Damn," Wil sighed, turning to face the elevator, his stunner at the ready.

Nic spun in time to deflect a blaster bolt that would have struck Wil in the chest.

From what was now the back of the group, Bennie shouted, "You're fired. You jinxed it!"

"You can't fire me!" Nic shouted back, dropping to a knee to deflect another bolt of supercharged plasma. Cynthia and Zephyr shoved past Wil to grab their clients, shoving them toward the nearest of their rooms, Bennie still leading the way.

"Move, move, move!" Maxim shouted. He fired his stunner, sending diffuse yellow bolts down the hallway. Wil's fire joined his, lighting up the darkened corridor.

Their attackers fell back briefly, giving the three defenders time to retreat.

Slamming the door to the room closed, Wil said, "They won't fall for that again."

"Stupid planet and their rules about personal weapons," Maxim growled, holding his stunner up to check the remaining charge.

Bennie clucked, holding out his beam saber hilt.

"Lucky you, your weapon looks like a sex toy," the big Palorian said.

"How's that help us?" Cynthia asked before Bennie could reply to Maxim. "No offense, but I'm not sure you two can take out a trained hit team."

Nic nodded. "Deflecting single shots is one thing. If they concentrate their fire, no way."

The team's Brailack hacker sighed, igniting his saber. He made a shooing gesture then plunged the blade into the floor.

"Like with drunk wizard guy," Wil said, nodding his approval.

"Sir Jarek Ruus," Bennie corrected, as a meter-wide circle

fell into the room below. Someone down there screamed. Bennie leaned over the hole. "Sorry." He motioned the others toward the hole.

"Who are you people?" a terrified Ruknak woman said, sitting up in bed.

"Sorry, ma'am," Wil said.

"Excuse me!"

Zephyr sighed. "Sorry, sir. We'll see ourselves out."

Nic bowed. "If you could call the local security forces, that'd be swell."

As Wil reached the door, the Ruknak man shouted, "Of course I'll call the authorities! You just cut a hole in the ceiling."

A blaster bolt struck the floor. Maxim and Zephyr each fired up into the room above, flooding the space with yellow stunner blasts. There was a muffled shout and a thud.

Wil had the door open and was waving everyone out. Cynthia went first.

More weapons fire rained down, sending the Ruknak man scrambling from his bed.

"Nice pj's." Bennie smirked. He turned to head for the door but yelped as Maxim lifted him off his feet.

"Time to go on the offensive." He nodded to Zephyr, who fired her stunner into the room above once more.

Maxim stepped under the hole with a wriggling and cursing Bennie firmly in his grasp. She stopped firing. He tossed. Bennie screamed.

"I hate you!" Bennie shouted as he flew up into the room they'd just left.

Everyone looked up as the sound of a beam saber activating preceded frantic screaming and the occasional blaster shot.

The screaming subsided, and nothing happened. Finally, Bennie poked his head over the edge of the hole to glare at Maxim. "I hate you."

"You did it." Blu'T'Ohm exhaled.

Bennie shrugged. "Turned out a beam-saber-wielding Brailack flying through the air is pretty distracting." He saw Maxim's mouth open. "But you still suck." He pointed at the big man. "Catch me." He vanished from the hole only to appear, falling through it, a second later. Maxim caught him.

"They're dead?" Wil asked.

Bennie shook his head. "Ran...well, limped, off."

Several hours later, after paying to relocate the shaken Ruknak insurance salesman to a suite several floors up, moving Blu'T'Ohm and Gul'P'Ulo to a room without a hole in the floor, and giving their statements to the local authorities, the team was crowded into the room Wil and Cynthia shared.

Wil pulled a glove out from under the bed, holding it up for the others to see.

"Where'd you get that?" Cynthia took the glove.

He nodded toward Bennie. "When we got back to Blue and Gulp's room, I saw it by the door. One of the attackers must have dropped it."

"Please don't call me that," the young Harrith woman said.

"There wasn't a hand in it?" Nic asked. When everyone turned to her, expressions of revulsion on their faces, she said, "He has a habit of cutting off hands and arms." She nodded to Bennie. The Brailack looked up from the tablet he was fiddling with and shrugged.

Cynthia offered it to Zephyr. "Looks PK." The other woman turned the piece of clothing over in her hand and few times.

Maxim shook his head. "Wrong sidearms." Everyone turned

to him. "Whoever these folks were, they weren't Peacekeepers." He nodded to Zephyr's hand. "Despite the cosplay."

Blu'T'Ohm put his face in his hands. "But they wanted us to think it was the Peacekeepers." He looked up. "Let me guess, the sidearms were Harrith designs."

Maxim shook his head. "I'm good, but not that good. Never got a good enough look at them. I just know they weren't standard PK gear. Could have been from anywhere." He looked at Bennie.

The Brailack shook his head. "Too dark, and there was too much movement. Never got a good look."

Zephyr set the glove down. "I think it's time we got to the bottom of this."

Wil stifled a yawn. "What've you got in mind?"

"Max and I go to Harrith Prime. We've got the tech from the gun boat. We track down the manufacturer."

Without looking up from what he was doing, Bennie said, "Makes sense. Probably the only way we stop playing defense."

Everyone looked at him, then at each other, sharing a collective shrug. Wil said, "He's right. You should take him and Nic. Get back to Fury, pick up the *Rocinante*."

This time Bennie looked up. "*Rocky Nontee*."

Wil shook his head. "Not calling it that. That's nonsense."

Blu'T'Ohm raised his hand. "If it's all the same, I'd feel safer with the Knight and his apprentice protecting me."

Wil rolled his eyes, spotting Bennie's ear-hole-to-ear-hole grin. "Fine. Take Gabe." He glared at Bennie. "They're still taking your shit heap."

The Brailack grumbled. "Fine."

Wil looked around. "Okay. Cyn and I will stick with green bean and Nic, keeping Blue and Gulp safe."

"Gul'P'Ulo," the young Harrith woman corrected. She sighed when she saw that Wil had ignored her.

He continued. "Be careful. If we're right, and it's someone on Harrith Prime, they're not gonna want to be exposed." The two Palorians nodded.

Wil looked at their Harrith clients. "Okay, let's hit the sack. Team 2 can take off in the morning. I don't want to pull Gabe off supervising the engineers any earlier than we need to. We're leaving day after tomorrow, so that should be fine. I can't see them making a run at us twice." He looked around. "I'll take first watch."

Bennie looked at Nic. "We'll take the next."

"We will?" Nic asked.

Bennie nodded.

Maxim stood. "We'll walk you to your room," he said to Blu'T'Ohm and Gul'P'Ulo.

The pair nodded their thanks and exited Wil and Cynthia's room.

The next morning, Zephyr and Max set off back to the spaceport. They booked passage on the fastest shuttle they could find. Unlike their previous outings via public transportation, the trip wouldn't take long and the odds of a child spilling sticky food on Zephyr was nil. Fury wasn't far from Caldicoldicot, so fast shuttles making the trip back and forth were abundant.

Gabe met them at the boarding terminal. "Good morning. I take it there were no further incidents?"

Zephyr shook her head. "Nope. Whoever our friends are, they're trying to point fingers without attracting too much attention."

Max nodded. "Everything good with the *Ghost*?"

The twice redesigned ex-engineering droid made a shrugging motion. This iteration of his body had better range of motion, so while not perfect, the shrug at least looked like a shrug. "The odds of the ship falling apart midflight are now closer to zero."

The two Palorians exchanged a look. Zephyr said, "Uh...But not actually zero?"

Gabe stared at her. "I am not a miracle worker." He turned and entered the terminal.

Zephyr turned to Maxim, eyes wide. His expression matched hers.

"What about your little friends?" Maxim called after the droid.

Without turning, Gabe said, "Both Tleb are still alive." He paused. "That...was a struggle."

They followed their mechanical friend into the public boarding terminal. "I hope no one drops a snack food on me this time," Zephyr said, sighing as the terminal doors slid closed behind them.

The terminal was like just about every other spaceport terminal in, and outside of, the GC. Outbound travelers went through simple security screenings. Inbound travelers were off to the side, passing through customs.

The rest of the cavernous space was food, drink, concession vendors, and seating. The trio found seats off to the side to wait for their shuttle.

Zephyr checked the large display high up on the wall above the various departure doors. "Only about ten microtocks."

Maxim looked up Gabe. "So, how're things back on Arcadia? You haven't visited in a while."

Gabe emitted a rattling sigh. "Tiring. I have discovered that I have no appetite for politics or power."

"You'd be the perfect leader, then," Zephyr said, smiling.

The droid tilted his head to the side. "While that may be true, and my colleagues on Arcadia have certainly put in the effort...No."

Maxim nodded. "Fair enough. Sometimes just having a homeworld you never see is enough." His smile didn't reach his eyes.

A day after Gabe and the Palorians departed Caldicoldicot, Wil and the others were looking at the *Ghost.* The little Tleb engineers had done an admirable job. The pair was excitedly bouncing from paw to paw as they walked Wil and the others around the ship.

"You even cleaned her," Wil said. He leaned down to offer his hand to the nearest of the little canid aliens. When the engineer—he had yet to determine the genders of the two engineers—didn't move to answer his invite to high five, he lowered his hand.

Bennie smirked. "You suck." Wil scowled at him.

The engineer nodded their head. "It looked like no one had ever washed her. We felt bad."

"So gross," the other added, head bobbing up and down.

Wil frowned and stood back up. "Anyhow. You got everything done?" He knew the answer already; Gabe had sent a comprehensive update before boarding the shuttle for Fury. Thankfully, the droid included a summary, which was all Wil read.

The first dwarfish engineer nodded. They had one ear that didn't stand up and it bobbed in time with their head. "Yes. Mostly. The ordinance you ordered is in the hold. We do not deal with weapons systems."

Wil nodded. "No problem."

The tiny being looked at its wristcomm, then leaned over to show its partner the screen. The second one nodded. The first swiped on the screen. "Your bill."

Wil's wristcomm beeped. Looking at it, his eyes grew to the size of saucers, and he coughed. "Oh my."

Bennie reached up and pulled Wil's arm down to look at the screen. He turned to the two small engineers, easily a head shorter than him. "I didn't realize they let criminals set up shop in the ports here on Caldicoldicot."

The two little people tittered to themselves in yips and growls that Wil's translation nanites couldn't comprehend. Finally, the nearer said, "We could offer a ten percent discount. On account of the uniqueness of your ship and adding its class to our list of ship types serviced."

"Fifteen," Bennie replied.

More hushed yipping and growling. "Acceptable." The pair bowed in unison.

Bennie smiled and looked up at Wil. "Pay the man."

"That one's a man?" Wil asked. Bennie nodded. He accessed the company account on his wristcomm, and paid two mini engineers. "You'll tow her out?"

"Of course." The one he now knew was male scampered off to hop into the gravlift vehicle used to move spacecraft into and out of the repair bay. A low rumble filled the bay as the forceful gravlifts powered up.

Twenty minutes later, the *Ghost* was leaving Caldicoldicot's atmosphere.

Alone on the bridge, Wil watched the stars flicker into the rainbow lines of FTL. After securing their departure clearance, Cynthia went down the corridor to the common deck to get lunch started. Wil had no idea where Nic and Bennie, or their two Harrith guests, were.

He looked around the bridge. The four stations that lined the perimeter, two to a side, were dark. Standby mode. Technically, the ship could be operated solely from the pilot and command station. After doing for that for almost two years, Wil still shivered thinking about those days, by far the darkest of his life.

"So much has changed," he said in a low voice. He looked over his left shoulder to the station Cynthia had claimed as her own. To think that when they met, she worked for two of the more dangerous criminals in the GC. She'd tried to kill him... two, or was it three, times? He couldn't recall, and he didn't care.

He sat up straighter, inhaling. "What a ride." He leaned forward, activating the autoflight system, watching as his station dimmed and the flight controls receded back into their housings. "I hope she made spam sandwiches."

Wil joined the others in the lounge. He inhaled. "Spam sandwiches."

Cynthia turned from the cooktop. "Last two cans."

Blu'T'Ohm looked up from the tablet he and Gul'P'Ulo were hunched over. "I'm sorry, what is *spam*?"

From the sofa, Bennie said, "No one knows. It's an Earth thing." He rubbed his stomach. "But it's delicious."

The Harrith man turned to Wil. "You're exporting Earth delicacies before your people have joined the GC?" He raised an eyebrow, causing the scar that ran down the side of his face to crinkle. "Mercenary."

Stepping off the shuttle, Zephyr looked over her shoulder. "This is some muhgrolacking boo dren."

Behind her, Maxim was doing his best to stifle the grin that threatened to split his face. Two tocks into their trip, the Malkorite child in front of them had stood up to check out her new seatmates and stumbled, sending her slush ice all over Zephyr's shirt.

"I don't recall crossing paths with any witches. Did I accidentally insult one somewhere? Is this a curse?" She plucked at the now dried and crinkly garment.

Gabe followed the pair off the shuttle. "The odds of something like this happening twice in as many shuttle trips are truly astounding."

"That doesn't make me feel better," she growled.

Flagging down a hover taxi, Gabe said, "It was not meant to."

Maxim, nearly in tears, slid in after his partner. "We'll be home in ten microtocks. You can shower while Gabe and I prep the *Nontee*."

She scowled, but nodded. Maxim looked at Gabe, who made a point of looking at the cab's ceiling.

Ten microtocks later, Maxim and Gabe were in the *Rocky Nontee*'s cargo hold, moving crates to the ship's side to secure them.

"This should be enough to get us by. It's not a long trip to Harrith Prime," Maxim said, securing a medium sized cargo module labeled *perishables*. The *Nontee*'s kitchen area was even smaller than the *Ghost*'s, so food had to be stored in crates in the hold.

Gabe nodded, both arms over his head, working on a bundle of thick cables. "Indeed. Unless you and Zephyr plan to double your body mass enroute, that should be sufficient."

Zephyr's voice came over the ceiling-mounted speakers. "We all set?"

Maxim looked up. "Yup."

The forward cargo ramp released a pained squeal as it rose.

Maxim looked at Gabe. The droid shrugged. "Bennie does not take care of his possessions." He headed for the rear of the cargo hold toward the small engineering space.

Maxim grabbed the ladder at the front of the ship. The *Nontee* was only two decks, so whoever originally built her decided a ladder was sufficient. Bennie had added a small lift platform to the ladder, but it wasn't rated for much more than the Brailack's weight.

He leaned into the flight deck, spying Zephyr half sitting, half straddling the pilot's chair. "That looks...well, something."

She looked over her shoulder. "Don't start."

*PART 4*

## CHAPTER 17

"Captain, these air cars are expensive," Blu'T'Ohm said, climbing into the backseat of the latest rental.

"They're also more flexible than ground vehicles," Cynthia said. She appreciated Wil's more tactical thinking but suspected it was less tactical and more *air car so shiny*. She shrugged. It didn't really matter to her. For all she cared, he could just be doing it to milk the expense account.

Nic looked over to the young Harrith woman next to her. "You doing okay?"

"I mean, I've never been almost killed this many times," Gul'P'Ulo answered. "But I believe in the movement." She shrugged. "So..."

Nic was silent a moment, chewing her lower lip as she fidgeted with her beam saber hilt. This was version three of her design and didn't suffer from the faults her previous design did, like randomly activating. "Because Harrith was already independent?"

The other woman shrugged. "Partially. I mean Harrith is a good example of a thriving society that doesn't rely on the GC for security, safety, or anything else." She inhaled. "But also because the GC is just so rotten. The Tarsi rule it like their own massive empire. Sure, they let other societies have seats on the council, but at the end of the day, it's the Tarsi and the Palorians telling everyone else how to live."

Nic nodded. She wasn't sure yet how she felt about all this. "I hadn't really thought about it like that," she admitted. Olop was a member of the GC and seemed fine.

"We'll be at the rally in a minute," Wil announced. Ahead of the air car, a large open-air arena was growing in size.

He guided the vehicle to the private landing pad that hung off the side of the arena. Several other vehicles were already parked on the football-field-sized platform.

He looked over his shoulder. "This a solo appearance and one of your forums?"

Blu'T'Ohm straightened his shirt, brushing invisible crumbs from one sleeve. "A forum. Myself, a representative of the GC, the planetary governor, and..." He shrugged. "I can't recall who the fourth guest is." He was in a bespoke suit with a sash draped across his right shoulder that landed perfectly on his left hip. Several little doodads adorned the sash, none of which Wil could discern the purpose or value of.

The air car set down on the pad, the side door sliding open before the vehicle's repulsorlifts finished powering down. Gul'P'Ulo followed Blu'T'Ohm out. The pair was greeted by a nervous looking Trollack woman in a neon blue sari-type garment with a hole in the back that allowed her stubby tail to move freely.

The organizer of the event bowed to her two guests and looked askance at the others, her transparent eyelids flicking. Turning back to Blu'T'Ohm, she said, "Welcome, welcome. We're so glad to have you join us. Especially in light of your recent troubles. So terrifying." She turned to Gul'P'Ulo.

"Thank you for keeping us posted on your availability." The young Harrith woman nodded.

Wil cleared his throat. "We should probably move indoors."

"Of course, of course," the Trollack woman agreed, waving an arm toward the building's entry.

Following the Trollack woman and their clients, Wil said, "Bennie, you and Nic stick close to Blue and Guido."

From the front of the procession, the younger of the two Harrith said, "Gul'P'Ulo."

Wil nodded. "That's what I said."

"It's not."

He waved a hand. "Cyn and I will work the crowd. You two, be visible."

Bennie nodded. "Can do." It still caught Wil off guard when the usually surly and argumentative Brailack agreed peacefully with something. It worried him.

"Been a while," Maxim said, stepping off the *Rocky Nontee*'s forward cargo ramp. He looked up into the bustling sky overhead. Ships and planetary craft buzzed all over.

He rubbed his lower back as he looked around the spaceport. The two-day trip from Fury had been anything but comfortable. Nic and Bennie had replaced the more standard-sized beds, chairs, and just about everything else in the ship, with smaller Brailack- and Olop-sized fixtures.

It had been a long two days.

"We're gonna need to have Gabe install some standard-sized gear in this bucket?" Zephyr asked, joining him at the foot of the short ramp. The *Rocky Nontee* had two other cargo deck openings, one each port and starboard, but they didn't have ramps.

"I guess we're lucky the interior isn't floor-to-ceiling carpet with glitter balls on every deck," Maxim said. Zephyr shuddered, nodding her head.

Gabe joined them. "The ship is in standby." He nodded to an approaching ground car. "I took the liberty of contacting an old friend."

The matte black vehicle slid to a stop on nearly silent gravlifts. As it settled onto subtle skids that deployed as it lowered to the duracrete, the side door rose like a wing.

Maxim and Zephyr both broke into smiles as they spied who exited the vehicle.

"Commander Shre' Ta'n," Zephyr said, meeting the woman halfway between the *Nontee* and the ground car.

The Harrith woman inclined her head as her large eyes blinked. "It's Admiral now." She smiled. "It's good to see you both." She looked past the two Palorians to Gabe. "Gabe?" She squinted. "You look...different."

Zephyr chuckled. "You should've seen the last version. Like Wil and Maxim had a chrome love child."

"You said it was not offensive," Gabe said, stepping forward to offer his arm to the Harrith woman.

The Admiral opened her mouth, but closed it when Zephyr said, "Long story. Another time." Admiral Shre' Ta'n nodded.

The Harrith woman held out a hand toward the ground car. "Gabe said it was urgent?"

Riding back into the downtown core of Drotu, the planetary capital, Zephyr looked around. "So. Admiral?"

The other woman smiled a big, toothy smile. "Thanks in no small part to you and the rest of your team."

Maxim returned the smile. "Us?"

"After the...what did GNO keep calling it? The Harrith Incident? The Harrith Navy was in tatters."

Zephyr smiled. "I remember. We spent half a cycle as privateers picking up the slack." Maxim nodded at the memory. Gabe remained motionless.

The Harrith woman nodded. "Well, it took a few cycles, but after our forces got back on their feet, we needed experienced commanders." She leaned back and shrugged. "My part in the final act of that whole thing was remembered." She reached up, running a hand along the rank insignia on her left shoulder board.

"You miss it? Being on the bridge of a ship?" Maxim asked.

Shre' Ta'n nodded. "Every day." She shrugged. "Such is life." She grinned. "It's not the forward screen of a bridge, but the view from my office doesn't suck."

The vehicle pulled to a stop outside a massive glass building.

"Nice digs," Maxim observed, straining to look up to see the entire building.

Gabe leaned over Maxim to peer up at the building. "Impressive."

"Harrith Naval Command moved here two cycles ago." The side door rose. As they all filed out, she added, "The original complex was bombed early in our conflict with the Quilant. They broke through our orbital defenses. Thankfully, the casualties were minimal. By the grace of the many gods."

She pointed to the large front doors. "Come on. I can order lunch."

Max cocked his head. "I could eat."

They followed her inside and through several security check points before stepping into an immaculate elevator.

Admiral Shre' Ta'n's office was three floors from the top of the building. Reaching her office, she pointed out the window. "You can see my house from up here."

"You can see all the houses from up there," Maxim said, taking in the view. The naval command tour was at least two hundred stories tall and dwarfed all of its immediate neighbors. "You know. I don't think I ever really stopped to appreciate the architecture of the city," he added, gesturing to a building a few blocks away that took up an entire block and reached almost as tall as the command building. Its dark gray with red-streaked stone set it apart from the more modern buildings of the district.

The Admiral nodded. "Drotu is one of our oldest cities. Most of the old buildings were replaced over time, but a few," she nodded to the dark gray and red building, "like the Tulf Dalmo, are set aside as historic structures." She moved to take a seat behind her desk. "I was born in Inid, just to the north." She looked at the trio sitting across from her. "But you didn't come here to discuss Harrith architecture."

Gabe inclined his head. "Correct."

"This is boring," Nic said over the shared team channel.

Across the stage, Bennie scowled. "Apprentice..."

She clucked. "Don't you 'apprentice' me. This is boring. I saw you over there sleeping."

"I was not sleeping."

"Yes, you were. You drooled."

"Children," Cynthia chided.

The panel on stage was, as far as Wil could tell, going well. The panelists were all calm and collected and interacting with each other respectfully. Nothing like the last few presidential debates Wil watched before his untimely departure from Earth and the Sol system. Given the turmoil on Earth lately, he could only imagine what more recent debates looked like. Probably closer to cage matches.

Cynthia and Wil were moving through the crowd from opposite sides. The arena was like those on Earth, except that there were wide walkways in front of each row of seats. Guess it was only humans that tried to make enjoying things in arenas miserable. Wil scoffed. "Downright luxurious." He was on the second level, moving section to section. It was hard to spot shady or ill intent when every other face was one Wil had never even seen before.

Wil was moving to the next section of seats when a face caught his attention. It wasn't a race he had encountered before, which wasn't saying much. The GC spanned thousands of light years, and even with the number of jobs the team had done over the last ten years or so, they really had only traversed a small portion of it. Add in the new members, affiliate members, and nonaligned societies like Harrith, and well...It was more common to not recognize the race.

He raised his wristcomm and snapped a pic. "What is this and are they giving off shady vibes or not shady vibes?"

Cynthia sighed. "She's a Klini, and no, not shady vibes." She chuckled, listening to the panel. "Her expression makes me think she isn't a fan of Blue."

"Can't blame her," Nic said.

Wil smiled and looked across the arena to the stage. He could see the young Olop shuffling from foot to foot at the back of the stage.

Wil continued on to the next section.

"Hey, Cynthia," Bennie said. "I've got a weird looking Rigellian making his way toward the stage. Stage left."

"Which side is that? My left?" she asked as she started to slide through the crowd.

"No, my left. I'm on stage. Hence, stage left." He rolled his eyes. "His hand is in his jacket."

"Someone was a theater kid," Wil quipped, trying to spot

the suspicious alien. He glanced to the stage to see Bennie make a sort of subtle rude gesture.

"I think I see him." From the crowd, she looked up at the stage, meeting Bennie's gaze and nodding toward the tall, pale, red-skinned man in the jacket. The Brailack gave a subtle nod.

The Rigellian man ahead of her was slowly making his way toward the stage, weaving between onlookers. She slid up to the man, her hand moving to rest on the forearm inside the jacket.

"Hi there," she purred.

"What the...Who?" The man's pupil-less eyes went wide.

She eased his hand out of the jacket. "Not really important." She gave him a gentle nudge away from the stage. "Why don't we take this outside?"

"No. I need. But, no..." he stammered.

"No, you don't." The claws in the fingers of the hand on his elbow slid out of the sheaths in her fingertips, just enough to push through the fabric of his jacket sleeve.

He winced. Then he nodded and let her guide him to the edge of the arena floor.

In her ear, Wil said, "Security is on the other side of the doors to your right."

"Copy that," she said, guiding her new friend to the doors.

## CHAPTER 18

The Rigellian man turned out to be just an upset employee of one of the panelists that wasn't Blu'T'Ohm. He wasn't carrying a gun but did have a vial of some type of foul-smelling ointment he intended to splash all over his ex-employer.

The panelists never noticed Cynthia's intercept, and the rest of the event went smoothly. She patted the man's upper-most shoulder and sent him on his way.

Cynthia reached the stage in time to hear the organizer insist that the panelists all join her at a reception for them and VIPs from the community. Wil gave Blu'T'Ohm a slight nod.

The gathering was in the large private party space at the top of the arena. "At least the food is good," Bennie said around a mouth full of what looked to Wil like an egg roll.

Cynthia turned from watching Blu'T'Ohm chatting with a Kilden man in a bright pink suit. "Save some for the rest of us."

He stuck his egg-roll-covered tongue out. "Snooze, you lose."

Wil glanced over to the local security team standing near the door. They had butted heads with the locals upon entering the arena. Having to let him and the team into the mixer had galled them. Bennie and Nic wouldn't relinquish their beam sabers, nor would Wil and Cynthia hand over the stunner pistols they were carrying. That had galled them further.

He hated not carrying his trusty old pulse pistol, but with everything going on in the GC, worlds that were normally pretty tolerant of personal weapons being everywhere were taking a sterner stance.

It didn't help that, with Blue as a customer, they were frequenting more Tier 2 worlds than he was comfortable with. He found Tier 2 planets to be too snooty. Too heavily monitored. Too well protected. Tier 2 worlds were no fun.

"Just don't embarrass us. Please," he said to Bennie as the Brailack shoved another egg roll thing into his mouth. He sighed.

Nic and Gul'P'Ulo were in the opposite corner, by far the youngest people in the room. Nic watched the crowd, then said, "Ever worry you'll get killed during these things?"

The Harrith woman turned to the younger Olop. "Well, not until just now. Thanks for that." Nic's face fell. Gul'P'Ulo continued, "I try to not think about that. The cause is so important. I mean, I don't want to be a martyr, but I also think it's worthwhile to show GC worlds that life without the GC's fingers in every aspect of things is possible." She gave a mirthless chuckle. "It's only until recently that this job felt dangerous."

"I admire your conviction," Nic said.

"You seem pretty into your Knight thing. That takes conviction, no?"

Nic shrugged. "I guess. It's less exciting than I thought it'd be."

"Being shot at, more than once, since I've met you isn't exciting enough?" The other woman shook her head. "I think once is more than enough, thank you."

Nic nodded. "Is it weird that I'm getting used to it?"

"Yes. Very."

Lunch was a delicious catered affair from a local restaurant down the road from the naval command building. Gabe, per usual, took up position off to one side of the room, staring out the floor-to-ceiling windows.

After taking a bite of something she had called adeel, Shre' Ta'n said, "I'm honestly surprised you all are still alive." She shook her head. "After the thing here, the privateering, the thing with that monster ship that wanted to wipe all biological life out, and whatever else. You're defying some serious odds."

Maxim dipped his head. "I don't know if it's a human thing, or a Wil thing, but I think he's a good luck charm."

Zephyr looked over to him. "You can never tell him that."

"Oh, gods no. He'd never let it go."

Watching the two Palorians, the Harrith woman chuckled as she shook her head. "So, time hasn't dulled our human friend any?"

Zephyr clucked. "Not even a little. He's married now but seems to be corrupting his partner more than she's blunting his nonsense."

The other woman's eyes bugged wider. "That's... surprising."

Both Palorians nodded their agreement.

Maxim offered, "We didn't see it coming, either."

"Especially since the first time they met she tried to kill him," Zephyr added.

"And us," Maxim said, nodding along.

The Admiral shook her head. "Sounds exciting."

From his place near the window, Gabe said, "Exhausting would be more accurate."

The trio exchanged a look, smiling. They enjoyed their

meals for a bit until Shre' Ta'n finally broke the amicable silence. "So. What brings you three here? Guessing it's not to catch up."

"It is not," Gabe confirmed.

Maxim shook his head. "We're hoping not a massive life or death thing. We're working with a Harrith guy, name of Blu'T'Ohm. Scar along his face." His finger traced the path Blu'T'Ohm's scar followed.

Shre' Ta'n nodded. "I know him. He actually served with me aboard the *Baxu Ahvil*. He was a sublieutenant, if I recall."

"He's a popular voice for the separatist movement now," Zephyr offered.

The other woman sighed, looking up at the ceiling. "I'm aware." She shook her head. "It tracks."

"Oh?"

The Admiral nodded. "After the Harrith Incident, he—and hundreds of thousands of others—were...let's say...angry with the GC."

Zephyr shrugged. "Pretty understandable. They tried to destabilize this sector by driving you to war with your neighbors so you'd be forced to join the GC."

"Or be consumed in a war that the Peacekeepers could later put an end to," Gabe added.

"Pretty grolacked, for sure," Maxim said.

The Harrith woman nodded her agreement. "Yeah. That didn't really fade, well...ever. Most folks have at least moved on. Our society is thriving. Our military is fully recovered. All things being equal, the Harrith people are doing okay. The Harrith Incident is a bad memory."

She took a bite of her meal, then continued, "The few that haven't gotten over it, Blu'T'Ohm among them, have been staunch anti-GC provocateurs. They split time here speaking out against joining and abroad encouraging others to withdraw."

"So, he's a true believer," Maxim said.

She nodded. "In every possible way. He won't stop until the GC collapses."

"Or he's killed," Maxim said.

"What, now?" The Harrith woman leaned forward.

The two Palorians shared a look. Zephyr broke the silence. "Guess the news hasn't reached here. There have been several attempts on his life."

"Really? By whom?"

"That is the question," Gabe offered from his place near the window. He turned to the others. "The initial attacks were carried out to point the finger at the Peacekeepers."

"Point the finger?" the Harrith woman repeated. She tilted her head. "Meaning?"

Gabe looked at his friends, who nodded as one. He said, "We believe the attacks originated here on Harrith Prime."

The woman across the table reared back as if struck. "What? How? Who?" She looked from the two Palorians to Gabe. "Really?"

He stepped forward, a series of whirs and clicks emanating from behind him. He reached up and over his shoulder, producing a small case. Maxim and Zephyr cleared space on the table as Gabe laid out random bits of technology.

"What's all this?" Shre' Ta'n asked. Her eyes roamed the various items scattered across the table.

Gabe proceeded to identify each piece of tech, highlighting the Harrith details as he got to them.

The Admiral swore.

"Can you believe that rent-a-cop? Getting in my face like that?" Wil complained. The team was walking through the public lobby of the spaceport. After one of the arena security officers got into a shouting match with Wil, he insisted they all—including Blu'T'Ohm and Gul'P'Ulo—leave.

"This gonna be a thing now?" Bennie asked.

Wil made to swipe at him, but the team hacker dodged out of reach, then wagged a finger at his friend as he made a *tsk* noise.

"It's just rude. I mean, we're not rent-a-cops, but we are running security. He could have not treated us like we didn't belong."

Cynthia shrugged. "Who cares?"

"Wil, obviously," Nic said.

Wil scowled at all of them. "Whatever." He looked around. "This way."

Blu'T'Ohm fell in next to Cynthia. "You all *have* done this before, right?"

She looked over at him.

The group exited the lobby into a short hallway, then stepped out into the main open area of the spaceport. The roar of a midsized freighter lifting off drowned out any conversation.

When the ship was far enough overhead that shouting wasn't required, Cynthia replied, "Security? Sure. Here and there. Sometimes."

"Sometimes?" Blu'T'Ohm asked.

"Here and there?" Gul'P'Ulo asked.

Wil, Bennie, and Nic continued out into the open air of the landing field. The sky overhead had been darkening all day. Thunder rumbled off in the distance. Wil looked up just as the first drops began to strike the duracrete. He turned to the others, exiting the ring wall structure. "Gonna rain, hurry up," he called.

Cynthia and the two Harrith exited the structure. The *Ghost* was parked a couple hundred meters away along curve of the spaceport's interior wall. Shorter term parking was out near the center.

As Wil, Bennie, and Nic approached the *Ghost*, a being in what looked like Peacekeeper armor stepped out from behind a sleek lime green and pale blue personal yacht parked next to their ship.

Wil tensed. Bennie nodded to the armored individual. "Nice ship. You pick the color scheme? This year's Peacekeeper chic?" His hand dropped to the beam saber hilt on his hip.

Nic fell back a step or two, her own hand on the hilt of her weapon. She turned enough to meet Cynthia's gaze, stopping the other woman in her tracks. Cynthia gave her young friend a fractional nod.

Three more armored individuals stepped out from behind the yacht. Wil glanced at the *Ghost*, only twenty meters away. So close, but so far. No one except the two Knights had any real weapons. Well, the two Knights and the three fake Peacekeepers.

The lead fake Peacekeeper raised their rifle and fired. The plasma bolt struck a purple energy blade meters before it would have struck Blu'T'Ohm in the chest.

The Rogue Enterprises team sprang into action. Cynthia forced the two Harrith next to her down to the duracrete, her stunner drawn and aiming at the nearest attacker. Stun bolts rippled off the nearest fake Peacekeeper's armor.

Bennie dropped to a crouch and sprinted to close the gap between him and the shooter before the attacker could process what was happening. The bright magenta energy blade slashed up, carving a glowing slice into the duracrete before arcing up into the midsection of the shooter, bisecting him from hip to arm pit.

Wil dropped to one knee, unleashing a volley of stun blasts that rippled as they washed over the armored attackers.

"This will be easy," one of them said, raising their rifle to take aim at Wil, only to be hit in the helmet by a red-hued bolt of energy that burned through the face plate.

"Easy, huh?" Nic smirked from several meters away.

"Go!" Wil shouted to Cynthia, who nodded and, in a crouch, ushered the two Harrith with her around the far side of the garishly painted yacht, toward the *Ghost.*

Wil tapped an icon on his wristcomm. "Self-Defense Protocol 2, engage. Cynthia has guests."

"Acknowledged," the ship's computer replied. Wil darted behind a trash receptacle as the remaining armored attacker opened fire.

From several compartments lining the underside of the *Ghost,* antipersonnel blasters deployed. The fighting was out of the range of the weapons, but Protocol 2 was designed to protect the crew and guests. As soon as Cynthia, Gul'P'Ulo, and Blu'T'Ohm came within the ship's small arms weapons' range, the various weapons would protect them.

Wil looked at Bennie crouched behind a similar trash can. He pointed to his stunner, then to Bennie, then made a flailing motion with both arms.

The Brailack raised an eyebrow ridge, mouthing the word *what.*

Wil repeated the gesture, mouthing the word *distraction.* He waved both arms in the air.

Three more fake Peacekeepers stepped from behind the flashy yacht.

Nic, several paces behind them, took aim at another of their attackers and toggled her beam saber hilt to blaster mode. The blasts were the same high energy plasma that created the weapon's blade. It took several seconds between charges for the capacitor to recharge.

She watched her two colleagues bicker and gesticulate while her weapon charged. When the small light she'd added to it in her last round of improvements lit up, she darted to her feet, roared, and fired at the nearest fake Peacekeeper. The blast struck the attacker in the shoulder.

Wil and Bennie watched in awe, then joined her. The best Wil could manage was sending mildly distracting stun blasts rippling across their attacker's armor.

The distraction was enough for Bennie to dart into the crowd and slash ankles and the backs of legs, crippling attackers one after another. Nic joined him, her beam saber back in sword mode.

"Haven't we done this already?" Gul'P'Ulo sighed from the bench she was sharing with Nic, Bennie, and Cynthia.

Nic shrugged. "You get used to it."

Wil and Blu'T'Ohm were speaking with the local security captain about the attack.

Like every other attack so far, when the attackers realized they weren't going to be able to complete their mission, they gathered their wounded and fled. Five minutes before the locals arrived, a nondescript but clearly military transport roared out of the spaceport and burned hard for orbit, followed by the garishly painted yacht. According to the security forces, the two ships made it to FTL before they could intercept.

Bennie leaned back against the wall. They were in the security office in the sublevel of the spaceport's ring wall office structure. "We didn't do anything wrong. It's fine."

The younger Harrith looked at him. "Some of us aren't accustomed to being detained by security."

"You get used to it," he said without looking over.

She looked at Wil, then Nic. "Doubtful," she said, crossing her arms.

Wil and Blu'T'Ohm walked over. "We're good," the former said.

"About time," Bennie said, hopping off the bench. He looked at Nic. "Come on."

As the group exited the ring wall and headed for the *Ghost*, Wil fell back to walk next to Blu'T'Ohm. "So, Blue. We should probably talk about next steps."

"What do you mean? I can keep paying your," he coughed, "exorbitant fees." He glared toward Bennie ahead of them.

Wil shook his head. "It's not that. Well, partly. Glad you can pay the bill. But this isn't a permanent solution."

The other man shrugged. "Well, I assume the rate is halved for now."

From ahead of them, Bennie looked over his shoulder. "What makes you think that?"

The other man quirked a salt and pepper eyebrow. "Well, your team is currently cut in half. I have no intention of paying for the half not actively working toward my safety."

Bennie spun on his heel. "No way. Our fee isn't based on the size of the team."

"Why not?" the Harrith man replied. "Whether you count team members or capabilities, either way you're diminished."

Bennie flapped his arm, spluttering. "No! I mean." He turned to Wil. "Wiiiiil!"

Wil shook his head. "He's got ya there, tiny green used car salesman."

They reached the *Ghost*, her antipersonnel weapons still

deployed and tracking the group as they approached the lowered cargo ramp.

Bennie stopped at the top and watched Wil and Blu'T'Ohm approach. "You know what? We've got other things to do than be your full time forever protectors, anyway."

The other man cocked his head to the side. The scar that ran down the left side reflected the overhead lights. "Isn't that literally what the Knights of Plentallus are about?"

Bennie scrunched up his face.

Nic stifled a chuckle.

Bennie stormed off toward the stairs leading up to the common deck.

Cynthia cleared her throat. "Let's get airborne."

Wil nodded. "Yeah, I'll get us going." He looked toward the stairs and shouted, "Green asshole, you're with me."

"Why?" Bennie shouted.

"Because I said so." He headed off after the cranky Brailack.

Cynthia looked at the other women. "Why don't we do a little sparring?"

"Me?" Gul'P'Ulo stammered.

"Why not?" Cynthia shrugged. "Whether we're with you two or not, looks like some self-defense might not be a bad skill." She looked at Blu'T'Ohm. "That okay?"

"She's a grown a woman," the Harrith man said, waving a hand. "I'll be in my quarters."

"Good evening. This is GNO Newsbreak. I'm Gulbar' Te." The Burzzad journalist dipped his head. "Tonight's top story comes from Pakma Tiri, where a riot broke out in the capital city of Inkon. Pro-GC separatists engaged with loyalists in the streets outside a forum featuring known separatist spokesbeing Durga Dala Maca, who gave an impassioned performance at a forum on the state of democracy in the galaxy." He turned, adjusting in his seat. "We're told the violence has claimed several hundred lives so far. Local authorities have cordoned off several square ploriths of downtown Inkon to attempt to contain the violence."

After a pause to let that sink in, he said, "We'll keep you posted on developments on Pakma Tiri."

## CHAPTER 19

The black combat shuttle settled to the ground in the public landing area of the Cardu industrial district.

Admiral Shre' Ta'n pointed. "The fabrication complex we're looking for is that way about half a plorith." After reviewing Gabe's findings in her office, the Admiral tasked her best analysis team with tracking down exactly which fab plants had manufactured the pieces of tech. To everyone's surprise, the various pieces Gabe presented all came from one plant.

Maxim took point. During the flight, the two Palorians had availed themselves of the transport's armory. Both were beyond excited to have something more powerful than a stunner.

"No shooting," Shre' Ta'n called after him, stepping out of the shuttle.

"Admiral. According to public records, the fabrication facility we're heading for is an ongoing business," Gabe said.

She nodded. "According to my team, yes. It's owned by a small consortium, producing various technology parts and pieces for different things. Nothing obviously illegal, but plenty of things that share common components with armor and weapons."

The droid turned to look at her. "Nothing so obvious as fake Peacekeeper technology, I assume?" he offered.

She shook her head in agreement. "Unfortunately, no."

The Cardu district was divided into sixteen square blocks. The Laakiee Province was an island in the middle of Harrith Prime's largest ocean and home to eight districts the size of Cardu. Long ago, the Harrith realized the value of putting their most volatile industries as far away from their populace as possible.

Each district had a small civil landing pad where workers caught shuttles back and forth between shifts. Due the nature of the facilities on the island, it had no full-time residents but was occupied all year round.

Zephyr checked the charge on her pulse rifle. "How many people work in one of these plants?"

Shre' Ta'n shrugged. "It varies, but I'd assume two tens or so. They're largely automated."

They reached the building, and the Admiral pushed on the door. The reception space inside was a small room with two potted plants on either side of a small desk near the far side of the room. Behind the desk set in the corner was a door leading back to the rest of the fabrication plant.

An older Harrith man looked up from a tablet. "Hello. How may I help you?"

Shre' Ta'n smiled. "Admiral Shre' Ta'n Narel." The man nodded. "I'd like to speak with the manager of the fab plant."

"Of course." He grinned, running a hand over his bald pate. He looked behind the Admiral to the two Palorians and droid of unknown design. "One microtock." He departed through the rear door.

Maxim and Zephyr moved to the edges of the room. The latter turned. "Remind you of anything?"

Gabe made a clicking noise. "Unfortunately."

The two Palorians looked at each other, then at their mechanical friend, smiling. A cycle ago, the team had infiltrated a warehouse on Tyr to rescue Cynthia from a secret extra-governmental agency of trained assassins. She was being held in a warehouse not too dissimilar from this one.

In the fighting, Gabe had taken significant damage to his previous body. It was enough that he had been forced to reconfigure himself. After his ordeal aboard the *Siege Perilous* nearly ten cycles ago, Gabe's core processing routines were loaded into a custom droid frame that had the ability to reconfigure itself at a nearly atomic level.

His previous frame was larger, built like Maxim. It had powerful shoulder-mounted cannons, wrist-mounted blasters, and the ability to fly. This body, his third in all, was slimmer, not designed for combat. It was a visual cousin of his original form: all long legs and thin primary arms with a smaller secondary set of limbs meant for working with small engineering components. When not in use, the smaller arms were almost impossible to notice.

Maxim ran his hand along the frame of a picture. "Nice lobby." Everyone nodded. He turned to Gabe. "Can you..."

The droid nodded. His optic sensors flickered from their normal yellow to a pale blue. The team knew the color they turned when his internal sensor suite was fully active and drawing maximum power.

"There are six beings heading this way. A total of twenty-four beings are in the plant." He turned to the others. "They aren't moving this way. It's presumable that they are plant technicians. There is significant shielding in use, making it impossible to scan certain parts of the building." There was a pause as Gabe continued his scans. He turned to the door. "I have lost track of our targ —"

The door at the rear of the lobby exploded inward. Two

beings in fake Peacekeeper armor rushed in, rifles up, super-charged plasma racing from the barrels to scorch the front wall of the small space, igniting small fires. One of the plants near the reception desk caught a plasma round and burst into flames.

Gabe's warning almost gave Maxim and Zephyr enough time. Both of them were nearly to the ground when the door exploded inward. Training and cycles of working with Gabe had honed their instincts. Their borrowed pulse pistols spat supercharged plasma at their attackers.

The two new fake Peacekeepers dove behind the reception desk, firing as they moved. One of them snapped off a shot at Admiral Shre' Ta'n, who was drawing her own sidearm. A plasma round burned into her torso. She grunted, stumbling sideways, her pistol still near her hip.

Gabe's eyes were now combat mode red. His internal targeting system tracked the first two attackers as they dove behind the reception desk, picking up two more in the hallway. While he had abandoned the more powerful shoulder-mounted weaponry of his old frame, he kept the forearm blasters that could deploy with a series of whirs and clicks from each arm.

He fired a volley into the desk, melting through the cheap plastoid material. The screams from behind the desk were confirmation enough that his shots had made contact. Peace-keeper armor was tough and durable but no match for his weapons.

"Down!" Maxim shouted as two more armored beings ran into the small room from the plant proper.

The shielding in the hallway was interfering with Gabe's sensors. He spotted the two new arrivals barely a moment before they entered the lobby. He had lost track of the last two he sensed earlier.

Calling the city of Osil picturesque would be putting it mildly. After leaving Cleblon and again having time until Blu'T'Ohm's next appearance, Wil selected the Nilop city as a place to lay low.

"And here I thought you only knew the lower rent spots in the galaxy," Blu'T'Ohm quipped as the *Ghost* came in low over the lake where Osil sat nestled along the shore.

Wil looked over his shoulder for a moment. "Only the best for you, Blue." He turned back to bring the ship in to land at a spaceport that wasn't the main one for the city. After the last few hassles with the mysterious fake Peacekeepers, the team agreed that keeping a lower profile was advisable.

Osil's smaller secondary port was not the usual tall duracrete ring wall design. Rather, this one was set below ground a short way from the lake, looking like a manmade crate two kilometers wide and half a kilometer deep.

Once the ship was settled and locked down, the team split up on a mix of assignments. Wil and Cynthia took grocery shopping before Bennie could claim the errand. Blu'T'Ohm's next engagement wasn't that far off, so they didn't have time to linger, unfortunately.

"I feel kinda bad. Did you see little green's face when you called dibs on shopping?" Cynthia asked as the pair made their way from the sky bus stop in the main commercial district of Osil.

Wil smiled. "Ask if I care." He pointed to what looked like a tourist trap disguised as a dive bar overlooking the lake. "It's five o'clock somewhere. We can grab groceries on our way back." Cynthia slipped her arm through his, and they walked into Boobo Goop's Zergling Ranch.

It never stopped being jarring to Wil just how many things that felt so Earthlike were seemingly universal. The inside of Boobo Goop's was like every sit-down low end casual eatery he'd ever been in on Earth. Random crap was affixed to the walls. Generic music played just loud enough to provide atmosphere but not so loud that patrons had to shout at each other. Beings of all shapes and sizes occupied tables scattered throughout the main dining room. Other than the tables and chairs designed for different physical layouts, the place could have been an Applebee's in Ohio.

Since four-star hotels didn't seem to offer any more protection than any place else, Wil insisted they stick closer to the spaceport. Bennie found them a low-rent dive that catered mostly to spacers that needed a place to crash while their freighters were parked at the port.

"You people seem to have a limitless ability to shock me," Blu'T'Ohm said, making a circuit of the suite Bennie rented. This time everyone had a room off the same central living space. While Wil hoped to not have to defend the space, this would be easier than a series of disconnected rooms.

Bennie shrugged. "Don't post your location to social media, and we can stay at nicer places." He hopped down into the central conversation lounge, a sunken pit ringed with plush seating. He had two tablets that he was balancing on each knee.

Nic watched her mentor get settled, then said to anyone who might care, "I'm going to walk the floor."

Gul'P'Ulo smiled. "We'll be here." She looked at her boss. "We should work on your remarks for the Future of Governance Summit. It's coming up fast."

Blu'T'Ohm sighed. "You're right." He took the tablet she was offering. "Might as well work on that now."

The two moved to the dining table, producing several tablets that they arrayed around the table.

Nic stepped out into the hall and looked to each side. As far as the team knew, they were the only guests on this floor. She headed to the right.

It did not take long for the two missing signals Gabe had sensed earlier to make themselves known. From halfway down the corridor to which the rear door connected, they were laying down covering fire.

"Left!" Max shouted, taking aim at the two armor-clad arrivals that just stepped into the lobby, ignoring their friends down the hall. Zephyr followed his lead, her plasma bolts following his. The armored attacker fell as their shots found weak spots in the armor.

From his position in the room, Gabe took aim at the last two targets. One fell before the other turned and fled, shouting something as he did. The remaining fake Peacekeeper in the lobby turned and fled back down the sensor-shielded corridor after his colleague.

Standing, Maxim said, "That was fun." He moved to the last attacker to fall, nudging the body with his boot, confirming it wasn't going to get up again. Satisfied, he looked at the hallway and then Gabe. "Cover that?"

The droid nodded, stalked to the open doorway, and kicked aside a piece of the door, training both of his outstretched arms down the short hallway. Anyone unwise enough to poke their head around the corner wouldn't make the same mistake. Ever again. While his sensors struggled with the material of the corridor, his optics were more than enough at the moment.

Zephyr joined Shre' Ta'n. "You're hurt."

The Admiral was slumped against the wall, holding her

side. She removed her hand to see that it was covered in pale red blood. "Flesh wound." Her almost perfectly round eyes met Zephyr's. "I'm fine. We need to call in reinforcements." With Zephyr's help, she inched into a seated position. She looked at her wristcomm, tapped a few icons and lowered her arm. "On their way."

Maxim turned. "We had backup this whole time?" He leaned over the reception desk, confirming the two attackers behind it were dead. They were.

"I had a rapid response team holding in orbit. Just in case," Shre' Ta'n said, then winced, looking at her side. Her shirt was soaked with blood. "I might need a medic after all."

The rapid response team lived up to its name. A dozen armored and well-armed troopers descended on the fabrication plant.

The first team through the front door took in the scene and immediately summoned a medical team. Gabe relinquished his position as sentry and stood down. His optics flicked from their normal yellow to blue as he powered up his sensors. "I am not detecting anyone else in proximity to the hallway. However, I believe the remaining fake Peacekeeper is moving the plant's workforce toward the rear of the building."

The team leader looked at Shre' Ta'n. The Admiral nodded. She looked at her people, pointing to the hallway. "Go!" She raised her wristcomm. "Teams 3 and 5, move on the rear of the building!"

Shre' Ta'n looked at the two Palorians. "Go with 'em."

Nic looked up from her wristcomm. Her patrol had turned into browsing the internex in the hotel's lobby. She was used to having no privacy; the *Ghost* wasn't very big. Adding the two Harrith had not helped. Gul'P'Ulo was nice enough, only a few cycles older than Nic, but still, some quiet time to herself was nice.

The hotel's lobby was dimly lit and empty. In other words, perfect.

That is, until two Tleb walked in. Two suspicious looking Tleb. Doing her best to look like she wasn't watching them, she watched them. The one covered in pale brown fur loitered near the door while the one that was covered in fur that was white with brown spots approached her.

"Excuse me, miss," he said. He had an overstuffed backpack on, and it looked to her like there was a camera drone sticking out from under the flap. When Nic looked up at him, he asked, "Have you by any chance seen a pair of Harrith with a Multonae, or something that looks like a Multonae, come through here? Maybe with a Tygran woman?" Most of the GC still had no idea what a human was, but their close resemblance to Multonae lead to lots of misidentifying. Wil once told her that he had been attacked in bars numerous times when someone thought he was a Multonae they knew and didn't like.

She sighed inwardly. More reporters. Max and Zephyr had told them all about their encounter earlier. She shook her head. "Nope, sorry."

The little man that, according to Wil, resembled something called a chihuahua, squinted at her. "Okay," he drawled. "Thanks."

As the Tleb journalist reached his companion, a trio of Brailack entered, two of them struggling under the weight of a camera drone that was ridiculously too large.

Nic watched as the two Tleb and three Brailack exchanged what looked like unkind words. She caught bits and pieces, mostly centered around the Tleb claiming they were there first.

One of the Brailack's faces contorted much like Bennie's did when confronted with someone he thought too stupid to deal with. The pale blue reporter waved a dismissive hand at his competition and approached the reception desk. The bored looking Quilant that was watching the entire exchange perked up as the Brailack approached.

Nic raised her wristcomm, punching the icon for the team channel. "We might have an issue," she whispered as she hopped off the chair and made her way to the elevator.

Up in the suite, Bennie looked up from his tablets. "You're kidding."

Nic's voice came from the small speaker. "Nope. At least five in the lobby right now. I'm guessing more are incoming. Did they post their location again?"

Bennie looked at the door to the room the two Harrith political agitators were sharing, then down to his wristcomm, bringing up Blu'T'Ohm's social media account. "Doesn't look like it."

He hopped off the sofa and was almost to the door to their room when he spotted something outside the suite's floor-to-ceiling window. It turned into two camera drones. He swore and rushed to the windows to activate the privacy mode. The transparent material turned opaque.

Forgetting the two clients, he rushed back to his tablets, grabbing one and scanning the room for the building network access panel. He had seen it earlier—where was it? Spotting it, he smiled and ran to the hallway that led to the refresher.

The suite's door slid open. "Where are you?" Nic shouted.

"Hallway," Bennie replied. He had two thin wires connected to the network access junction inside the panel. His wristcomm screen was flashing as various custom software tools penetrated the building's network. "I'm trying to reroute the elevators."

"Too late," she said, rounding the corner. "I don't know how they got past me in the lobby but there are two Tragalallans skulking around the elevator bay. I told them I was traveling with my stupid family on a family vacation that was stupid." She smirked.

Bennie sighed. "Dren." He glared. "Let's go see if we can't distract them." He moved the wires from his wristcomm to the tablet and tapped a few commands in. "I just created five fake reservations that match us to varying degrees on the floors below, plus one on the other end of the hall." He disconnected. "Time to sell it."

The pair left the suite.

The fabrication plant was crawling with Harrith military, police, and more than a few well-dressed special agents of some sort or other within an hour.

The last two fake Peacekeepers had vanished, likely ditching the armor and blending in with the workers. Wil looked at the group cordoned off in the corner, wondering which one he or she was. He shrugged. Maybe they'd figure it out when they debriefed them all.

"Ma'am." A junior naval officer approached. He had a gauntlet in his hand. It was matte gray. Maxim recognized it immediately: Peacekeeper.

Shre' Ta'n took the piece of armor and turned it over in her hand. She nodded to the officer, sending him back into the rear of the building. The medics had treated her wound as best they could, then bound her torso until she could get to a medical facility. She still winced when she turned.

Handing the piece to Maxim, she asked, "Thoughts?"

After examining it, he handed the piece of armor to Zephyr. "Definitely the right place. That's PK armor, alright."

Zephyr tossed the gauntlet in the air, then caught it. "Well made, but not quite right." She turned it over. "Even after applying the paint coat, it's just a bit too light." She offered it to Gabe.

His eyes flashed from yellow to blue, turning the gauntlet over slowly. He looked at Zephyr. "You are correct. This piece is close but has several molecular deviations from standard Peace-keeper armor. That explains why it did not hold up to our fire." He passed the gauntlet to a passing naval officer. "It shares circuit and fabrication design telltales that match the pieces of equipment we found among the debris left behind by the ship that attacked us."

"Well, this is interesting," Shre' Ta'n said, looking up from the tablet one of her people handed her.

"What's that?" Zephyr asked. The other woman offered the device. "Oh. Well, now."

Maxim sighed. "Are you two trying to be opaque?" His life partner smiled, offering the tablet. "Dren." He looked up and to the Admiral. "This place was popular." On the screen was the building's access and visitor log. While names were redacted, several of the unique identifiers had been to the fab plant several dozen times in the last few months.

Shre' Ta'n nodded, taking the tablet back from Maxim. "I wonder if we can decrypt these identifiers? My guess is they're a who's who of upper echelon Harrith Navy and Governing Council."

Gabe tilted his head. "I do not understand. Why would your government and military want to kill Blu'T'Ohm?"

Shre' Ta'n said nothing for a bit. Finally, "I don't know. I don't love the path his life has taken, but I can't see why the government or military would want him dead."

Maxim raised a hand. "We're ignoring one thing." When both women looked at him with matching raised eyebrows, he said, "Perhaps Blue isn't the target or even the point?"

Gabe picked up the thread. "Maxim has a point. Regardless of the reason, these people are framing the GC and Peacekeepers. The GC and Peacekeepers are the targets. Blu'T'Ohm could be nothing more than a convenient martyr."

"Dren," both women hissed.

Zephyr ran both hands through her hair, adjusting her ponytail. "I saw on GNO that word finally got out about that part. Wil and the others wouldn't have shared it, so…"

"So, things are escalating," Maxim finished.

Two more troopers came from the rear of the building. The senior-most said, "Ma'am, you should see this."

"Of course," Maxim said under his breath.

The group followed the two Harrith Navy officers deeper into the fabrication plant.

The rear of the building where the manufacturing took place was separated into several large areas, each crowded with machinery of all shapes and sizes. None of it made sense to Zephyr or Max, but Gabe seemed to be able to identify each piece of equipment. He narrated each piece as they worked their way to the rear wall of the cavernous building.

"Must be the main office," Maxim said when their guides stopped outside the door to a complex consisting of three stories of offices connected by a spiral staircase set against the far wall. He looked up. Three offices per floor, filling most of the rear wall of the building.

"Lots of offices," Shre' Ta'n commented.

One of the troopers nodded. "Most seem to be unused. There's one on the third floor that was set up as a break room and two on this floor."

Inside the office, clearly the main administrative space for the operation, another Harrith Naval officer was looking at a half dozen assorted tablets on a central work table. He looked up. Seeing the Admiral, he saluted.

She returned the gesture. "What've you got?"

He shrugged. "Honestly, ma'am, I'm not sure. There are thousands, likely hundreds of thousands, of files." He waved a hand over the tablets and racks of processing cores. "It's going to take some time."

"Perhaps I can assist?" Gabe asked.

Shre' Ta'n looked at the two Palorians as the Naval officer looked at her.

Zephyr nodded. "Can't hurt to try."

The Admiral nodded to Gabe, who moved to stand next to the other Harrith man. As he moved his hands over the arrayed tablets, thin data tendrils snaked from his fingertips. The tip of each tendril glowed with pale blue light.

The younger Harrith man took a step back. The tendrils slithered over the tablets, snaking their way into seams. Pulses of light traveled up and down each tendril.

The Admiral looked at Max and Zephyr. "So...what now?" She glanced at Gabe. His optic sensors were dim.

The quartet of non-droids were starting to get uncomfortable in the silence when Gabe's optic sensors blinked back to their full intensity.

"Interesting," he said.

## CHAPTER 20

"What do you mean, they're gone?" Bennie demanded.

He and Nic had returned from their game of cat and mouse with the invading journalists, alternating between leading them on wild goose chases across multiple floors and scaring them off with their beam sabers.

When they returned to the shared suite, Blu'T'Ohm and Gul'P'Ulo were gone.

The young Olop planted her hands on her hips. "Which words or series of words were unclear?"

"You're fired!" Bennie threw both arms into the air.

Nic scowled. "You can't fire me. Come on, let's find them before Wil and Cynthia get back and yell at us." She looked over at him. "Besides. You're the one that left them alone."

Bennie scowled but chose to ignore that last barb. "Any ideas?"

She shrugged as she grabbed a tablet from dining table. "Let's see if he posted to social media."

"We should be so lucky," Bennie groused. He hopped up into the chair next to the one Nic had climbed up into.

Thankfully, the myriad journalists had given up on the

building when it became clear that the two sword wielding mystery beings were not going to stop harassing them.

Nic swiped on the screen a few times. "Nothing." Bennie held out a hand, little green fingers wiggling. She scowled. "I know how to swipe on a screen. Use your own." She scrutinized the tablet. "Wait." She held the tablet so he could see the screen. "Posted their exact location." On the screen was Gul'P'Ulo sipping a drink on the pool deck several hours earlier. "You said they didn't post."

Bennie swore. "I don't know what the pool deck looks like!"

"You thought she just had a pic from another day at the pool stored and ready for use later?"

He waved his hands. "I don't know what young people do!"

She shook her head. "Whatever, where do you think they would have gone?"

Bennie looked at his wristcomm. "Oh, grolack."

"What?" Nic leaned toward Bennie.

"Those stupid krebnacks," he grated. He offered his wrist-comm to her.

"Oh no," she sighed.

He nodded and hopped off the seat. "Let's go."

They arrived outside the nondescript and, by the look of it, closed-for-the-evening used bookstore a few minutes later. Bennie shook his head. "What the wurrin is this?"

Nic clucked. "No books on Brai?"

Bennie pitched his voice high. "No books on Brai." He turned, glaring. "I meant, it's closed."

They reached the door. He pushed on it, and it swung open. "Or looks like it is." He lowered his voice. "Spooky." He went in.

Nic rolled her eyes and followed him into the building. The lights were out, so she fell back on the training that Bennie drilled into her daily since she convinced him to take her on as his apprentice. She could hear voices. Several voices, in fact. She looked over to Bennie, who nodded. He heard them too.

They crept closer to the rear of the bookstore, passing shelf upon shelf of old books from across the GC. The store was divided by race and language, and further, by genre within each.

"Quite the collection," Bennie whispered as they neared the back of the building. He looked at Nic. "By the way, Wil doesn't need to know a bookstore was involved."

She nodded.

The voices were getting louder.

Nic unclipped her beam saber as she looked at Bennie. He nodded, doing the same. He made a gesture. She nodded, moving off to the other side of the store.

The voices were louder. Blu'T'Ohm's was clear, rising above the rest. Neither of them could make out what was being said yet, but the volume made it sound like an argument.

The rear of the bookstore had only one door, and the voices were on the other side. The pair reached the back wall, turned following the wall, and reached the door at the same time.

Bennie looked at Nic, ensuring that she was ready. With one hand, he reached over to the door handle. Like everything in the building, it was old: a latch, wood, hinges. His finger on the activation switch of his beam saber, he pushed the door open.

Nic rushed in first. The *snap-hiss* of her beam saber activating caused the room to fall silent.

Bennie came in behind her, his beam saber humming as it cast its purple tint on the room.

Two dozen faces turned to look at the intruders. To a person, their mouths were hanging open. Blu'T'Ohm was glaring at the new arrivals.

Bennie took in the scene. Blu'T'Ohm was at the front of the room at a lectern. "The wurrin is going on here?"

"Grandpa thought it was a book signing," Nic told the group.

Bennie glared at his apprentice. "We had an agreement."

She shrugged, a grin spread across her face.

Cynthia shook her head, looking at Wil. "Books again? This gonna be a thing?"

The pair had returned to the hotel to find Bennie, Nic, and the Harrith social agitators missing. Since there wasn't any sign of foul play, Wil had assumed an unauthorized field trip. A quick check of his wristcomm and the Find My Crew app Bennie wrote, and he located his crewmates' signal.

"Books are essential," Wil protested. He turned to Bennie. "You got some 'splaining to do, Lucy."

Bennie's face scrunched up. "I don't—" He waved a hand. "I don't care."

Wil nodded. "Good call." He looked Blue and Gul'P'Ullo. "Come on. Let's go."

Wil spent the entire cab ride back to the hotel scolding the two Harrith and their guardians. Once they arrived, he sent the two Harrith to their room while the crew planned their next moves.

Wil had just opened a bottle of grum when his wristcomm erupted into the chorus of "Who Let the Dogs Out?" He looked down at the screen, then looked around the room for Bennie. He answered the call. "One second." He snapped the fingers of his other hand at Bennie. "How do I wake the screen?"

Bennie looked over. "What?" Wil pointed at the entertainment display on the wall. "Oh." He snatched a tablet off the coffee table and tapped a few commands.

The screen came to life. Wil flicked the screen of his wristcomm, sending the call to the large wall-mounted display. "Okay, go ahead."

From the small kitchenette space, Nic waved. "Hi, Max!"

The big Palorian man smiled and winked. He made room for Zephyr in the frame.

"So, things have gotten interesting out here," she said.

Bennie leaned forward. "How so?"

"We found the source of the parts," Maxim offered.

"And the weapons," Gabe added from off screen.

"Where's Gabe?" Nic asked.

Maxim smiled. "He's how we're making the call. He's a wristcomm now."

From offscreen came Gabe's exasperated metallic rattle noise.

This time Wil leaned forward. "Back on topic. Really?" Nods on the screen. "Shit." More nods.

"I think you all should come to Harrith Prime," the big Palorian said.

The door to Blue and Gul's room opened. The young Harrith woman said, "We have a rally and forum on worlds nowhere near the home sector."

Wil spared her a look, then turned back the screen. "Can't Shre' Ta'n shut it down?" The look his teammates exchanged said all he needed to hear. "Gotcha."

"She's an admiral now," Maxim offered.

Wil smiled. "Good for her!"

Bennie tapped his wristcomm screen a few times. "If we leave now, we can be there in two days."

"We have a schedule to keep," Gul'P'Ulo protested. She had entered the room followed by her boss. Both were now with Nic in the small kitchenette space at the table. She turned to Blu'T'Ohm. "Sir, we're making inroads on several Tier 1 and 2 worlds. If we vanish, again, that momentum is lost."

The older of the two Harrith looked at the Rogue Enterprises team. "Surely we can head home later?" He spread his arms. "When there's more time?"

His aide nodded her agreement.

Cynthia looked at her teammates on screen, then to the two Harrith in the kitchen area. "This doesn't end by continuing to go about business as usual." She met Blu'T'Ohm's gaze. "Someone is trying to kill you." She looked at Gul'P'Ulo. "Both of you. The answers are on Harrith Prime, not at your next rally."

Wil nodded. "She's right." He hitched a thumb toward the screen on the wall. "We're going to Harrith Prime."

"We can't!" Gul'P'Ulo shouted. She looked around the room, her cheeks darkened. Finally, turning to her boss, she said, "You'd turn your back on the cause?"

Wil stood. "For what it's worth, it's not his choice, really. We're going. You two can stay here, and almost certainly get killed, or come with us."

Nic added, "Don't forget, you leaked your location—intentionally." She shrugged. "I'm kinda surprised your friends haven't already attacked us."

Cynthia inclined her head to the young Olop woman. "She's got a point."

"Luckily, the bookstore is empty now," Bennie offered.

Wil turned to the screen. "We'll see you three soon. Don't get killed."

Maxim grinned. "Do our best."

The screen flickered and went black.

Wil twirled a finger in the air. "Pack it up."

Gul'P'Ulo glared at him but moved into her shared room.

"I still can't believe it," Admiral Shre' Ta'n said from her seat in the assault shuttle. They were on their way back to the Admiral's office after she handed over on-site management of the forensic clean up to one of her trusted aides. They managed to keep the raid under wraps, ensuring that those involved weren't yet aware that their fabrication plant had been taken.

Sitting next to her, Gabe nodded. As the shuttle took off, he had filled them in on the broad strokes of what he uncovered from the data in the plant's computers. "Keep in mind, my search routines are best suited for summarization. There is likely much more nuance to the data and what it means. A more purpose-built droid or other computational device may be able to provide a much clearer picture."

Across from them, Zephyr shrugged. "But the end result isn't different, right?" Gabe inclined his head in agreement. She went on, "A cabal consisting of some of the most powerful people in Harrith's military-industrial complex are linked to that fabrication plant."

The shuttle bucked as it hit a bit of turbulence the gravlifts couldn't fully compensate for.

Maxim said, "Which means they're behind the attempts on Blue's life, and the many, many deaths at that first rally. But why would they want to kill him? He's Harrith. He's speaking out against the GC. Both of those seem like pluses." He looked to the Admiral. "I assume your people haven't changed their minds with regard to the GC and membership? Harrith thing and all."

The other woman nodded. "The—what's it called out there? Harrith thing?"

"Harrith Incident," the two Palorians said as one.

Shre' Ta'n nodded. "Yeah, that. After that, my people were even more united in our stance to not be pulled into a galaxy-spanning government." Sighing, she added, "Which means I can't think of a reason to want to kill someone as popular as

Blu'T'Ohm Ka-tan. I mean, I'm not a fan of how he's going about this, and while I'm no fan of the GC, a more controlled dissolution would be better for everyone. He was pushing things to dangerous levels."

Gabe raised a hand. "You are correct that a controlled collapse of the Commonwealth would be better for those in the GC." He made a hand waving motion that he had seen Wil make more than once when explaining some finer point of Earth media. "A chaotic collapse could benefit parties outside the GC."

The silence in the passenger compartment of the assault shuttle stretched into awkward territory before Shre' Ta'n said, "I need to take this to the authorities."

"You sure that's wise?" Maxim asked.

The overhead speaker clicked. "Admiral, we'll be at the command center in ten microtocks."

Shre' Ta'n nodded but wasn't sure if she was being honest. The names that Gabe revealed were some of the most famous tech businesses and political giants on the planet. The rest of the trip passed in silence, which suited her fine. She needed to mull over what her next steps would be.

The next morning, the quartet was standing in the lobby of the Drotu government complex. It served as both the municipal capital of Drotu but also the home of the planetary government. The city's administrative offices occupied the first floor. The offices of the Circle took up the remaining floors.

"I know I asked this already, but..." Maxim spread his arms wide. "Sure about this?"

Shre' Ta'n nodded. "No backing out now. I've got an appointment. Not showing up would raise eyebrows."

Maxim took a deep breath. "Then, let's go."

Zephyr fell in next to the Admiral. "We'll follow your lead."

They met an officious young woman who smiled. "Admiral Narel." She gave a minuscule bow. "The Circle is ready to see you," she looked at the others, "and your colleagues?"

They fell in behind the younger woman.

"The Circle?" Maxim whispered to Zephyr.

"Stop reading joining ceremony magazines, my love," she clucked. "The Circle is the governing body of the Harrith sector. Each colony and Harrith Prime has a pair of elected representatives."

"A pair?"

She nodded. "The two candidates that get the most votes in the election are sent. The one with the most is the primary representative, and the other is the secondary. It seems to work pretty well for them. The pair has to agree on how they will vote, which means making two parties back home happy, or not."

Maxim nodded along as she explained. "I can see why they might not be keen to get involved with the GC. Their system works and doesn't cause much strife."

"And the GC's political class feeds on strife," Zephyr chuckled.

They reached a pair of three-meter-tall wooden doors embossed with scenes from Harrith history.

On either side of the massive doors was a Harrith Navel trooper in ceremonial armor, complete with a power lance in one hand and small shield in the other.

The chamber of the Circle was, in fact, a sphere. A massive several-dozen-meter-diameter sphere. The huge doors were situated along the equator of the great shape. The lower hemisphere was a tiered amphitheater, while the upper hemisphere was home to a single large structure that hung from the center of the dome. All around that were light fixtures and other pieces of rigging.

Maxim pointed. "What's up there?"

Shre' Ta'n followed his finger. "The media office. Sessions of the Circle are streamed to the entire sector." Zephyr opened her mouth. The Admiral shook her head. "I requested a closed session. As an admiral, I have that right. State secrets."

Zephyr nodded. "Had me worried."

Directly below the media office in the lower portion of the space, a single lectern stood in a five-meter-wide circle. The tiers that ringed the central stage consisted of workstations, each with two chairs.

Gabe took in the space. "How are the seating arrangements assigned?"

Their young guide brought them to an open lift platform that followed a track down the curve of the bowl to the floor below.

As the lift began its soundless glide downward, the Admiral said, "Random assignment. At some point in the distant past, journalists implied that being closer to the lectern was a reflection of power and prestige, so the Circle voted to assign workstations at random at the beginning of each legislative session."

As they stepped off the lift, Zephyr said, "Maybe the GC should look to the Harrith for guidance versus trying to absorb them?"

"Indeed," Gabe agreed.

As the foursome reached the lectern, an almost invisible hatch opened on the tier in the midpoint of the bowl. Well-dressed Harrith men and women filed in, taking similar lifts up and down the sides of the amphitheater.

Shre' Ta'n watched until those entering the space trickled. Barely a third of the seats were occupied.

Zephyr saw her friend's expression and leaned in. "This normal?"

The other woman gave a slight shake of her head. "This is the security council, a subset of the full Circle." She frowned. "The senior speaker isn't coming."

One of the seated representatives stood and made her way to the bottom of the bowl and the lectern there. When she reached it, she looked at Shre' Ta'n and her guests. "Admiral Narel, a pleasure." She dipped her head.

Shre' Ta'n inclined her head in return. "An honor." She coughed. "I was under the impression this would be the full Circle."

The other woman smiled, not kindly. "It was decided that the security council should first hear your report."

"I, uh...I see."

The representative stepped from behind the lectern, her hand extended, offering it to the Admiral.

Shre' Ta'n moved to the lectern, introducing the two Palorians and droid. Gabe joined her. There was a dataport in the podium that Gabe's data tendrils slid into. A holoprojector mounted below the media office came to life.

Maxim leaned close to Zephyr. "Do we know if any of these people are bad guys?"

Zephyr shook her head. "No idea. But I'm hoping not."

They watched faces as their friends presented the findings and summaries of the data from the fabrication plant.

As Gabe presented data, Shre' Ta'n explained what was being displayed.

Once Gabe and the Admiral finished their presentation,

moving to join Maxim and Zephyr, the chair of the security council moved back to the podium. "Thank you, Admiral. That's quite the story."

Shre' Ta'n barely contained her grimace. By the sheer grace of the many gods, no one on the security council was, as far as Gabe had found, involved in the cabal.

The lead representative stepped from the lectern and made a slow circle as she spoke to those gathered. "You've heard the report and seen the data."

From several tiers up, a middle-aged Harrith woman said, "We move that an exploratory committee be formed to investigate this."

"Seconded," another representative said from behind the Rogue Enterprises group.

The chair of the security council nodded. "A vote."

Zephyr looked at the woman next to her. "A committee?"

Shre' Ta'n gave a single terse nod as reply. She held up a hand. "If I may?" She didn't wait for permission. "With all due respect, this situation is more urgent than forming a committee. The names we uncovered are—"

"Are pillars of our society," one representative interrupted.

"Several of our colleagues," another shouted.

"And major donors," yet another said.

Shre' Ta'n shook her head. "Be that as it may. They're part of a cabal that, for whatever reason, is trying to destabilize the GC."

"Is that so bad?" someone demanded.

"It is if they murder Harrith citizens, if they frame the GC's own peacekeeping force for the act. It is if the goal is the deaths of millions of innocents who find themselves alone in the galaxy with enemies at the door." She turned a slow circle, trying to meet as many eyes as possible. "That's not who we are."

Wil looked around the bridge. With Maxim and Zephyr gone, the bridge felt less complete. He looked at Zephyr's station, occupied by Gul'P'Ulo. "Don't touch that." He snapped. Her hand stopped just above the console.

She looked up. "So many controls and such—in just this one console."

Bennie looked over. "Just don't blow us up."

The younger woman raised both hands, leaning back in the seat, her eyes wide.

Wil shook his head, turning a glare to Bennie. "He's fucking with you."

She turned to Bennie. "Little krebnack."

He winked.

Wil rolled his eyes, then turned to face the main display. Over his shoulder, he asked, "We cleared?"

Cynthia nodded. "Yeah. No inbound traffic warnings. No holds. Cleared for FTL."

He pushed the FTL control slider forward. The sea of stars on the display stretched into rainbow lines.

Cynthia put her earpiece on the console in the custom indentation that charged it. "I'm thinking the racing game. With the fungus people."

"Loogie racers," Bennie said, nodding.

"Mario Kart," Wil corrected, adding, "loogie racers?" He shook his head. He looked at the ceiling. "Hey, Ga—" He shook his head. Gabe wasn't aboard the ship either.

The team had split up numerous times in the past, but for whatever reason, this time, Wil was just feeling weird. He didn't know why; the job wasn't that different than others they'd done. He shrugged, stood up. "Let's game."

The common deck was awash in the chiptune beats of go-cart-driving cartoon characters doing their best to knock each other off a rainbow racetrack in deep space.

A motorcycle riding man in a green overalls hurled a turtle shell at the woman in a pink ball gown riding her own motorcycle.

"You lopar!" Cynthia shouted.

Blu'T'Ohm smirked. "I like this game."

While they argued, another shell came from behind, sending Blue's character spinning.

Bennie chuckled. "Eyes on the prize. Eyes. On. The. Prize." His character blew past the others.

Cynthia snarled. "You'll pay for that." She looked at Blu'T'Ohm. "Both of you."

Shre' Ta'n slammed her palm against the wall in the hallway outside the Circle chamber. "Dren!"

"Guess politicians are politicians no matter the sector," Maxim sighed.

"They told me to stand down and you three to leave," the Admiral growled.

The security council had voted to begin an investigation, then politely but forcefully asked the off-worlders to leave. Of the Admiral, the request was less polite. She was ordered to return to her duties, which did not include investigations, or anything else, planetside.

The Council would enlist the services of the planetary security division if and when they deemed it appropriate.

"I have remotely activated the *Rocky Nontee*," Gabe offered.

"The preflight sequence will be complete by the time we arrive at the spaceport."

The trip to the spaceport was quiet. The Admiral was fuming, and neither Max nor Zephyr knew what to say. They were outsiders—those were her people.

Once at the spaceport, the Admiral ushered them through security, waving her wristcomm with secure credentials at every checkpoint.

The *Nontee* was sitting right where they'd left it. Next to her was a new ship, a freighter of similar size, much newer and cleaner than Bennie's dilapidated bucket.

"Called the tower, and the *Nontee* is already cleared." Shre' Ta'n looked at Zephyr. "What does that mean anyway? Nontee?"

"I will prepare the ship," Gabe said, moving ahead of the group.

The Palorian woman shrugged. "Beats me. Bennie misunderstood the name of..." She waved a hand. "Long and stupid story."

Maxim nodded. "As most stories involving Wil or Bennie tend to be."

The three of them chuckled until Gabe turned, his eyes red. "Get down."

Maxim and Zephyr each barely avoided plasma bolts, diving hard to the duracrete. Six beings in Peacekeeper—but almost certainly fake—armor came around the ship next to the *Nontee*, firing their rifles at the quartet.

Shre' Ta'n was on the ground a few meters away, her shoulder sporting a slight singe.

Caught out in the opening, the two Palorians and Harrith woman had little to no cover.

After issuing his warning, Gabe broke into a run, hoping to draw the enemy's fire as he reached the *Nontee*'s side. His sensors confirmed he had been partially successful. Two fake Peacekeepers were heading for his friends, while the remaining four were moving toward Bennie's ship, and him.

He spun, firing several rounds from his right arm blaster, striking one of the attackers' center mass. They fell to the ground, but his sensors knew they were still alive. The remaining three scrambled, sending super charged plasma splashing against the *Nontee*'s hull, adding to the carbon scoring already decorating it.

Maxim rolled along the permacrete, already warm from the sun and absorbed heat from the thrusters of dozens, if not hundreds, of ships that had already come and gone from the port. As he rolled, he pulled his borrowed pistol, thankful Shre' Ta'n hadn't taken it back yet. Maybe she'd forgotten he had it?

He opened fire, doing little beyond scattering the attackers. Zephyr did the same, rolling in the opposite direction. Shre' Ta'n did her best to scoot back the way they all came, her wrist-comm raised, calling for reinforcements.

"Gabe! Can you get to higher ground?" Zephyr shouted.

"Acknowledged," he sent over their comms. He had given up his prolonged flight capabilities when he chose his current physical configuration but made sure he retained limited thrust capabilities to enable what Wil called "long jumps." He leaped up, miniature repulsorlifts in the soles of his feet ignited, providing just enough boost to reach the upper hull of the *Rocky Nontee*.

Maxim rolled up against an overflowing trash receptacle. He got to his feet, scuttling around the bin to open fire. "Anyone have eyes on the Admiral?" he said. He ducked just as several pieces of trash caught plasma rounds and burst into flames.

"Negative," Zephyr said. She was crouched next to an abandoned cargo crate that had seen better days. Something corrosive had eaten most of one side. A hundred meters separated the two Palorians.

"The Admiral has found shelter," Gabe said. He fired both of his arm-mounted blasters as two attackers came around the side of the *Nontee,* trying to line up shots at Maxim. His first rounds struck the attackers, sending them to the ground. His subsequent shots targeted weak spots in their armor, killing or crippling them.

"There are three left," Gabe sent over the team's comm channel. He glanced at the first attacker he shot, noticing that they were no longer lying on the duracrete. "Make that four."

Maxim looked out around his cover, coughing from the caustic fumes spreading in every direction. "I'm going to—" He stopped as the sound of sirens rose over the sound of weapons' fire. Looking up, he saw the first of many civil security and Harrith Navy assault transports rise over the wall of the spaceport.

The remaining attackers grabbed their fallen comrades and beat a hasty retreat. He watched them drop into an open sewer drain near the center of the wide circle of the spaceport's landing field. He looked to the *Nontee.* "Gabe, you saw that?"

"I did."

Zephyr stood up from her cover and made her way to the Admiral, helping the other woman to her feet. "We're not leaving," she said.

"No, you're not," the other woman agreed.

"We are not?" Gabe asked, touching down a few meters from the two women as Maxim reached them.

"No," Zephyr said.

"I had my doubts, but this erases them," Shre' Ta'n said.

Zephyr nodded. "Someone in the Circle is involved. Someone clever enough to not be linked in the records we found."

Maxim made a clucking noise. "Yeah, that tracks."

"Indeed, it does," Gabe agreed.

"Hello, this is GNO Newstime, and I'm Klor'Tillen," the pale green Brailack newscaster said. "We're hearing of more attacks on separatist spokesbeings." He took a deep breath. "Frilluh Swa of Burrziia was killed in what looks like a Peacekeeper raid. The details are still incredibly fuzzy, but we have several eyewitness accounts claiming that beings in Peacekeeper armor boarded the Burzzad woman's transport, killing everyone—or almost everyone, as it turns out—on board."

Behind him, a display came to life showing the remains of a private yacht. The ship was open to space as a result of dozens of hull breaches with black scorch marks around them.

"A spokesbeing for the Peacekeepers said that they could not comment on an ongoing investigation, which tells me that this may not be what it seems." He shook his head. "So soon after rogue elements in the Peacekeepers attempted to forcibly annex the Harrith sector, I'm sure getting to the bottom of this is priority one."

He smiled. "In other news, a delegation from the newly welcomed associate member world, Mearth..." Frowning, Klor'Tillen said, "No, that's not right. My apologies. Earth. A delegation from Earth is now enroute to Tarsis to meet with members of the Governing Council."

PART 5

Bennie reached the bottom of the *Ghost*'s cargo ramp and said, "What did they do to my ship?" He pointed to the nearby *Rocky Nontee*.

Wil joined him. "It looks just as shitty as it did before."

The Brailack hacker looked up at Wil. "There's new scorch marks on her hull." He pointed. "There. There. And, gods! There!"

Wil leaned forward and squinted. "You can tell?"

Bennie glared at Wil. He snorted and stormed off toward the *Rocky Nontee* mumbling about humans having no sense.

Wil watched his weird little friend run a hand along the bumpy hull of his ship. He sighed and nodded to the Palorian members of the team standing a few hundred meters away with Admiral Shre' Ta'n. The group started toward the *Ghost*.

Cynthia, Nic, and their clients came down the ramp to join Wil.

Wil smiled. "Captain Shre' Ta'n."

"Admiral now," she corrected, offering her arm.

Taking her forearm in his hand, Wil smiled. "Glad they recognized your worth."

She grinned, a flush creeping across her cheeks. "Indeed." She reached up to straighten her hair.

Gabe, standing behind her, tilted his head, his optic sensors whirring and clicking as he took in the scene.

The Admiral's smile shifted. Not to a frown, exactly, but definitely to something less warm as she looked past Wil. "Blu'T'Ohm."

The Harrith man inclined his head. "Admiral."

Wil coughed. "Admiral." He extended an arm to Cynthia. "My wife. Cynthia Luar."

The two women exchanged pleasantries. Wil watched, smiling. Cynthia hadn't been with the team when they'd more or less single-handedly saved the Harrith sector from being coerced into joining the GC.

The Rogue Enterprises team hadn't been to Harrith Prime since they were government sanctioned privateers. Wil couldn't even remember how long ago that was, now. After what became popularly known as the Harrith Incident, the team helped out while the Harrith Navy rebuilt itself.

The first few months of privateering had been exciting for the newly formed team. Local criminals had sensed the opening and tried to grab as much territory as possible. Many went to war with their rivals, civilians in the crossfire be damned. Others sought new markets. Wil and his team brought them all in, or if they proved uncooperative, took them out.

The crew of the *Ghost* had melded as a team hunting pirates and smugglers less clever than themselves. He smiled remembering their first adventure, long before they had an official team name.

Prior to the Harrith Incident, he had been working alone for Xarrix Cruthup as a smuggler after finding himself alone with what was essentially a tiny warship. His one ask of the now-long-dead crime boss had been to find him a crew. The reptilian criminal had delivered, providing the transport schedule for a pair of disgraced Peacekeepers being quietly disposed of aboard a Partherian military transport.

After springing Maxim and Zephyr, the team grew again when Bennie, hired to code new idents for the Palorian couple, came under attack from Peacekeepers.

The new foursome, needing cash and resources, took another Xarrix job. A supposedly—

but anything but—simple heist later, and the team grew again when they stole a crate that contained an engineering droid, Gabe.

So many adventures.

Wil's reverie broke as Blu'T'Ohm shouted, "That can't be!" He shook his head.

"I'm afraid so," the Admiral said. She looked around the assembled group. "We shut down the fabrication plant linked to the components Gabe scanned, but there's no telling how many more might be involved."

"We're relatively certain some of the security council are involved, despite their names not being in the records," Maxim added.

"But why?" Blu'T'Ohm asked, unable to fathom a reason his own people—let alone the actual government—would want to kill him...

"Perhaps we should continue this elsewhere?" Gabe offered.

"Trouble?" Wil asked. He looked around the spaceport. It was a smaller port on the outskirts of the capital city.

"No. We moved the *Nontee* without issue after the ambush at the main port. But still..." Zephyr said.

"From a tactical standpoint, we are exposed," Gabe insisted, adding, "We do not know the extent of our enemy's capabilities."

"Whoever is bankrolling this operation has power, reach,

and influence. Better to play it safe," Maxim said, nodding to his mechanical friend.

"I have someplace we can go," Shre' Ta'n offered.

Blu'T'Ohm turned to her. "You'd protect us?"

She shrugged. "I don't like your politics on this, Blue. But something is happening that's bigger than you. We have to find out what."

"Very well," the older of the pair sighed.

Gul'P'Ulo turned to her boss. "Sir. We're not influencing votes here on Harrith Prime."

"I'd say you're also safer, but that seems debatable at this point," Wil offered.

The safe house Shre' Ta'n brought them to was a two-story affair in a suburb on the outskirts of Drotu. She insisted that they change vehicles three times between the small spaceport the team's ships were docked in and the bedroom community they were now driving through.

The last vehicle they switched to was from a private vehicle rental service. The Admiral drove.

As the vehicle pulled to a stop in front of the house, Wil craned his neck to see around Maxim. "My parents had a minivan like this when I was kid." He started unfolding himself from the third-row seat he, Cynthia, and Bennie had been wedged into for the better part of an hour. "It sucked about the same but didn't have gravlifts."

"Just move your ass," Bennie said, shoving Wil's behind, causing him to collide with Maxim. The big man growled.

Shre' Ta'n came around the front of the vehicle. "I'm afraid you'll need to get creative with the sleeping arrangements. This is the only safe house I remember the access credentials for." She shrugged. "That said, it has the benefit of only myself and my aide knowing you're using it."

"Hopefully we won't need it long," Zephyr said, grasping the other woman's arm. "We'll see you tomorrow?"

Shre' Ta'n nodded. "Probably not until after lunch. I have a staff meeting I can't move. Plus, I should probably be seen going about my usual business."

Everyone nodded their agreement. After being told to stand down by the security council, attracting attention was low on everyone's list.

The next day, the Admiral brought lunch from a Ruknak fast food place she knew in the city.

"Damn!" Wil said around a mouthful of something he couldn't pronounce. "Who knew those rock heads could craft something this..." He took another bite. "This...better-than-good."

The Harrith woman nodded. "I eat there once a week, at least."

"Wonder if they can do bulk orders," Bennie said, several crumbs tumbling from his mouth.

Cynthia rolled her eyes. "Okay, so we're all rested, and Max and Zee filled us in on what you all have been up to here." She looked around the room. The team, plus their clients and the Admiral, were all in the sunken conversation pit in the living room space. Myriad takeout containers littered the low central coffee table. "Now what?"

"Now we figure out what the wurrin is going on," the Admiral answered. She took a bite of lunch.

"How?" Nic asked. She looked around at the adults in the room, noticing their blank expressions.

"Records." Everyone turned to Bennie. "What?" He reached up to pick at his teeth. "Something in my teeth?" No one looked.

"What do you mean, records?" Maxim asked.

The Brailack hacker looked around and sighed. "Come on. You can't be serious."

"Pretend we're dumb," Wil said, his voice flat.

"Pretend?" Bennie replied, smirking. He held up both hands, one still clutching his lunch wrap. "Something like this. As big as you all say this is, there's no way there aren't records somewhere. I mean, more than what you already found at the factory." He spread his arms, sending chunks of his lunch flying. "This is bigger than a factory selling knockoff PK gear. This isn't a few shady government types or military or anything. This is everyone."

"Not. Everyone," Shre' Ta'n growled.

Bennie dipped his head. "You know what I mean." He waved his free hand while taking a bite of his meal. Around it, he said, "This has to go pretty high up. You don't run something this large on napkins and in scratch pads. Someone, somewhere has a ledger."

"We did not find a ledger or any other accounting record at the fabrication plant," Gabe said.

Zephyr looked at Shre' Ta'n. "The Dystum?"

The other woman shrugged. "Maybe? Our appointment was made with his office. Someone pushed us off to the security council." She shook her head. "Dren."

"Okay. So...what? We break into the..." Bennie looked at the Admiral. "White House? Parliament? Whatever your government's main building is called."

She shook her head. "The Circle, but no. Too well protected." She looked at the ceiling. Bennie opened his mouth; she extended a hand, finger held upright. "Thinking." He closed his mouth as Maxim grinned, nudging him. She looked at the group. "Sovereignty Day."

After a few moments, Zephyr couldn't hold it any longer. "And, that is?"

Wil leaned toward Cynthia. "Glad she asked. I was about to." Cynthia rolled her eyes and took a bite of her lunch.

Shre' Ta'n smiled. "The anniversary of you five thwarting the GC's plan to absorb the Harrith sector."

Wil looked at the others. "Oh, shit. You made that a holiday? Are we...like, heroes?" He leaned forward. "Are there statues?"

"Oh no," Cynthia groaned.

"My likeness isn't cheap," Bennie said around another mouthful of food.

"Your likeness is extra cheap," Nic said. Bennie glared.

The Admiral waved a hand. "Calm down. We don't have any monuments to you or anything. But yeah, you have some star power we might be able to leverage." Everyone leaned forward. She said, "The Dystum's estate will have the access we need and always has one of the larger Sovereignty Day parties. It's a who's who of political, corporate, and military power within the sector." She smiled. "And about a thousand or so party guests of no consequence."

"That sounds promising," Cynthia said.

Shre' Ta'n held up a hand. "A few hurdles." She nodded to the Palorian couple opposite her in the conversation pit. "The Dystum and the rest of the Circle, no doubt, have heard at least some version of the security council's report. They'll know you've been sent away." She turned to Gabe. "You too."

The droid inclined his head. "Our remaining on the planet could be a strategic advantage."

"Dren," Maxim groaned. "She's right. Guessing showing up the party would be a dead giveaway."

The Harrith woman nodded her agreement. "We did go to great lengths to hide your ship after the attack." She cocked her head. "It won't hold up to much scrutiny, but I was able to fabricate your departure records."

"How soon is this Sovereignty Day?" Bennie asked.

"This week's end."

"So, three days," Zephyr said.

Nic wiped her short muzzle to make sure her lunch hadn't left anything behind. "So what? We sneak into the head person's estate and what? Hack his computer?"

Bennie shrugged. "Sounds like it. His terminal will, for sure, have the access we need to find out who's involved in all this. With what Gabe and the others collected, we should be able to connect the threads."

In the kitchen area, Gul'P'Ulo looked at her boss. "Sir, we're losing ground every day we're here." She checked her wristcomm. "Chulak held a vote yesterday on a referendum to leave the GC. It lost, by less than two percent of voters." She looked him in the eye. "We...You could have swayed them. Opened their eyes to potential of true independence."

The senior of the pair sighed. "You're right. We'll make arrangements to leave tomorrow. If they want to stay here, we can hire security elsewhere. Maybe the Navy will lend us a squad." He turned to the others in the lounge area. After clearing his throat, he said, "We'll be leaving."

Everyone turned to look at him. Wil said, "I don't think that's a good idea."

Gul'P'Ulo shook her head. "You don't understand. The separatist movement can't do our work here on Harrith Prime. We need to be where the debates are. Where societies are discussing their future."

"Until we figure this out, your safety cannot be guaranteed off-world," Gabe said.

Blu'T'Ohm shook his head. "She's right, though. We can't be here. The societies of the GC are discussing their futures, and I and other separatists have to be part of those conversations. We have to counter the Tarsi's propaganda." He sighed. "If you're set on remaining here, we'll hire security elsewhere."

Around another mouthful of food, Bennie said, "Shpeeking off."

"What?" Cynthia asked, turning to the Brailack hacker.

He chewed and swallowed, then said, "Speaking. Of." Enunciation was easier once his mouth was less full. "We should discuss your funding."

"Why?" Gul'P'Ulo asked, a bit too quickly.

Bennie raised an eyebrow ridge. "Well, for one, so you can pay us. But also, to see if there's anything honky." He looked at Wil.

"Hinky," the human offered.

Bennie nodded. "Hinky, in your finances. I did some digging earlier. Do you know where your money comes from?"

Blu'T'Ohm shook his head. "Donations and sponsors."

Gul'P'Ulo offered, "The separatist movement has benefactors across the GC and beyond its borders."

Wil and Bennie exchanged a look.

"Why?" Blu repeated.

Bennie shrugged. "You've never asked where it comes from? Who actually is donating?"

Blu looked at his aide, who shook her head a little too quickly.

The team busied themselves with prepping for the upcoming job until Shre' Ta'n arrived the next night with dinner from a Harrith restaurant near her home that she swore the team needed to try. Blu'T'Ohm and Gul'P'Ulo reluctantly gave their approval of her menu choices after trying them. The two were still pouting over being told that leaving the planet right then wasn't a good or feasible plan.

Wil broke the companionable silence that had settled over the meal. "Okay, so I've been thinking."

"Did it hurt?" Bennie quipped, ducking before the last word left his mouth, narrowly avoiding Wil's outstretched palm.

Wil said. "The way I see it, our primary objective is to get into the Destro's—"

"Dystum," Shre' Ta'n and Blu'T'Ohm corrected in unison.

"Yeah, him. We get into his estate and get access to his computer terminal."

"Oh, is that all?" Cynthia asked, smiling.

Wil ignored her. "Find the evidence, hopefully with a list of names, and get out."

"Then what?" Nic asked.

The room fell silent.

Wil looked around. "We burn it all down, and I guess save the GC..."

"Or at least slow its death down to a manageable pace," Maxim added.

Shre' Ta'n looked at the group sitting around the lounge's conversation pit, eating dinner and discussing the collapse of the largest governing body in the galaxy like it was just another day. She knew from firsthand experience and reports funneled through Harrith Naval Intelligence that these people did the right thing in the most ham-fisted way possible, but always for the right reasons.

She'd been on the receiving end of that once, and it looked like she—and her people, her world—would be again. She wasn't sure what to think of that, in all honesty, but also wasn't sure her thoughts mattered at this point. The mass transit vehicle was leaving the station.

Zephyr set her plate down. "Okay, so what's this look like?"

Wil set his plate down and took a sip of his drink. Something fruity and sweeter than he preferred, but the safe house refrigeration unit had been mostly empty when they arrived, save for these sugar drinks.

He looked at the others. "Max, Zephyr, and Gabe, you're gonna have to lay low for this."

Gabe raised his hand. "Actually. I have an alternative." His optic sensors dimmed as several mechanical noises began to come from various parts of his body. His torso split down the middle, panels revealing themselves, folding like origami. His arms clicked several times as his upper and forearms lengthened, cylindrical sections fitting back into place. His legs followed his arms. The final change was his neck retracting and angling forward so that his head stuck out at a ninety-degree angle from his torso.

"Okay, that's disconcerting," Shre' Ta'n said. Everyone nodded.

"Ew," Nic said.

"You don't get used to it," Wil said. He nodded to Gabe. "Okay. Gabe is still in play."

Maxim shook his head. "No way. This is too big an op."

Shre' Ta'n sighed. "I'm afraid we don't have a lot of options. If you show up at the party, the Dystum will know that you, and I, ignored the security council's instructions." She looked over to Zephyr, then back to Maxim. "Sorry, you two." She held up a hand to forestall the big Palorian's retort. "I have an idea, though. I can requisition a command vehicle. I know it's not boots on the ground, but you can run overwatch from the vehicle." She grinned. "We have some fun toys you might enjoy."

Maxim frowned. "We could just use the image inducers. Look like any other Harrith."

Bennie coughed. "Oh, um. We can't."

Everyone turned to the shrinking Brailack. His face was turning a deeper shade of green.

Wil inhaled slowly. "Explain."

Bennie glanced to Nic, who held up a hand. "Don't look at me."

He swallowed. "I was trying to reverse engineer them. See if I could fabricate knockoffs. Those krebnacks at the Draplin Combine built in some impressive safeties. I kept thinking I was about to circumvent them when new ones activated, slagging the device."

Cynthia rubbed her face as she shook her head. "You broke them all trying to make knockoffs?"

"Well..."

Zephyr sighed and rubbed her forehead. "To do what? Sell?"

Bennie pulled a face. "Yes..."

Maxim lunged for his much smaller teammate. "You little..." Zephyr had her arms around his waist.

Bennie scrambled up and out of the circular seating area.

The Harrith admiral cleared her throat. "So, I should requisition the command vehicle?"

Maxim sighed, dropping back to sit next to Zephyr. "Yes."

Nic watched the adults a moment. "What about me?"

Wil pointed to Cynthia, then Nic. "You two." He grinned. "You two are Blue's security escort."

"Sweet," Nic cheered. She pumped a furry little arm in the air.

"What?" Cynthia groaned.

Wil shrugged. "We can't let him out of our sight."

"I'm not a child," Blu'T'Ohm complained from the kitchen area.

Wil ignored him. "Since we'll be at the party, they need to be at the party."

Cynthia looked at Bennie's Olop apprentice. "Okay. Sure, I guess that tracks."

Wil shrugged. "I know it's not ideal, but the more assets we have on the inside, the better." Cynthia nodded her agreement.

"This is so insulting," Blu'T'Ohm complained. He turned to Gul'P'Ulo. "We should at least make the most of our time on Prime." She nodded her reluctant agreement.

Gabe made his disgusted-with-biologicals noise, hoping to get his colleagues back on track. "I believe I can attain an invite in this guise that will keep my identity secret," Gabe offered.

Wil smiled. "How?"

"I will go to the capital as an envoy of Arcadia." Gabe's new head turned to take them all in. "I will ask for an invite to the Dystum's Sovereignty Day party in order to observe a mature and powerful nonaligned government."

Wil nodded. "Okay. Good call. The more angles we have, the better."

Bennie looked at Wil. "What about us?" He was still loitering between the conversation pit and kitchen area. He pointed to himself, then Wil.

Wil grinned. "We go in as us. I'm thinking I can pay a visit to the Dystum and wrangle an invite. Local celebrity and all that."

Bennie rubbed his little green hands together. "Can I be Libido Carbone again?"

"Lando Calrissian, and no. We're going to be ourselves."

Zephyr nodded. "So, we have a plan."

"Sounds like," Cynthia agreed.

The next morning, Bennie, Wil, and Gabe took separate public transport into the capital complex to secure invites to the Dystum's Sovereignty Day celebration. Gabe loitered nearby until Wil and Bennie went in, then followed, taking a seat in the waiting room.

"Captain Calder. What an honor." The Dystum of the Harrith Circle rose from behind his desk, coming around to offer his arm to Wil. He seemed genuinely thrilled to meet Wil.

Wil grasped the offered forearm. "Pleasure's all mine." He looked down at Bennie. "You remember my teammate, Ben-Ari Vulvo."

The three had never met. During his recovery after the Harrith Incident, the sitting Dystum had stopped by for a brief photo op, but this new one had only been elected two or three cycles ago. Thanks to Shre' Ta'n, he knew this man would at least know of the team.

The Dystum nodded and exchanged pleasantries with Bennie. The older Harrith man moved back behind his desk. "What brings you to Harrith Prime?" He sat and pointed to the two guest chairs in front of his desk.

Bennie opened his mouth a moment before Wil dropped his hand over the little hacker's mouth. He smiled. "Bennie and I were making a cargo run to one of the colonies in Quilant space and saw on GNO that you all have a holiday around our little, you know..." He made a rolling motion with his hand. He pushed Bennie toward a seat, sitting as he did, in the other.

"Sovereignty Day, yes, indeed." The Dystum beamed. "Sovereignty Day celebrates Harrith's victory against those who sought to destroy our sovereignty." He frowned to himself hearing how that sounded but said nothing.

"Neat!" Wil grinned.

The other man cocked his head to the side. "Curious. You know your Palorian crew members were recently here? With the droid."

Bennie affected a shocked look on his face. "Really?"

"Indeed. You didn't know?" The other man's gaze was locked on Wil's.

Wil shrugged. "We've grown our business. Two ships." He never let his gaze drift. "They still here?"

The Dystum shook his head. "I don't believe so. My understanding is that they departed two days ago." He sighed. "I didn't get a chance to meet with them, but I'm told they met with Admiral Narel."

"Who?" Wil asked.

"Oh, of course. She was Captain when you last saw her. Shre' Ta'n Narel."

Wil snapped his fingers. "Oh, right! She's an admiral now? That's awesome!"

"They're gonna be jealous they missed the party," Bennie put in.

The Harrith leader regarded the Brailack, then turned to Wil. "I'd be honored to have you both join me at my estate for the Sovereignty Day celebration this week's end."

Wil and Bennie smiled. The latter said, "We'd be honored."

The pair made small talk for another thirty minutes before making their exit.

Down the street, Gabe walked into the main administration building in Drotu. The building spanned several blocks and featured more than a few multistory spires connected by sky bridges. Busy civil servants bustled all around him as he moved toward the welcome desk.

The young Harrith woman looked up, then back down to her terminal, then quickly back up at the approaching droid. When the strange looking droid reached her desk, she smiled. "How can I help you?"

Gabe inclined his more angular head. "I would like to speak with someone from your state department. I am an envoy from Arcadia." He transmitted his fake credentials to her terminal.

"From..." she stammered.

"Arcadia."

She nodded. "Yes, Arcadia. The..."

"Sovereign droid homeworld," Gabe offered. He gestured to her terminal, where his identity and pertinent details were onscreen.

Her already round eyes somehow grew wider.

Gabe nodded. "Yes."

She swallowed. "Let me call someone."

"Thank you."

A moment later, a middle-aged Harrith man came out of an office down the hall. He hurried around the welcome desk, offering his arm in greeting. "Hello there. I'm Deputy Secretary of State Gil'Bart Wemli."

Gabe dipped his head. "Hello. I am...Mitch."

The man in front of Gabe smiled. "What can I do for you, envoy...Mitch?"

"I am here to learn more about your society. With everything going on, my people have decided to look to stable examples of non-GC cultures in order to best ensure our young government survives this current turmoil."

The Deputy Secretary of State's eyes widened. He nodded his head enough to dislodge a tuft of hair on top of his head, sending it fluttering back and forth. "Of course. Of course! In fact, your timing is excellent. Our annual celebration of being a free society is coming up. Tomorrow, in fact!"

Gabe tilted his head. "Is that so?"

More aggressive nodding. "Indeed. Sovereignty Day. It recognizes the victory of the Harrith people over those who sought to undermine our government and force us into Galactic Commonwealth membership."

"I see," Gabe replied. "I would like to know more."

"Of course." The officious Harrith motioned back toward his office. "Please."

Gabe followed him.

As the door closed, the official said, "One of the biggest parties is at our head of state's residence. I'm sure I can get you on the guest list."

## CHAPTER 22

While Wil, Bennie, and Gabe were in the city and Maxim and Zephyr were with the Admiral, Cynthia and Nic were at the safe house going over their part of the operation.

The two were in the house's rear yard. The older woman had run her young colleague through a series of martial arts flexibility drills while the two talked.

"So, what's it like in green bean's Tower?" Cynthia asked.

Nic dropped into a crouch, then sprung up over the brickwork fireplace in the yard's center without touching it, landing in a roll before vaulting to her feet and leaping into the air again, this time spinning end over end before sticking a three-point landing.

She stood. "It's okay. Kinda lonely and haunted-like. Most of it's shut down. C7K2 is doing his best to bring life back to the place, but..." She shrugged. "The upside is that security is pretty weak. I've explored the entire Tower, even the parts they don't want me to see."

Cynthia leaned against a patio chair. "Nice moves. Tell me more about sneaking around the Tower."

Nic spent an hour telling the other woman about her first

time in the Tower of Plentallus on Nexum, about the ducts and poor security features on the doors.

When the young Olop woman finished, Cynthia made an approving face. "Okay, so you don't need as much training as I thought." She smiled. "You're sneaky."

Nic grinned, bearing her tiny, pointed teeth. "I got game."

"Don't get cocky," the other woman quipped. "Bennie and the Admiral got us the blueprints for the estate. Let's go over those."

Nic rubbed her little hands together, grinning. A gesture she picked up from Bennie, Cynthia assumed.

Maxim whistled. He and Zephyr were with Admiral Shre' Ta'n in an unmarked warehouse several blocks from the naval command building. "These are nice."

The trio was standing in front of four state of the art mobile command vehicles. Each was painted a flat gray with cowlings over the gravlifts to minimize vulnerable spots. A series of antennae and sensor arrays covered the vehicles' roofs, some hanging over the sides.

Shre' Ta'n moved to one of the vehicles, placing her palm on a piece of the body that looked like the rest of the vehicle. A panel under her palm glowed blue, then green. The side door made a low popping sound as it separated from the body, receding slightly, then sliding backward. She stood aside holding an arm out. "After you."

The pair walked up the stairs into the vehicle's main cabin work space. Lights came on as they entered; displays woke, showing city and orbital tracking data. A narrow situation table in the center lit up with a holographic view of what Maxim assumed was the Dystum's estate.

"Each of these vehicles can coordinate a major land and air operation. Full planetary data network access, including the military and all commercial networks."

Zephyr looked over her shoulder. The other woman was trying, not successfully, to hide her pride in the vehicle's capabilities. "Her name?"

"What?" Maxim and Shre' Ta'n said as one.

Maxim turned to look at the other woman and stepped aside, smiling.

The Admiral blushed. "This one is Lycoria." She grinned.

"I approve," Zephyr said.

Maxim meandered further to the rear of the vehicle. "Staff?" He counted six workstations.

Shre' Ta'n looked around. "I'll see what I can do. I don't have six analysts that I trust or can wrangle into service, but I can probably get three that understand discretion."

The big Palorian nodded. "That'll work."

Zephyr was eyeing the forward section. "Driver?" She leaned in to look at the small cab. There was a single seat surrounded by monitors. She couldn't find any kind of control system.

"Self-driven," Shre' Ta'n said. She nodded to the compartment. "Manual control is an option, of course, but..." She rapped a knuckle on one of the side panels near the ceiling. "After all, this isn't a combat vehicle."

Zephyr nodded, grinning. "This should be fun."

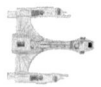

The estate of the Dystum of the Circle was more like a palace, in Wil's opinion. It sat atop a low hill several kilometers outside Drotu proper. The hilltop district was concentric ring after ring of mansions winding toward the Dystum's estate at the peak. The neighborhood was a who's who of Drotu's wealthiest and most powerful, each ring smaller than the one below it.

Sovereignty Day celebrations were taking place all across Harrith Prime and the numerous Harrith colony worlds in the sector. The Dystum's party was the party to end all parties, starting around midday and ending sometime the following morning. Technology mavens, celebrities of stage and vid, politicians from all parties—everyone made an appearance at the Dystum's party.

"Damn," Wil said under his breath. He and Bennie were in a luxury ground car, gliding up the hill. Searchlights were arrayed around the property throwing beams of light stabbing into the low clouds.

Bennie looked up from picking at the lapel of his hastily purchased bespoke suit. "These folks sure can party." He adjusted his sleeve, making sure his wristcomm was concealed.

The ground car came to a stop at the gates. Beyond them, thousands of mostly Harrith partygoers were already milling about the grounds.

The naval officer at the gate checked Wil and Bennie's faces against his tablet. "Welcome." He smiled. "And, thank you."

Wil returned the smile. "Uh, you're welcome." The vehicle continued up the hill to the drop-off lot. He looked at Bennie. "You ready?"

As the vehicle came to a stop, both passenger doors rose. As the team hacker stepped out, he looked at Wil and winked, pulling at each sleeve in turn. "Always."

Wil groaned. "Let's do this, Double Oh Dummy."

The pair walked toward the estate's main door. They were

met by a well-dressed Harrith man. "Greetings, Wil Calder and Ben-Ari Vulvo." He bowed. "Welcome. Please make yourselves at home. The Dystum will be making his address just before day's end." He pointed behind him toward a long hallway. "The bar and buffet are that way. The bulk of the festivities are on the rear lawn."

Wil smiled. "I could use a drink." He shoved Bennie ahead of him.

They made their way through the crowd of partygoers, several already on their way to a good hangover in the morning.

Bennie nudged Wil as they passed a staircase occupied by dozens of fashionably dressed socialites. In a low voice, he said, "The second floor is guest rooms, another ballroom, a few other things. There's a staircase in the rear to the private quarters and offices. That's where we need to go."

Wil nodded as they continued past the stairs. "Everyone get that?"

"Copy that," Maxim said from the mobile command center, parked near the base of the hill.

"We're approaching now. We'll be inside shortly," Cynthia added.

Bennie pointed. "Bar."

A cluster of Harrith Naval officers spotted the pair and waved for them to join their conversation. Wil sighed. "Get me a grum." He split off from Bennie and headed for the group. Bennie reached the bar and waved to get the young bartender's attention. "Two grum, please."

The young woman nodded. "Enjoying the party?" she asked as she leaned down to fetch two frosty bottles.

"Just got here, but I'm sure I'll find ways to entertain myself." He raised an eyebrow ridge. "You working all evening?"

She handed him the bottles. "I'm off in two tocks." She

smiled and made sure to not break eye contact. "Hope to see you later."

Bennie winked. "Oh. You will." She grinned, turning just as a blush crept up her neck.

The small earbud that was snugly tucked into his auditory canal clicked. "You know we can all hear you, right?" Nic said.

Bennie grinned. "Hate the game, not the player." He turned to see that Wil had broken off from the conversation he was having and was moving toward another group, this one made of what looked to Bennie like socialites. His and Wil's job right then was to be seen by as many partygoers as possible. Bennie joined him, offering one of the cold bottles of what passed for beer in the Galactic Commonwealth.

He looked up at the group of mostly Harrith. "I'm a Knight of Plentallus."

Wil rolled his eyes.

The military ground car left the guest drop-off area. Gabe watched, then turned to Admiral Shre' Ta'n. "Shall we?"

The Admiral was in her dress reds. She smiled to Gabe. "I'm still not clear on how this all worked out."

Walking to the front door, the droid said, "It was surprisingly easy to maneuver the deputy secretary into not only gifting me a guest pass to this party but insisting I have an escort of sufficiently high station accompany me. A few well-timed linguistic cues and your name was at the top of his list."

The doors swung open and the estate's majordomo ushered them inside, bidding them welcome and encouraging them to explore the grounds to the rear of the property.

The pair moved through the party. Several naval officers

stopped them as they made their way. They passed Wil and Bennie, engaged in a conversation with a gaggle of well-dressed socialites.

Both pairs passed each other without any type of acknowledgement of the other.

"So, tell me, Gabe." Shre' Ta'n looked up at him. "What kind of droid are you?"

He turned his head slightly, making optic sensor and eye contact as they exited the back of the estate. The lawn was full of hundreds of people gathered near tents and portable bars. A stage was set up in the far corner, likely where the Dystum would be making his remarks later that evening.

"I am unique," he said. "Shortly after thwarting Commander Janus and his co-conspirator's attempts to trick your society into joining the Galactic Commonwealth, I was killed."

Her breath caught. "Oh, is that all?" She made a face. "Did it hurt?"

They angled toward one side of the stage and a display that was set up showing Harrith historical moments.

Gabe said, "It was aboard the dreadnaught we discovered."

She nodded. "I remember hearing about that."

"The intelligence that ran the ship found me intriguing. After my body was destroyed, it kept my spark to interrogate."

"Your spark?"

"What biologicals might call their soul. Though that is not at all what it is for droids. It is our primary processing array, the core programming that makes each droid unique. The *Siege Perilous* had never encountered artificially created intelligences other than those of its society. It did not know what to make of us and needed to learn as much as it could." He stopped to examine a display—created, he hoped, by a child—depicting the battle over Harrith Prime. What he assumed was the *Ghost* was a grayish smudge with flames behind it.

He turned to the Admiral. "Not a very accurate re-creation."

She smiled, accepted a drink from a passing server, and said, "You were saying..."

"While the ship's intelligence explored my spark, I explored the ship's systems. In particular, the database. It was a wealth of information on the society that the ship originally came from. I was able to hijack several of the ship's systems in order to build a body from a design I found in the database." He placed a hand on his chest. "Well. Not this body. A mechanical frame capable of reconfiguring itself as needed."

Shre' Ta'n took a sip of her drink. "Amazing. You can change into anything?"

He shook his head. "No, I am bound by the physical boundaries of the initial form I selected. I cannot have four legs or two heads, but can, within reason, create any combination of humanoid designs."

"Incredible."

Gabe nodded. Using his internal communication suite, he sent, *Team 2 in position. We are near the stage.*

In the mobile command vehicle, Maxim and Zephyr exchanged a look and nodded to each other. There was no disguising the mobile command center, so they were parked out of the way at the base of the hill, in a lot that was scheduled to be a recreation center soon.

The two Palorians were side by side at the master command station. Three Harrith Naval officers were arrayed at other stations. Each had served aboard the *Baxu Ahvil* with then-Commander Narel. She vouched for each of them.

Zephyr turned to the youngest of the three, a woman. "Everyone ready?"

The younger woman turned in her chair. "Yes, ma'am. I've got full control over the local grid for the hilltop district."

Zephyr nodded. She tapped her commset. "Overwatch is ready."

"This is itchy," Nic complained. She was in a bespoke pantsuit that the Admiral helped source.

Cynthia looked at her. "You look good, though." She smiled. She, too, was in a custom-tailored pantsuit. Finding clothes that accommodated a tail on a world where the predominant species was tailless, was never easy. Both women had spent several hours the day prior at a tailor that had the personality of an angry Qwaptar.

Not only were the clothes Nic and Cynthia wore custom-tailored, but they were custom-tailored for fighters, with give in all the right places.

Cynthia checked her various pockets, then cracked her knuckles. To Blu'T'Ohm, she asked, "You ready?"

He stared at her, brows flat. "To attend a party? Yes, I think I can handle that."

Cynthia clucked. "You know it's more than that. If we're successful you can go about your business undermining the Commonwealth without fear of being murdered."

Nic scowled. "Or, you know, if not: get murdered."

The older man returned the scowl.

"We have arrived," the ground car's driving AI intoned. The vehicle slid to a halt, and both passenger doors opened.

Stepping out, Nic took in the sight. "Wow," she whispered. "Gul'P'Ulo is gonna be so jealous." The younger Harrith political agitator had opted to visit family while in Drotu, leaving the party and the networking to her boss.

Blu'T'Ohm nudged her out of the way. "No, she won't. Excuse me." He slid out around the young Olop, smoothing his suit shirt and jacket. "Let's get this over with."

Cynthia slid out of the vehicle, adjusting her own outfit as she did. "After you. Remember, we're your security detail. Talk to who you like, do what you will. We'll be around."

"Lucky me." He made a show of ignoring the two women as he stormed through the open front door.

Nic fell in next to Cynthia. "This is so exciting." She looked up, her grin stretching across her little teddy bear face. She reached inside her blazer, double checking that her beam saber was still safely attached to the shoulder harness she rigged up.

"Stop fidgeting. It's a dead giveaway."

"Oh, sorry." Her hands dropped to her side.

Up ahead, Blu'T'Ohm was already engaged in an animated discussion with a quartet of Harrith business people.

Cynthia slid a hand over to her wristcomm, tapping an icon to join the team's mesh communication network. "Team 3 onsite," she whispered.

The two women meandered around the room as Blu'T'Ohm chatted with guests. They were in a formal reception room with a few dozen other partygoers, all of whom were impeccably dressed. Cynthia looked at each face, committing them to memory. Just in case.

"What're you doing?" Nic asked, watching her taller colleague.

Cynthia smiled. "Fourth rule of—"

"I think we're on five now," Nic said.

"Don't interrupt," Cynthia scolded. She continued, "It's important to catalog faces. You never know when it'll be useful."

"All of them?" Nic looked around the room. Everyone in it

was Harrith, and she hated to say it, but they all looked the same to her.

Cynthia angled toward the edge of the room, opposite Blue and his conversation companions. "All of them." She pointed to a woman nursing a drink in the far corner. She was stylishly dressed and all alone. "She's an executive. Probably the head of one of Harrith's biggest companies. She's here because it's where everyone important is, but she doesn't want to be."

Nic looked across the room. The woman was beautiful, well dressed, and—now that Nic was really looking—was clearly annoyed with everyone in the room. Her eyes moved from person to person, never lingering more than a second or two.

Nic was looking from face to face, doing her best to catalog features, when she spied Blu'T'Ohm leaving the room. She nodded in the direction he had exited. The pair left the room and found their charge in the middle of another group of important looking Harrith.

Cynthia turned to Nic. "How many men were in the room we just left?"

Nic frowned. "How many? What?"

"Men. How many?"

Nic closed her eyes, reviewing faces from the previous room. "Nineteen?"

"That a question or a statement?"

"Statement."

"Wrong."

Nic's eyes went wide. "What? No. I counted."

Cynthia smiled. "You were close. Twenty-one."

Nic closed her eyes again. "Where were they?"

"Behind you, next to the door we came in."

The younger woman nodded. "Dren."

"Language."

"Don't get drunk." Wil took the fluted glass from Bennie as the hacker raised it to take a drink. "You still have a job to do."

"Spoil sport."

"You're a mean drunk."

"Am not."

"Come on, let's go explore the upstairs areas." Wil shoved his small teammate back toward the front of the estate and the grand staircase. "The Dystum should be making his speech soon."

In a low voice, Bennie said, "Team 1 moving upstairs."

Partygoers were moving up and down the pair of staircases in the main hall with ease. The two Rogue Enterprises team members fell in with the crowd.

The second floor of the Dystum's estate was far less grand than the main floor. Meant for guests and state business, it was luxurious without being over the top.

Bennie whistled. "Still nice."

Wil nodded his agreement.

Partygoers were wandering the halls same as below, but in far fewer numbers, mostly in discrete groups. Wil and Bennie found several people camped out in a conference room swapping stories about political wins and losses. Multiple bottles of colored liquor were scattered across the tabletop.

Passing the door, Wil said, "I think I'd like them."

Bennie pulled his sleeve up to reveal his wristcomm, consulting the screen. "I think what we're looking for is up the hall and to the right." He didn't wait for Wil.

Downstairs, a chiming tone drew everyone's attention toward hidden speakers in the ceiling. "Attention, honored guests. If you'll make your way to the south lawn, the Sovereignty Day celebration will continue with remarks from the Dystum of the Circle," a voice announced.

A discreet distance away from their charge, Nic looked up at Cynthia. The former said, "I'll get him." She headed toward the clump of people having an animated discussion with Blu'T'Ohm. She tapped his hip. He ignored her. She tapped him again. Ignored. She punched him on the rump. "Let's go," she growled.

Cynthia watched the younger woman. It was funny, when the young Olop didn't think anyone was watching, her self-consciousness washed away.

Nic and Blu'T'Ohm returned. The Harrith man nodded toward the crowd migrating toward the doors leading to the lawn. "Off we go." He turned on his heel and merged with the crowd. "Sel'Ardu Pilra? How good to see you!" Blu'T'Ohm and the man he was speaking with exchanged greetings as they flowed into the crowd.

Out on the lawn, Shre' Ta'n and Gabe watched partygoers file out of the estate, the crowd on the lawn growing. She turned to Gabe. "The others are ready?"

Gabe nodded. "They are moving into position now."

"I'm nervous. Is that weird? I mean I'm an admiral in one of the most powerful navies in the sector." She reached up and rubbed the back of her neck as they walked.

"Your nervousness is warranted."

"I'm sorry, what?" She pulled the taller droid toward one of the decorative shrubs that lined the lawn.

Gabe tilted his head. "Our plans have a tendency of going horribly sideways."

"That's..." She frowned. "Disconcerting."

"Indeed." His current disguise configuration lacked any type of functional mouth, opting instead for a more standard vocalizer. If he had a mouth, he would attempt a sympathetic smile. "I have had to come to terms with the uncertainty and chaos that surrounds my team. Else I would have long since gone rampant."

The Admiral pursed her lips. "I do not feel better."

Gabe pointed to Blu'T'Ohm, Nic, and Cynthia. "It would not be unusual or arouse suspicion for you to speak with Mr. Ka-tan, would it?"

Shre' Ta'n shook her head. "Not at all. Let's go say hello to my old colleague."

Leaning back in his seat to stare at the mobile command vehicle's ceiling, Maxim said, "This isn't as fun as I expected."

Zephyr offered him something in a greasy wrapper. "Food's good, though.

He unwrapped the draugluin—which Wil insisted on calling a space gyro, whatever a gyro was—and took a bite. "True."

He turned to look at the three Harrith analysts sharing the mobile command vehicle with them. "Eat up."

"Thank you, sir. We will," one of them—the team leader, if he recalled—said.

Maxim turned his attention back to the displays on his console. "Looks like everyone is ready. Wil and Bennie are moving toward the third floor. The ladies and Gabe are on the lawn."

Zephyr turned in her chair. "Teams 2 and 3, are we a go?"

Over the channel, Gabe's voice said, "The Dystum and other members of the Circle are taking the stage."

## CHAPTER 23

Wil looked around. He and Bennie had meandered their way to the staircase that connected the second floor to the third. The staircase was protected by a heavy security door that Wil figured was usually open, hidden in the wall. While Wil stood watch, Bennie made quick work of the door's security system.

In minutes they were on the third floor. The full floor was offices and conference rooms. The Dystum's office occupied the entire front half of the building.

"Who needs an office this big...in their home?" Bennie looked around the room.

"I think this is just the foyer," Wil said. He nodded toward an ornate wooden door at the back of the room, behind a modern looking desk with a nametag that read, Maxine.

Bennie strode to the door and shoved. He bounced off it, stumbling back a few steps when the door didn't budge. He nearly crashed into Wil. "Locked," he grumbled.

Wil raised an eyebrow, looking first at Bennie, then the door. His gaze fell on a darkened panel set in the wooden frame. "Have at it."

Bennie went back to the door and examined the panel.

After a few pokes and prods, he slid a thin piece of metal out of his wristcomm. He slid the probe along the edge of the panel until it caught. "Mango."

"Bingo," Wil said.

"That's what I said." Bennie didn't look up. He slid the probe deeper into the panel, then gave it a yank. The front of the panel popped out of its housing. He peered into the guts of the control panel. "Quality work."

While the little green hacker went about his work, Wil examined the space. Over his shoulder, he said, "Appreciate the craftsmanship later." He examined the drawers of Maxine's desk. Several of what he assumed were knickknacks littered the top of the desk. The flag of the Harrith Collective stood in the corner near the door back out into the hallway. On the other side of the door was a flag for what Wil assumed was the state or region that Drotu was in.

"Got it," Bennie said as a click sounded from inside the pair of thick wooden doors. He stood and pushed against one. It swung inward on silent hinges. Walking in, he took a look around. "I should run for office. This is nice."

Wil followed him in. "Yeah, you should do that."

From behind a desk that wouldn't fit in any of the *Ghost's* crew quarters, Bennie said, "Really?"

"Not at all, no. You'd be horrible, and no one would elect you once they discovered all the super shady shit you do. You're evil." Wil came around the desk, whistling in appreciation. "This is a nice desk, though."

Wil sat down in one of the guest chairs while Bennie got to work.

The team's hacker looked at the desk. "Huh."

Wil turned his full attention to Bennie. "Huh, what?"

Over their comm units, Cynthia said, "The Dystum is taking the stage."

Wil's gaze never left Bennie. "Huh, what?"

The Brailack ran his hands along the desk's surface. "Do you see a terminal?"

Wil frowned. "I assumed it was some type of fancy holographic interface or something." He knocked a knuckle on the desk. "Maybe folds out of the desk?" He looked at the ceiling then the walls. Bennie ducked out of sight under the desk. "What're you doing?"

"Looking for change. What do you think, krebnack?" came the slightly muffled retort. "Maybe it folds out of the desk," Bennie mocked.

Wil slammed a fist on the desk, smiling when he was rewarded with a loud thunk and a string of expletives. He got up and moved around behind the desk, pulling on drawers. All he could see was Bennie's rear end and tiny dress shoes.

Bennie turned around under the desk. Peering out at Wil, he asked, "What're you doing?"

"Helping?"

"Stop it. Go sit down or something." He crawled out from under the desk. "There's definitely a terminal in here somewhere." He got to his feet. "Where are you?" He ran his little green hands along the top of the desk. Wil chuckled at the contrast of green against the dark wood.

Wil went back to his chair and dropped into it. He looked at his wristcomm, pulling up a game that Cynthia introduced him to. He still wasn't sure he was playing it correctly, but he enjoyed tapping the screen and making the animated thing that looked like Oscar the Grouch mixed with an ice cream cone, dance around the screen gobbling up the fleeing Smurf-like creatures.

Bennie whooped. "There we go."

Wil looked up as he was withdrawing his hands, as a thin display slid up out of the desk nearer to Wil. Holographic keys formed over the wooden surface. Next to the ephemeral keyboard, a piece of the desk slid away to reveal a data port.

Bennie set about his task, fingers flying along the virtual keyboard.

Wil smirked. "See, holographic."

"Are you done?" Wil was next to the door leaning out to look into the outer room, convinced he heard something in the reception area.

"I just started. Do you…You know what? No." Bennie didn't even look up from his work. On the desk's deployable screen, more windows than Wil could count were popping into and out of existence as Bennie sifted through the Harrith governmental network.

Wil watched the hacker work, then turned back to the door.

Bennie's fingers worked the holographic keyboard as if it were a real, tangible thing. The Dystum's office had a direct and unthrottled connection to the planet's data network.

Wil was nervous. They knew security was walking this floor but didn't know the pattern or timing since the building's security system was closed off from the planetary network.

He looked over his shoulder. "You confirmed the security team wouldn't be by any time soon, right?"

"What?" Bennie looked up. "Oh. Forgot."

Wil turned. "You little shithead."

Bennie held up a hand. "Oh, this is interesting."

Wil sighed. "What?"

Bennie looked up. "Oh, nothing."

Wil glared at his friend. "Focus."

After the Dystum finished his remarks and left the stage, a band playing long metal wind instruments took over. Nic was watching the show when she heard a loud voice. "Blu'T'Ohm Ka-tan!" She turned to see an overweight Harrith woman stumbling toward her and Cynthia's charge. She stepped in front of the much larger woman. "Excuse me." She held a hand up to slow the woman.

It was as if the large woman did not even see Nic. She steamrolled right over the much smaller Olop girl in front of her, only stopping when Cynthia slid in front of her, hand out to collide with the woman's chest. "Hello." She smiled, showing her incisors.

The woman looked past Cynthia. "You're a disgrace, Blu'T'Ohm Ka-tan!

The Harrith man turned slowly toward the woman.

Standing, Nic said, "Not a fan of the separatists?"

Seeming to notice Nic for the first time, the woman said, "What? No. The GC has plenty of problems. People like him," she jabbed an accusatory finger, manicured nail glinting in the light, toward their client, "are speeding up a process that should take cycles, and the repercussions will be immense, even for the Harrith Collective. He and his ilk will bring ruin on the galaxy."

Blu'T'Ohm stared at the woman, his mouth slowly opening and closing. Eventually, he regained his composure. "Madame, I and others who feel the same are simply sharing with GC worlds what we Harrith have known all along, that they don't need the Tarsi watching over them. That they can live peacefully in a galaxy without corrupt oversight."

The woman harrumphed. "You'll bring ruin on us all, I tell you. Do you think your friends who leave the GC won't still need protection? Our sector will become swamped with refugees! What then?" She was waving both arms as if she were guiding an aircraft in for a landing.

Nic and Cynthia remained between the two Harrith, the latter offering, "Perhaps we can continue this discussion at a lower volume over there?" She pointed to a less crowded piece of the lawn, further from the stage and the still performing band.

"Someone's coming!" Wil hissed, stepping back into the Dystum's office.

Bennie looked up. "I'm not done."

Wil reached the desk, looking around. "Shut it all down or put it to sleep or something. If they see the desk is active, they'll get suspicious."

Bennie frantically worked the keyboard. The display flickered and went dark before retracting back into the desktop.

Outside the door, voices could be heard.

"Hurry up!" Wil urged.

"I can't just disconnect," Bennie replied. "It'll corrupt the transfer." He gestured to the data cables tethering his wristcomm to the computer.

Wil looked around the room. "Under." He pushed Bennie down, shoving the hacker under the desk. The data cables running from his wristcomm to the desk's data ports were visible, but the rest of the terminal was now back to its sleep mode configuration, the desk looking like nothing more than an ornate piece of office furniture. "Stay quiet." He took in the room again. Not a lot of hiding places.

The voices were getting louder.

Wil spied a door that he had missed until now. It was designed to blend into the wall and did so almost perfectly. He darted to the door, pulling it open. A restroom. "Of course," he whispered to himself, easing the door closed behind him.

The restroom was nice, for a restroom. He couldn't hear what was or wasn't happening on the other side of the door; the builder of the room had ensured it was soundproof. Wil wished the Ankarrans had thought of that with the *Ghost*'s heads.

He tapped his earpiece. "We might have a wrinkle. Security patrol in the Dystum's office."

"They're wondering why the lights are on," Bennie provided in an almost-too-low-to-hear voice from under the desk.

"Need help?" Maxim asked. He was bored out of his mind in the mobile command vehicle.

"Not yet," Bennie answered. A moment later, "Okay, yes. Distraction, please."

Maxim looked at Zephyr, who said, "Trigger an alert on the far side of the property."

"Ma'am, I don't—" one of the loaner analysts started to protest.

She cut him off. "Do it." Turning to the other two, she said, "One of you. Now. Nothing big or crazy, just trigger a fault in a motion sensor or something."

All three Harrith went to work, hunching over their terminals, mumbling to each other as they worked.

Maxim looked at the screen before him showing the locations of the team. No one was close enough to do anything to help Wil and Bennie.

"Got it," one of the Harrith said.

On comms, Bennie said, "Thanks. Whatever you did, both security goons just made a quick exit."

"This might be a good time to make your own exit," Zephyr said.

"Agreed," Wil answered.

Maxim turned to the analysts. "What'd you do?"

The team leader smiled, rubbing her hands together. "We had access only to certain things, so we made the best use we could. Every security agent on the property was alerted to multiple faults in the perimeter wall, indicating intrusion."

"Party crashers." Maxim smiled. She nodded.

Zephyr turned to add her thanks but was stopped by every system in the vehicle shutting down. Instead, she said, "What the grolack?"

The main hatch slid away, letting the light from shoulder-mounted light units flood the vehicle's interior. Several armored forms entered, the leader shouting, "Harrith Guard, don't move."

Max, Zephyr, and their three loaner analysts all raised their hands.

"What's the meaning of this?" Zephyr demanded.

"Shut the grolack up," the leader of the assault team shouted.

Bennie let the data cables slide into their storage compartment on his wristcomm. The desk's data port retracted back into the desk. "Done."

Wil was back at the office door, keeping an eye out for security. Whatever Max and Zee did to call the two security officers away, it worked. The hallway leading back to the stairs was empty and silent. He looked back to his friend. "Okay, let's go."

Bennie followed him out into the hallway and toward the stairs. The sounds of the party drifted up to meet them. Bennie looked at the time on his wristcomm. "These people party hard."

Wil clucked. "Celebrating their freedom."

The pair reached the ground floor as a quartet of Harrith Guard troopers walked through the estate's front door. Wil swore and shoved Bennie down the hallway that led to the bar and rear lawn.

"Hey!" the Brailack hacker protested.

"Shut up," Wil hissed, pushing his friend to walk faster. He reached up to his ear. "Something is wrong. Harrith Guard are here. In armor."

"What?" Cynthia said. "How? Max, Zephyr, you have anything? Gabe?"

When no reply came back, Wil swore again. He and Bennie reached the rear lawn as two more quartets of Harrith Guard troops came around the sides of the estate. He spotted Nic and Cynthia near the stage. "You two get out of here, now."

He saw Nic shake her head. "No way. We can't—"

Bennie shoved past Wil. "Apprentice. You have your orders!" Bennie snapped. "Go."

Across the lawn, she scowled as she nodded once.

Wil watched as the crowd began to realize that the planetary special forces were moving in from several directions. He turned to Bennie and shoved him toward a shrub. "Get this data back to the safe house. You and Gabe figure this out." He turned and strode into the crowd.

On the far side of the lawn, Nic looked at Cynthia, then Blu'T'Ohm. "We gotta go."

Cynthia nodded her agreement. To Blu'T'Ohm, she asked,

"Can you create a diversion?" Over his shoulder she spied a pair of Harrith Guard heading their way.

He nodded. "Go. I'll get to the safe house on my own."

"We're trusting you."

"I know." He turned to the pair of armored troops. "Excuse me! Excuse me, what's going on?" He waved his arms to ensure the two troopers' attention was squarely on him. He glanced back as the two troopers intercepted him, forcing his hands behind his back. The two women were gone.

Wil looked up as the door opened. "You too, huh?"

Admiral Shre' Ta'n nodded. She looked around the room, spotting Maxim and Zephyr on either side of Wil in the small conference room.

The guard that stepped in behind the Admiral shoved her inside the room, then stepped back, slamming the door shut behind him.

Taking a seat at the table, she asked, "Where's my analyst team?"

Maxim tilted his head. "Far as we know, they released them. Blu'T'Ohm too."

Zephyr nodded. "They brought them all in with us but separated us when we got here, wherever here is."

The Admiral huffed. "Still the Dystum's estate. The security wing is my guess." She shook her head. "This has to be the cabal." At the look the other three gave her, she said, "This isn't a holding cell." She gestured to the corners of the room. There were no cameras or visible recording equipment. "We're here until they clear the grounds, then they'll relocate us."

Wil nodded. "I saw them talking to Blue. Gabe?"

The Admiral inclined her head. "In the clear."

Wil released a sigh of relief.

Zephyr leaned back in her chair. "If it is the cabal, they certainly wouldn't want their sacrificial uillop tucked away where no one sees him. He can't die a martyr's death behind closed doors."

"Dark," Wil said.

"True, though," Maxim replied.

The door opened, and a Harrith woman walked in. "Okay, come on."

"See anything?" Nic whispered.

Cynthia shook her head. "Not seeing any signs of pinkyness."

From behind them, Bennie said, "I think it's hunky. Hunky-ness." The two women jumped, turning to glare at the Brailack that had snuck up on them. He grinned. "That's right. Snuck up on the two of you. Like a ninja assassin. Or..." He made a show out of dramatically pausing. "Like a Knight of Plentallus."

Cynthia turned back to look at the house. "Shoulda stopped before the last part. More impressive."

Bennie made a choking noise. "No, it's not. Being a Knight is way better."

They were all looking at the safe house from across the street. In the half hour since Nic and Cynthia arrived, no one had come or gone from the darkened residence.

"If you say so." Cynthia stood and crossed the street toward the house. She smiled hearing Bennie splutter.

Nic shook her head. "You're so easy to bait."

"You suck as an apprentice."

"Good comeback." She followed Cynthia across the street.

Bennie scowled and followed the two women across the street. "By the way! None of my security monitors were tripped. No one has entered."

Cynthia reached the front door. It was closed. She raised her wristcomm, sending the unlock command. The door clicked and swung open.

Bennie looked up from his own wristcomm. "No sign anyone bypassed the house's or my security systems."

Cynthia nodded. "Just to be safe." She motioned inside the house, pointing in different directions. Nic and Bennie each produced their beam sabers, thumbs resting on the activator switches.

A few minutes later, the three of them met in the lounge space.

"However they found out about us, guess it didn't include the safe house," Bennie said. He stepped up onto a stool and opened a cupboard to fetch a drinking glass. Over his shoulder, he asked, "Any idea who else got away?"

From the entryway, a voice said, "The Admiral was taken into custody."

"Gabe!" Nic shouted running over to hug the droid. As she did, his body shifted back into his most current configuration amid a cacophony of whirs and clicks.

"Greetings," he said, looking up from his small furry attacker to Bennie and Cynthia. "I believe Captain, Maxim, and Zephyr are all in custody with the Admiral."

Bennie sighed. "Well, first things first." He raised his wristcomm. "You and I need to parse the data we got from the fab plant against what I got from the Dystum's office."

Gabe inclined his head. "We should start immediately."

"What about us?" Nic asked.

Cynthia looked at the young woman. "We train."

While Gabe set up a workstation using components Admiral Narel had procured and stored in the vehicle parking bay—what Wil called a garage—the others slept. Their respective flights from the Dystum's estate had taken hours. Bennie helped for a while, but when he fell asleep on his feet, his mechanical friend sent him to bed.

The next morning, Bennie was the first to stumble into the main living space of the house. "Hi," he said, rubbing his large black eyes. The skin under each was a darker shade of green.

"You do not look rested," Gabe said.

Bennie made his way to the kitchen space and woke up the chlormax machine, thankful the house had one. "That's good. I don't feel rested."

"That explains a lot," Cynthia quipped, exiting the hallway from the bedrooms. Bennie turned to her and stuck out his tongue as he held up a mug of chlormax for her. "Thanks." She turned to Gabe. "Anything?"

"I am afraid I have only just finished assembling the workstation." He paused, accessing the terminal wirelessly. "The data will be copied over in three more microtocks." He turned to Bennie, who was examining the workstation. "Then we can begin." The Brailack absently nodded. "We are fortunate that the Admiral was able to procure equipment ahead of time."

Cynthia took a sip of her drink, welcoming the flush of heat and energy. She hadn't really slept. Even with the techniques she'd learned as a child assassin in the Yadro Collective, sleep mostly eluded her. Every tock that passed likely put Wil and the others further from their reach. It was all too fresh in her mind the lengths her friends had gone to rescue her on Tyr not long ago.

The front door opened. Cynthia's hand dropped to her hip and the butt of her stunner. Bennie's hand was resting on his beam saber hilt and Gabe's eyes were bright crimson.

Blu'T'Ohm came around the corner and stopped short. "Oh." He raised his hands over his head.

Everyone relaxed, including the startled Harrith political instigator. "I'm glad to see you all." He looked around. "Where are the others?" He turned to Cynthia.

She shook her head. "In custody. Nic and I made our escape, barely. While you distracted those guards, we made our way to the far wall. The Harrith Guard were prepared, though. We spent the better part of two tocks sneaking between decorative shrubs and statues until we got an opening to get up and over the wall."

He nodded. "I see."

"You did not see the others?" Gabe pressed.

Blu'T'Ohm shook his head. "No. They took me into custody, *for my protection*, but that was nothing more than spending three tocks in a small office on the first floor with a Harrith Guard trooper just outside. I never saw or heard the others but heard several of the Guard talking about other detainees."

"Morning," Nic said from the hallway. She took in the scene, then turned to Bennie. "What'd I miss? Why didn't you wake me?"

"I'm not your alarm clock." He tossed a dismissive hand in the air. "Besides, there's nothing you can do right now, so you might as well be rested." He turned to Gabe. "Ready?"

The droid inclined his head and offered a chair to Bennie. The two got to work. Neither knew what they were looking for or if it was present. They had a fair amount of incriminating evidence from the data they took from the fabrication plant, but the hope was that they could identify links in the government network to tie the various threads together. As Wil said, it was a crap shoot.

Nic watched her mentor and Gabe get to work, then looked at Cynthia and Blu'T'Ohm. What do we do?"

The front door opened again.

Gul'P'Ulo came around the corner and stopped short. "Oh, gods," she gasped, hands flying up, the package she was holding, falling to the ground with a dull thud.

Bennie squinted. "Where've you been?"

The young Harrith woman lowered her hands. "With my family. I told you that." She reached down to pick up the package and took a tentative step further into the room. "I heard about the raid." She looked down at the bag in her hand. "I brought breakfast." She made an uneasy face.

Gabe tilted his head. "Interesting. I have been monitoring the local newsnet, and there has been no mention of the raid."

She ran her long thin fingers through her hair, earrings in each ear catching the morning light. "Oh, uh. One of Blu'T'Ohm's contacts reached out to me."

The older Harrith man looked up. "Who? I've not been in contact with anyone since they released me." He looked at the others. "I was afraid anything I did would jeopardize you all."

Cynthia smiled, nodding.

Bennie leaned around Gabe. "What'd you bring?" He nodded toward the bag.

"Oh. Uh. Pastries."

Bennie squinted across the room. "Filling?"

Cynthia scowled. "Is that the important thing here?"

Bennie shrugged. "To me."

The younger of the two Harrith looked around. "Where are the others?"

"In custody," Cynthia said, turning her attention back to Gul'P'Ulo from Bennie.

"Oh no. So, the mission, or whatever, didn't go as planned?"

"They never do," Bennie said. "But we still got the data. We're going over it now." He waved her over to him.

She turned to her boss. "Then we should let them get to it. I can have us booked on a shuttle off-world by tonight." She handed Bennie the bag of pastries.

"What's the rush?" Bennie asked around a mouthful of baked good, still squinting at the young Harrith woman.

Gul'P'Ulo shrugged. "I'm sorry your friends are in custody, but there's nothing Blu'T'Ohm or I can do. Vice Admiral Wuan has them, and neither of us have any clearance that would help."

"Who?" Bennie leaned in.

Cynthia took a step toward the other woman. "How would you know who has them?"

The Harrith woman took an involuntary step back, bumping into the wall.

"Your heart rate is now three times Harrith normal," Gabe said, sparing a glance at the conversation taking place on the other side of the workstation.

Nic looked to the young woman she thought of as a friend. "Gul...?"

The young woman looked around the space. Bennie and Cynthia's hands had drifted toward their weapons. Bennie hopped out of his seat.

Nic stepped between them and the young woman, free hand held out toward her friends. "Gul, what's going on?"

Gul'P'Ulo looked at her boss, eyes wide. A flush crept up her cheeks, turning her pale skin pink. "Sir?"

Blu'T'Ohm looked at her from where he was sitting at the dining table. "I think you have some explaining to do. The raid at the Dystum's estate has been kept quiet. The guests were ushered off the property before I was released. They wouldn't have known what was happening." He looked from his aide to the others in the room. "I know Vice Admiral Wuan. Clar'V'Al Wuan is in charge of Clandestine Operations." His gaze fell onto his aide, the woman he had worked closely, tirelessly, beside. Someone he had thought was on the same side as him. Now, though...

Gul'P'Ulo looked around the room again. Nic was still right in front of her. She shoved the younger woman toward Cynthia and Bennie, turning to bolt for the door in the same motion.

She had the door open when a beam saber hilt hit her in the back of the head, dropping her to the floor, unconscious.

Everyone turned to look at Nic. She looked up from the prone form of her friend, facial fur flattening. "What?"

"Good shot," Cynthia said, moving to the unconscious Harrith woman. She kneeled down, picking up the beam saber hilt. "Here." Nic joined her, taking her weapon back.

Bennie came over with a dish towel. "All I could find."

Cynthia took the towel and secured Gul'P'Ulo's hands behind her back.

## CHAPTER 24

"Who else is involved?" the stern-faced Harrith man asked, leaning on the table.

Wil looked at Zee and Max, then the man opposite them. "Actually, that was my question."

The team had been moved from the Dystum's estate to a secure conference room a few floors below the Admiral's office in the naval command tower in downtown Drotu.

"I can't believe you convinced the Dystum we wanted to kill him," Maxim said.

The man in the vice admiral's uniform smirked. "You didn't give me much time to plan a better story. I had to improvise." He cocked his head at the three of them, turning his focus on Zephyr. "You were supposed to be off-world. You two and your droid friend. He left you here?"

Both Palorians shrugged. The Vice Admiral squinted. "If he's here, we'll find him."

"Doubt it," Zephyr said.

"So, he's still here?"

"I didn't say that. I just don't think you're very competent."

She shrugged. "He could be down the street or back on Arcadia. Who knows?"

The Vice Admiral shook his head. "He's unimportant." He turned to Wil. "Your life partner, on the other hand...Congratulations, by the way. She must be here somewhere?"

Wil shrugged. "Thanks. We like to vacation separately."

The other man smirked. "I don't believe that. Finding a Tygran shouldn't be hard. I have people on it."

Wil's eyes narrowed. "If you hurt her..."

"You're in no position to make threats, Captain Calder."

Wil didn't look away. "There's a saying on my planet."

"Oh?"

Wil nodded. "Fuck around and find out."

"Quaint."

Breaking her silence, Shre' Ta'n said, "Clar'V'Al, you know you can't keep me here. For one thing, I outrank you. For another, I've done nothing wrong." She looked at her fellow detainees. "Neither have they, for that matter."

The Harrith man shook his head. "Oh, Shre' Ta'n. You never were a political animal." He waved both arms to encompass the room. "No one knows you're here. I can do what I like." He shrugged. "We'll search, of course, but you'll have disappeared. Tragic, really."

Wil turned in his chair to face the Admiral. "Who is this turd?"

"Clar'V'Al Wuan. Vice admiral in charge of Planetary Intelligence." She glared at the man opposite them. "And, obviously, a traitor to the Harrith Collective."

Wuan scoffed. "Traitor?"

"Is 'grolacking traitor' better?"

Maxim cleared his throat. "You can't exactly just march us out of here as terrorists. Three of us are well known heroes—"

"Heroes that the Circle explicitly asked to leave the planet after making your wild accusations to the security council," the Vice Admiral interrupted.

"Be that as it may, we're still pretty well known here. Why would we intervene on Harrith's behalf only to, cycles later, do ..." She squinted. "What, exactly?" Zephyr asked.

Wuan shrugged. "I'm actually not sure yet. Like I said, I wasn't prepared for this. I planned for a lot of contingencies, but you weren't one of them."

Wil smiled. "We're touched."

The other man gave Wil a flat look, saying, "Don't be. I didn't think you were worth planning for."

Maxim huffed a laugh. "That'll teach you."

Wuan waved a hand. "I've time though, no worries. Back to you all. Where's your little Brailack? He here, too, somewhere?" The Rogue Enterprises team shrugged as one as if they had practiced it. He stood. "Maybe after a tock or two, you'll feel like talking." He left the room without another word or even a backward glance at his captives.

As the door's locks clicked, Wil looked at the others. "So, this is going well."

Zephyr nodded. "We've at least learned a few things."

Shre' Ta'n looked at her. "What?"

"The Dystum isn't involved," Zephyr said, adding, "If he were, Wuan wouldn't have to make up a story."

The other woman smiled. "I hadn't thought of that. You're right." She pursed her lips, pressing her tongue against the inside of her cheek. "What does that get us?"

Zephyr offered a half smile. "Not sure. But the more we know, the better."

"Talk. Now." Cynthia leaned in so that her face was inches from Gul'P'Ulo's wide flat nose. She bared her teeth.

Cynthia sat in one of the chairs from her bedroom. The young Harrith woman was in a similar chair from one of the other bedrooms. It wasn't perfect. The chair was amply padded and its arms were one piece, so they'd been forced to use bed sheets to tie her torso to the chair's back while towels secured her feet to the bulbous feet of the chair.

"I can't," the younger woman whimpered.

Cynthia shook her head. "Wrong answer." She looked over her shoulder. "Do you know what being bit by a Brailack feels like?"

"What?" Bennie shouted, looking from the workstation he and Gabe were hunched over.

"No..." Gul'P'Ulo said through sobs.

Cynthia smiled wide. "Pain like you wouldn't believe. Lesions, boils. Skin sloughs off." Seeing the look on the younger woman's face, she added, "That's just the first two tocks."

Bennie looked at Gabe. "That's not true at all."

"I do not care," the droid said, not looking away from the data streaming across the display.

He looked over the display at Cynthia. "I resent being used as a threat."

Nic, standing next to Cynthia, said, "It's true. I saw him bite a smuggler we apprehended on Thundera. By the time the authorities arrived, he was screaming incoherently as his skin hung in melted strips."

Gul'P'Ulo paled, tears running down her cheeks.

Gabe turned to Bennie. "You make an effective interrogation tool."

Bennie turned and drawled, "Yay."

Across the room, Blu'T'Ohm, looking like he'd just eaten a bug, gaped at Bennie.

Bennie glanced at the man and bared his teeth. Blu'T'Ohm recoiled.

Cynthia stood. "Just tell us what you know. We'll protect you."

The other woman shook her head. "I really don't know much. I was hired to keep an eye on Blu'T'Ohm and steer him where I was told."

"Excuse me!" Blu'T'Ohm was on his feet.

His probably-now-former aide shrank into the chair. "I was told where to book rallies and to make sure you went where you were supposed to. That's it, I swear!"

Gabe turned to Bennie. "Look at this." A window appeared on the display nearest Bennie.

"Well, dren." The hacker nodded. "This is promising."

"Indeed," Gabe said, his attention back on whatever virtual workspace he was seeing.

"Bennie, come here. Need your teeth," Cynthia called.

"Oh, god!" Gul'P'Ulo exhaled.

Bennie stood. "This is degrading."

Gabe turned to look at him. "It is, yes."

Bennie hadn't even made it around the makeshift workstation when the young Harrith woman shouted, "Okay! Okay! Vice Admiral Wuan—he's in charge. He's the one who hired me." She sniffled loudly. "Actually, it was someone that worked for him. I only met him—the Admiral, I mean—once." She glanced at Blu'T'Ohm. "Before we left Harrith. The rest of the time it was a...lieutenant, I think."

Blu'T'Ohm was still pacing. "I can't believe this."

Cynthia moved away from the chair with their Harrith captive in it. She looked over to Bennie and Gabe. "You two are certain the Dystum isn't involved?"

Bennie looked up. "Yeah. He's either clean or exceptionally good at covering his tracks."

She nodded. "We can't wait for the Dystum's help. We need to find this Vice Admiral Wuan and spring our friends." Looking up at the ceiling, she sighed. "I hate splitting us up more, but," she turned her gaze to Bennie, "little green, I think you need to go to the Dystum's estate and show him what you and Gabe have put together? At the end of the day, we're gonna need him on our side, but waiting for him or the Circle to act will almost certainly mean our friends vanish and we never see them again."

Bennie extended his arms, palms out, cracking his knuckles. "I'll find out when he's due back at the estate."

Cynthia nodded.

Nic tore her eyes from her still quietly sobbing friend. "What...what about the rest of us?"

"We break into..." She turned to Gabe and Bennie.

Gabe said, "According the public net, the Vice Admiral is in charge of Planetary Intelligence. His office is in the naval command building."

Bennie smiled to himself. "I'm downloading the schematics now."

The Dystum returned to his estate. All traces of the Sovereignty Day party the day prior were gone, the work of hundreds of staff laboring through the morning. As his government issued ground car glided silently to the storage garage, he walked through the two large doors.

He was still shaken by the report from Planetary Intelligence. To think those people could be caught up in trying to now undermine the society they'd saved. He shook his head.

"I've got a few things to do in my office before dinner," he called out, seemingly to no one.

"Very good, sir," came the reply as the majordomo slid out of a corner to startle the Dystum.

"I hate it when you do that," he growled.

"Sorry, sir."

The estate was a trapping of the office he didn't mind. It was beautiful, massive, and the pool in the west lawn was to die for. Stepping into his assistant's office from the hallway, he looked around. She rarely worked out of the estate unless he was planning to stay home for the day.

His office was dark, and when he walked in, the lights that should have turned on as he entered, didn't. He turned to the wall-mounted sensor switch next to the door frame and waved his hand in front of it. Nothing. He waved his hand more vigorously.

"I disabled it," a voice said from deeper inside the office.

The Dystum released a choked off scream as he spun. He couldn't see who was sitting at his desk. "Who...Who are you?" Behind him, the door clicked closed. The sound of the lock engaging made him jump once more. He spun, grabbing the handle.

A magenta beam of light rising from behind the desk preceded a *snap-hiss* sound. The room was bathed in a deep purple light. A Brailack, sitting behind the Dystum's desk said, "Hi. Have a seat."

"Who are you?" the Dystum repeated, squinting into the bright energy blade. He took a tentative step toward his desk. The purple beam of light pulsed faintly, a hum coming from it or something near it.

"I'm Ben-Ari Vulvo. Knight of Plentallus."

The Dystum shook his head. "I don't know what that

means. Is it a cult? I wasn't aware we had Brailack cults operating on Harrith Prime." He took a step back.

"What? No, it's not a cult!" He slapped his free hand palm down on the desktop. "It's an ancient order...You know what, never mind. I said, have a seat." His voice was deeper this time. "We need to talk." The magenta beam of light winked off and the office lights came on.

The Harrith man looked around the now brightly lit office. "How did you—"

"Would you just sit down, already!" the little Brailack demanded. He hopped off the chair, vanishing from sight. He came around the side of the desk. "I've got a lot to tell you." He pointed at the seat he had just vacated. "Sit."

The Harrith man looked around the office. With a sigh, he stepped closer to his desk. "You're not going to kill me, are you?"

The Brailack rubbed his face with both hands. "Knight. Of. Plentallus. No, I'm not going to kill you."

Falling into his well-worn chair, he asked, "How did you get in here, anyway? Security monitors every window and door. Especially after Planetary Intelligence apprehended those terrorists at the Sovereignty Day celebration last night." He gasped. "Wait, are you...?"

Bennie pointed to a corner of the room and the large, sort of circular hole in the wall. Through the hole, several trees were visible in the dim light of the evening.

The leader of the Harrith Collective's eyes bulged. He turned to Bennie, then the hole, and back again. "You?" He pointed to the hole. "That wall. This building is a thousand years old!"

"Explains why it wasn't easy to cut through." Bennie waved a hand. "We've got more important things to discuss than architecture."

"More important than..." The other man released an explosive sigh as he threw his hands in the air. "Unbelievable." Running his hands across the surface of his desk, he took a deep breath. He exhaled and looked the Brailack. "What is it that you need to talk to me about that couldn't wait until the morning and an appointment?" One his hands eased from the desktop, dropping to his lap before easing toward the silent alarm switch mounted under the desk.

Bennie cocked his head and clucked. "Come on. You think I didn't disable that?" He pointed to a sensor panel in the corner by the ceiling. "Sensors are spoofed too. Your majordomo, if he looks, will see that your office is occupied by one life sign. Yours." He waited for the Dystum's arm to return to the arm of the chair. "Can we get on with this?"

"Good afternoon. I'm Klor'Tillen, and this is GNO Newstime." The pale green Brailack journalist inhaled. "We've just learned that Acrar Two has been attacked by its neighbor Bormean. At this time, details are sparse, but what we're hearing is that the Acrarians have been almost entirely wiped out." He shifted in his seat. "It appears that the Bormeans, with assistance from an as yet unknown supplier, moved against their neighbors with the intent of cleansing the world ahead of future Bormean colonization."

Klor'Tillen turned to another camera pickup. "Acrar had only recently voted to leave the Galactic Commonwealth, which meant that when the attack came, no one was there to defend them. As far we know, the Acrar had little to no space defense force."

After taking a calming breath, he continued, "We'll do our best to keep you informed, but as of three tocks ago, the entire system was under siege, and no one was being allowed in or out. Our hearts go out for the Acrar."

## CHAPTER 25

"I'm not sure about this," Gul'P'Ulo said for what Cynthia thought was the ninth or maybe twentieth time since they untied her, she couldn't recall.

Cynthia, Nic, Gabe, and Blu'T'Ohm were standing outside the Harrith Naval command building with their captive. Before leaving the safe house, Cynthia convinced Gul'P'Ulo to call her handler and explain that Blu'T'Ohm caught on and wanted to meet someone to discuss ways the plan didn't result in his martyrdom.

"He did not sound happy that I'd been made." She looked around the street. This late in the evening, there wasn't much foot traffic.

"According to the building's network, neither your handler nor Vice Admiral Wuan have left the building all day," Gabe offered. Hacking into the Harrith nation's most secure network was beyond his capabilities, likely even Bennie's. The building's badge system, however, was unbelievably easy.

Cynthia looked around. "That means our friends have to still be in there."

"We hope," Nic said from a few feet up the sidewalk. She

was kicking something. Looking up at the others, she said, "They're definitely still up there. For sure." Her face made it clear how she really felt.

Cynthia looked at Gabe. "You ready?" He nodded. His body whirred and clicked. Holo emitters, similar to those the team previously owned, engaged, surrounding him in a hazy nimbus before fading.

"Woah," Nic said, watching Gabe be replaced by a lifelike, albeit slightly taller than average, holographic Harrith man in a military uniform. She looked at the others. "You all had those?"

Cynthia nodded. "Yup. Emphasis on *had*."

"Stupid Bennie," the young Olop said.

"Can say that again." Cynthia smiled.

"Stupid—"

Cynthia held up a hand. "It's an expression...from Earth."

Nic shrugged.

Cynthia nodded to Blu'T'Ohm and Gul'P'Ulo. "Okay, you two. Showtime."

They both nodded. The younger of the two was visibly sweating.

"Good luck," Nic said. "You got this."

Gabe followed the two Harrith into the building.

A Harrith woman in an ensign's uniform looked up. She spied Blu'T'Ohm and jumped to her feet. "Good evening. How may help you?"

Gul'P'Ulo cleared her throat. "I'm—I'm here to see Sublieu-tenant Pre'S'Oh."

After waiting forty-five seconds, Gabe entered and made a show of brushing past the two visitors. "Excuse me."

The ensign glanced at Gabe, noticing his rank—Captain—then turned back to the two Harrith visitors. "Of—of course. He's expecting you?"

Gabe continued past the lobby to the bank of lifts. He

slowed just enough to wirelessly access the security turnstile. It beeped and opened a moment before he reached it.

Gul'P'Ulo watched Gabe, then shook her head. "He is, yes."

The other woman nodded. "One moment, please."

The lift was part of the building's overall security infrastructure, making it unhackable from afar. As Gabe entered the lift, two of his holo emitters increased their output to project an empty lift car to the camera. Using his remaining emitters, he shifted from the Harrith captain to a junior grade lieutenant. He pressed the button for the floor Admiral Shre' Ta'n's office was on.

He had to wait only a moment after the lift reached the desired floor. He watched the doors slide closed as the lift went to its next destination, a secure floor below the admiralty levels. Moments later, the lift's doors slid apart again. A tired looking lieutenant stepped in without looking up. Spotting Gabe, he coughed. "Lieutenant."

Gabe nodded. "Sir." He stepped around the man, exiting the lift. As Gabe stepped past the other man, the holo emitters projecting the empty lift car disengaged. With any luck, anyone watching the feed would see the sudden appearance of the lieutenant and blurred departure of a second person as a minor glitch in the camera.

Without access to the building's security system, Gabe had no way to access the secure floors. However, the floors immediately above and below were easier to access. His eyes flickered to blue as he attempted to scan the area. The walls, floor, and ceiling were all shielded. He could sense a few life signs as vague impressions, but that was all. Hopefully the floor's layout had not changed from the plans Bennie was able to source. He moved to the agreed upon conference room and the window that offered an impressive view of the city.

Telltale whirs and clicks preceded the appearance of the

plasma cutter that replaced his left hand. He made a perfect circle in the transparent material.

*I am in position,* Gabe wirelessly sent to the team's close-range comms.

Outside on the sidewalk, Cynthia nodded. "Our turn." She looked up as Gabe leaned out from the hole he had just cut in the window of a conference room.

Cynthia produced a grappler pistol. She turned to Nic. "So glad I snatched this from that mobile command vehicle."

Nic looked at her friend. "You just..." She leaned to the side to look at Cynthia from a different angle. "On you, somewhere?"

Cynthia gave the younger woman a knowing grin. She looked up and took aim. With a pop, a thin dart shot straight up, trailing a nearly invisible monofilament line.

The women watched Gabe snatch the grappling hook out of the air and take it back inside the building.

*You may proceed,* he sent over their comms.

Cynthia gripped the pistol with both hands. "Hop on."

"This can't be," the Dystum of the Harrith Circle said for the third time.

Bennie shook his head. "You think I'd go through the trouble of sneaking in here to feed you dren?"

The other man glanced at the hole in his office wall, then shook his head. The pair had been at the Dystum's desk for twenty minutes. Bennie showed him screen after screen of data. Before he left the safe house, he and Gabe had built indexes, reports, and a few charts showing the interconnected web of crime that had deep roots on Harrith Prime.

After they showed the team their work, Wil had offered to contribute a short animation but withdrew the offer after the entire team laughed at him. For an uncomfortably long time.

The Dystum thumbed through a few more screens. "This can't..." He looked at Bennie across the desk. "Sorry." Sighing, he closed the chart he was looking at that showed the connection between the illicit fab plant and the Planetary Security division of the Navy. "What do you need me to do?"

Bennie smiled. "I've got a list." He produced a portable data drive. He reached across the desk to push the section of desktop aside, revealing the data ports.

The Dystum cocked his head. "How did you know that was there?"

Bennie retreated to his seat, making a face. "Good guess?"

"Okay, I kinda thought they'd have gotten here by now," Zephyr said from the slab of metal that passed for a bed in the detention cell they'd been shoved into. She thought the conference-turned-interrogation room was small, but the cell they were in had her longing to be in the other room.

Admiral Shre' Ta'n, leaning against the wall next to Wil, said, "I won't lie, I don't have a good feeling about this."

Maxim frowned. "You don't think he'd really kill you, do you?"

She shook her head. "Kill me, no. Fabricate enough evidence to get me sentenced to death for high crimes against the Harrith Collective, yes. Twice, if he could."

"Lovely guy," Maxim mumbled.

"Like all this positive thinking," Wil murmured through his swollen lip. When they refused to answer the Vice Admiral's questions, the Harrith man had taken his frustrations out on Wil. He looked around the cell. "They'll be here. They have to have figured out where we are by now."

Shre' Ta'n nodded. "The only good news is that Wuan will keep us here until he's ready to make his move. Whatever that is."

"More importantly, whenever that is," Wil said.

"And the bad?" Zephyr asked.

"When he's ready, he'll move fast. Wuan is a climber, and he's ruthless." She shook her head. "He's been making noise since his promotion into the admiralty. Expand the Collective by any means necessary. Eliminate threats preemptively. That included destabilizing the GC."

"What a peach," Wil said a moment before the lights in the cell dimmed, then turned red. From somewhere outside the cell, an alarm klaxon sounded. He smiled, wincing, reaching up to touch his lip. "Guess they're here."

Lieutenant Pre'S'Oh stepped off the lift and spotted Blu'T'Ohm and Gul'P'Ulo. He sighed, smoothing his rumpled uniform jacket.

"That's him?" Blu'T'Ohm asked. His aide nodded.

The Lieutenant slowed. "This needs to be quick. We're busy."

"Oh?" Blu'T'Ohm said. "What's going on upstairs?"

The other man stared at him, unblinking. He shook his head. "So, she screwed up and you want to be, what? Involved? How?"

Blu'T'Ohm drew himself up. "Well, for one, I'd rather not die. I believe in this cause, but not that much." When the other man continued to just stare at him, he continued, "Our goals are in alignment, and I believe I can do far more for the cause alive than as a martyr."

The Lieutenant sighed and looked at his wristcomm, then at the ensign sitting nearby. He held a hand out to guide the two visitors further from the reception desk.

Gul'P'Ulo shifted her weight, then said, "He's not wrong. Our audiences grow at every rally. Even with this current detour, we've got over two tens booking requests for Blu'T'Ohm alone. According to other aides in the network, other spokesbeings are seeing similar interest."

Blu'T'Ohm inclined his head. "A few tweaks to my message, some carefully worded insinuations..." He spread his arms. "How many fake Peacekeepers have you spent in this endeavor so far? Armored and hired goons."

The Lieutenant nodded slowly. "We'd need to find a way to still have our fake PKs be seen from time to time." He scowled. "Though using them more wisely is a good idea now that we have a finite amount of armor and equipment. Thanks to you, as I understand it." His look made it clear what he thought of that.

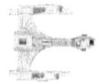

Upstairs, Gabe was helping Cynthia and Nic into the building. "I estimate we have fifteen microtocks at most. That number will be greatly impacted by Blu'T'Ohm and Gul'P'Ulo's ability to stall the Lieutenant."

Cynthia pulled up the limited floor plans that Bennie had been able to download. "If this is right, or even kinda right," she tapped the screen with her other hand, "there should be two secure cells here and two secure interrogation rooms across the hall." She looked at her two companions. "They have to be in one of them."

Gabe's optic sensors turned light blue, then back to their normal yellow. "My sensors are severely impaired. This and likely the floors above and below are heavily shielded."

Nic nodded. "Wouldn't want this to be too easy."

"You're too young to be so cynical," Cynthia quipped. Nice shrugged and started for conference room's door.

As good as Bennie was, the floor plans he'd found online were the original plans, and as an extra precaution, someone had removed the floor numbers, leaving only the department names for clusters of floors. Admiral Shre' Ta'n's office and the rest of the admiralty were the top four floors. Planetary Intelligence was the next three below those. Various other departments made up the remaining twenty floors of the building.

Nic rounded a corner up ahead and yelped. Before Gabe or Cynthia could react, she charged out of sight just as a blaster bolt struck the wall where she was standing a moment earlier.

As much as Nic enjoyed giving Bennie as much trouble as she could, her training as a Knight of Plentallus was going remarkably well. No thanks to Bennie, other than making sure DV-o had access to Nic via comms and was a remarkable remote educator.

Seeing the trooper at the end of the hall at this time of night had startled her, but in the time it took her to yelp, she had her beam saber in hand, thumb on the activation plate. By the time she'd taken three steps, her pinkish blade was thrumming, casting the dimly lit hallway in pale pink light.

As Nic closed the gap, her training further kicked in. While she had been surprised to see the trooper, it was obvious he was even more surprised to see a young Olop in the hall. He didn't even get his blaster out of the holster until she was three-quarters of the way to him.

As the first shot sailed past her, she leapt toward the wall to her left, planting her foot and pushing off to get even more height and speed. She hit the right-hand wall and repeated the maneuver. By the time the trooper brought his pistol to bear on her, her beam saber blade was slicing through the barrel.

As the barrel hit the carpeted floor, the startled guard stumbled backward, falling to the floor. Before Nic could bring her saber to bear, the man frantically slapped the screen of his wrist-comm. As she slammed the hilt into his face, an alarm klaxon rang out.

She looked around, seeing small recessed lights flash red along the length of the hall. "Well, dren."

Gabe and Cynthia turned the corner in time to see Nic knock the guard unconscious. She stood and clipped her beam saber to her belt. She coughed, her facial fur flattening. "Sorry."

Cynthia shook her head. "Nothing you could've done." She looked around. The hallway was pulsing red. "No time for stealth now."

Gabe nodded and approached the nearest door, placing his palm on the access panel. Data tendrils snaked out of his fingertips, slithering under the panel, little pulses of light trailing along them. He turned to look at his companions, who both nodded. He sent a command to the access panel. The door slid open.

Nic leaned around Gabe. "Nice office." She leaned back to look over the access panel. "Weird they don't put labels on people's offices. Seems a bit extra."

Cynthia shook her head as she rubbed her eyes.

"Our friends are not on this floor," Gabe said, letting the

door slide closed. "They would not have the detention cells and interrogation space on the same floor as their offices."

Cynthia nodded her agreement. "Up or down? We've got maybe five microtocks."

"Down." The droid nodded to a door at the end of the hallway.

"Stairs. Yay," Cynthia quipped.

"Okay, that's not a terrible idea," the Lieutenant said, nodding.

Blu'T'Ohm had just outlined what he envisioned as his first speech now that he was part of the cabal. It wasn't perfect, but it was the best he had been able to think up on the trip from the safe house without knowing exactly what the cabal wanted.

The Lieutenant looked at Blu'T'Ohm. "I have to give you some credit. You're certain you could pull that off?"

Blu'T'Ohm nodded. "I believe so. The first one might be a bit rough as I figure out the right notes to hit to plant the seed. Can't be too obvious."

The other man turned to Gul'P'Ulo. "If he's part of the operation, we don't really need you, now do we?"

The younger woman gasped. Eyes wide, she turned to the man who thought he was her boss up until yesterday.

Cutting off whatever the Lieutenant was about to say, a loud siren pierced the lobby space, startling everyone. He looked around, his face slack with surprise for a moment, before realization dawned on him. Drawing his blaster, he leveled it at both Blu'T'Ohm and Gul'P'Ulo. "What're you two up to?"

"Us? Nothing! What?" The younger of the two took an involuntary step away from the pistol.

"We've been here with you!" Blu'T'Ohm replied, doing his

best to sound shocked and indignant. He had hoped that the Rogue Enterprises team would be able to get in and out without raising an alarm. He cursed himself for trusting them that far.

"With me. Now." He motioned for them to move ahead of him toward the bank of lifts. Passing the front desk, he said, "Lock the building down."

The young ensign nodded.

## CHAPTER 26

The stairwell was bathed in harsh white light. Cynthia stepped in, looking up, then down, her pistol held at the ready. She moved further onto the landing, making room for Gabe and Nic. The droid took the lead heading down the stairs.

Nic fell in behind Gabe. "At least there aren't—"

Somewhere below them, a door slammed open.

The droid turned to look at his young friend, then continued down the steps, taking them two at a time.

They only had to reach the next landing down before the Harrith officers coming up did. Gabe rounded the corner as two Harrith Guard troopers reached the landing. They flinched; he did not. His forearms clicked and whirred, blasters sliding up and into place. The two troopers fell to the ground before either was able to raise their rifles.

Cynthia followed him to the landing, bending down to retrieve one of the rifles. "This is more like it."

Nic bent to grab the other weapon.

"You're too young for an energy rifle," Cynthia said.

The younger woman stood up, pointing at her hip. "I'm

carrying a beam saber that can cut through that rifle and shoots bolts of energy that burn through armor."

"You'll shoot your eye out," Cynthia insisted, reaching for the door.

Nic turned to Gabe, only to get a shrug.

Cynthia eased the door open. "I don't hear anyone." She stepped out into the hall and was immediately tackled from the side. Gabe rushed in behind her, Nic on his heels.

Three more Harrith Navy troopers were waiting. Gabe turned toward the nearest, trying to bring his blasters to bear but was knocked off his feet. Nic leaped over the droid and his two attackers to square off against the remaining trooper.

"A little girl?" the man scoffed. He looked beyond her. "Why do I get the little girl?"

Clipping her beam saber back onto her belt, Nic growled. "For that, it's gonna hurt." She sprung into the air before the offensive trooper realized what was happening. She tackled the man to the ground. One hand, claws extended, had a firm hold of his armor's chest piece. The other rained blows on his face and neck. "You're mean!" she screamed at the man beneath her.

Cynthia took two punches to the face before getting her legs under her attacker and flinging the armored woman up and off of her. The other woman landed with a grunt. Cynthia was on her feet in a flash, turning and leaping on top of the trooper, pinning both arms under her knees. She reached behind her for the other woman's stunner.

Gabe stood, holding his two flailing attackers at arm's length, then slamming them together. He examined both men, then slammed them together one more time. He dropped the two unconscious troopers and turned to Cynthia. "Do you require—"

She slugged the woman under her one more time, then stood up. "I'm good."

The pair turned to find Nic standing over a severely bloodied man. His face was a ruined mess. She wiped both hands on her pants. "What took you two so long?

Cynthia took in the sight and made a face. "I think we need to have talk later."

Gabe looked from Cynthia to Nic, and back again, then said, "I believe we need to go this way."

The older Harrith man released an explosive sigh. "I can't believe this."

Bennie shrugged and looked at his wristcomm. "Yeah, betrayal and all that. We should be getting a move on."

The other man made a face. "What? Where?"

"The naval command center. Where else?"

"Why?"

Bennie rubbed his face. He wasn't sure how much he should share of the team's plan. "I mean, you have to tell some-one, right? Involve those who aren't involved in this. You gotta bring this cabal to justice." He squinted. "Right?"

The other man nodded. "Yes, of course." He reached for a control on his desk. After tapping an icon and receiving an acknowledging beep, he said, "Ready my ground car."

Bennie pumped a little green fist.

The door to the outer office opened, and the Dystum's majordomo entered. "Your car should be ready momentarily, sir." Whatever the older man was going to say next was lost when he spotted Bennie sitting in one of the plush guest chairs opposite his boss. "I..." His head tilted. "I'm sorry, sir. I was unaware that you had a guest." He turned to Bennie. "One that did not come through the front door." The Dystum cleared his throat and nodded toward the hole in the wall. The majordomo fell into a spasm of some sort upon seeing the hole.

Bennie slid deeper into his seat.

The leader of the Harrith Collective watched the show a moment, then said, "We'll be heading for the Circle chambers. Please alert them to assemble."

Bennie's gaze snapped up, his mouth opening. A look from the other man halted whatever Bennie was planning to say.

"Yes, sir," the majordomo said, stepping back out into the reception foyer.

The Dystum stood and motioned for Bennie to follow him. "We'll use the front door if that is okay with you, Mr. Knight of Whatever-it-Was."

Bennie frowned but remained silent.

"Watch out!" Nic shouted, pushing Cynthia aside a split second before a blaster bolt sizzled past. After their last encounter at the stairwell, the remaining Navy and Harrith Guard troops were shooting first and worrying about prisoners second.

The Tygran woman regained her footing and leaped toward the two officers ahead of them. She fired twice while in the air, neither shot connecting. As she hit the ground, she dropped into a roll, coming up to fire point blank at the nearest woman. The stun blast rippled across the officer's body sending her bonelessly to the ground.

Cynthia was on her feet before the unconscious woman hit the carpet, landing two quick punches to the stomach of the man standing nearby. She felt the light body armor under his dress uniform and adjusted her third strike to land under his arm as he raised it to attack. He managed to squeeze off a shot, the energy bolt striking the wall behind her.

Gabe had his back to the two women, using his arm-mounted blasters to keep three other Harrith Naval Intelligence officers at bay. His glowing red optic sensors flicked from target to target, tracking them as they tried to get closer, ducking his precision fire. Two more joined their colleagues as one of the braver troopers fell to the floor.

"Why are there so many?" Nic shouted over the repeated whines of blaster fire. "Don't these people have home lives?" She ran past Cynthia and her sparring partner to reach the door that Gabe said was likely their destination.

The trio had fought their way to that door from the moment they stepped out of the stairwell onto this floor. Gabe assumed that one of the nearby floors must serve as a dormitory for officers on the night shift for the various departments.

Inside the detention block, Vice Admiral Wuan waved a blaster at his prisoners. "What did you do? How did you signal them?"

Wil shrugged, wincing as his shoulder reminded him of their most recent interrogation. "Who says we did anything? You've got our gear, and we're in a signal dampening cell."

Maxim smiled. "Maybe our people are just better than yours."

"No doubt there," Zephyr said. "Look, this is obviously unraveling around you. Cut your losses."

The man on the other side of the energy shield smirked. "Please. A couple of well-trained civilians are no match for the Harrith Navy and the Harrith Guard. The building is locked down, and reinforcements are on the way."

"It's cute you think that'll help," Wil said through his swollen lip. "I mean, sure, we—the well-trained civilians—single-handedly stopped the GC from absorbing your entire society at gunpoint, but yeah, I'm sure a few night shift Intelligence folks are more than a match."

"Don't forget the corporate monster army. We were kinda instrumental there too," Maxim added.

Wil snapped his fingers and pointed at his big friend.

The expression on Wuan's face shifted from contempt to rage and back again before settling on confusion.

Maxim watched all this, then said, "There it is." The others nodded.

Something struck the door to the detention center. The cell the team was in was the furthest from the main entry, so it was impossible to tell if it was a body or a blaster bolt.

It was a body.

Nic smirked. "Don't pick on people smaller than you." She wagged a little fur covered finger at the unconscious man.

From down the hall, Gabe said, "We have yet to encounter anyone that was not taller than you."

She looked at the droid. "Since when do you joke?"

Gabe was about to answer when the officers he was holding back with stun blasts got tired of waiting. The largest of the four took the lead, rushing toward the droid. As he absorbed repeated stun blasts, he first staggered, then his companions held him up using him as a human— or in this case, Harrith— shield. When he fell, the next trooper in line took up the role of shield.

Gabe's forearm-mounted blasters rotated back into his arms just as the remaining two Harrith Naval officers reached him. Up close, they both opted for hand-to-hand combat, deploying short fighting batons. Each lashed out with a flurry of kicks, punches, and baton swings.

After his most recent physical reconfiguration, Gabe's frame was better suited to unarmed combat, but it was still not his forte. Even with reflexes faster than most biologicals, half the blows of his attackers landed hit home, sending him stumbling backward toward his friends.

"You're the ruler of this planet. Why can't you divert traffic?" Bennie complained.

Next to him, the Dystum adjusted in his seat. "I'm not a ruler, and it's the entire sector. And, no, I can't just ignore traffic rules."

Since leaving the estate in the hilltop neighborhood, the Dystum's hover limo had been making its way across town. Once out of the neighborhood, at the other man's urging, Bennie hacked the guidance system to divert the car to the naval command tower. Neither was sure if the majordomo was part of the cabal or not but didn't want to take a chance.

The Dystum turned to look at Bennie. "Don't I know you?"

"Did you just have a stroke?" Bennie asked. He frowned at the other man. "I don't know how to help, if you did."

The other man waved his hand, as his eyed narrowed. "No, you rude little loa berry. I mean, now that I'm seeing you better light, weren't you at the Sovereignty Day festivities? At my estate?"

Bennie clucked. "Oh." He drew it out. "Yeah. I was."

Cynthia and Nic watched as Gabe fought his attackers, giving ground quickly. The former looked down. "He could use some help."

Nic nodded, a sly grin on her face. "I got this." She sprinted toward Gabe, his back to her. "Going high!" she shouted as she took two more steps, then vaulted up toward Gabe's back.

Gabe heard his newest colleague and leaned forward as he lunged in to both deflect several high kicks and land a punch that should have broken ribs to one of his opponents. Body armor kept the man in the fight.

A feral scream came from behind the droid as a furry blur in an earth-tone tunic launched over his head, bright pink energy sword slashing down in front of her.

Part of DV-o's training of late was nonlethal ways to use a beam saber. After Nic and Bennie's adventure on Multon, she had been keen to learn how to avoid severing limbs if not necessary.

Putting that training to use, she slashed her blade down between Gabe and his attackers, sending the two Harrith stumbling back far enough to create some distance. Switching her weapon off, she hurled the hilt at the furthest of the two faces. The same move she'd used against Gul'P'Ulo earlier.

Before her weapon struck its target, she landed, leaping onto the chest of the other man, her climbing claws digging into his uniform. With one hand holding on to the flailing man, she rained blows on his face with the other. When he succumbed to the repeated blows and fell to the ground, she dropped into a roll and snatched her beam saber hilt from its place next to the head of the other man.

"Nicely done," the tall droid said, dipping his head. "Far less gore than last time."

Nic looked up, beaming. "Thank you. I've been working on not cutting off arms."

The droid cocked his head. "A...worthy goal." He turned to Cynthia. "Do you require assistance?"

She stood up from the dismantled access panel. "Nope." The door slid open.

The door to the detention block slid open. Wuan and his prisoners turned as one to the now open hatch with Gabe standing among several bodies.

"Time's up," Zephyr said.

Everyone watched as two of the three Intelligence officers assigned to watch the space rushed the open door. A feline-featured blur leaped into the foyer past Gabe, landing atop one guard while her leg lashed out at the other, driving the man away from his colleague into the iron grip of Gabe's outstretched hand. He lifted the struggling woman off her feet.

By the time the tangle of Harrith and Tygran limbs hit the carpeted floor, the Harrith woman was out cold and Cynthia was crouching to tackle the other woman, only to pause as Gabe turned and threw the guard out into the corridor. From beyond came a loud crack, followed by Nic's excited shout. "I got that one before she hit the ground!"

Cynthia turned to the remaining guard. The man was halfway between the intruders and his boss. He looked at Cynthia, then Gabe, then turned to Vice Admiral Wuan. "Sir?" Before the Vice Admiral could answer, his body spasmed as a stun blast caught him in the back.

"He's gonna need something for that headache," Maxim said.

Zephyr nodded. "Stunner at that range. Ouch."

Spying the rest of the Rogue Enterprises team behind the remaining Harrith Naval officer, Nic waved. "Hi, guys!" She looked at Wuan and released a low growl.

Gabe and Cynthia joined her, each with a weapon aimed at Vice Admiral Wuan.

Wil clucked. "You know, I hate to say I told you so, but... well..." He spread his arms wide, shrugging.

The hover limo settled, and the passenger door was open before the vehicle finished fully resting on the ground. Bennie was on the sidewalk, tapping a foot. "Come on!"

The Dystum of the Harrith Collective stepped out. "I do not hop out of moving vehicles." He looked at the building and the strobing red lights visible through the large glass lobby doors. "That doesn't look good."

Bennie waved a dismissive hand. "That just means my friends are already here doing their thing."

The other man cocked his head. "Their thing? Their thing is causing a building-wide security alert in the command center of the Harrith Navy?"

Bennie shrugged. "On slow days." He turned and made for the doors.

"They'll be locked."

The Brailack Knight of Plentallus looked over his shoulder. "I have a key." He held his beam saber hilt up for the other man to see. The energy blade cracked into existence with a *snap-hiss*. In a single fluid motion, he drove the blade into the glasslike doors. The material bubbled and hissed as the blade sliced through it and whatever locking mechanisms were in the metal frame.

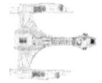

Wuan looked at Cynthia's group, then over his shoulder at Wil and the others.

Shre' Ta'n shook her head. "Clar'V'Al. Give up. It's over."

Wuan's face scrunched up, his skin darkening. Whatever he was about to do died with him. A stun blast rippled over his body, sending him twitching to the ground.

Wil looked past the unconscious man. "Babe, he was gonna monologue."

Cynthia looked down at Wuan, nudging him with the toe of her boot. "Sorry, were we going to do the monologue thing?" She stepped over the body to the cell's perimeter. "I can never tell. We should plan ahead of time if we're gonna let them do that."

"Maybe every other?" Maxim offered.

Wil shook his head. "But we can't know who'll be interesting ahead of time."

Nic, squatting down next to the stunned man, lifted one of his arms. "We could wait until he wakes up." She let the arm fall back to the floor.

The alert siren fell silent, and the room's lighting returned to normal.

Shre' Ta'n watched all this, then shook her head. "You people are mad." She looked at Cynthia, then nodded to the side of the cell opening. "Mind?"

Cynthia smiled and deactivated the force field that closed off the cell's opening. She ran to Wil, helping him up and kissing him at the same time. He made strained choking noises.

Nic ran over and leaped into a hug from Maxim.

The Admiral looked around. "Right under my nose."

"Under all our noses," a voice said from the room's door. The Dystum of the Circle stepped into the detention center over one of the unconscious naval officers. Bennie was right on his heels, hopping over the same unconscious form.

"Well done, little green." Cynthia nodded to the team's hacker.

The older Harrith man looked around. "I don't know what to say." His gaze stopped at Shre' Ta'n. "Admiral."

"Dystum." She inclined her head.

The two men reached the others, exchanging nods.

"I guess my promotion is coming early."

Everyone turned to the entry. Blu'T'Ohm and Gul'P'Ulo walked in, Sublieutenant Pre'S'Oh behind them, blasters in each hand.

"Blue!" Wil said, smiling. He looked past the two Harrith. "Guy that likes to punch prisoners."

The Sublieutenant looked around the room, his eyes falling on the Dystum. He cocked his head. "The Dystum of the Circle killed by heroes-turned-anti-Harrith terrorists." He looked at Shre' Ta'n. "They killed a decorated admiral as well, so tragic." He smiled. "We can stage some footage with our remaining PK armor. That'll be a great touch."

"What about us?" Blu'T'Ohm asked.

The man shrugged. "Two nobodies were caught in the carnage."

"Nobody!?" Gul'P'Ulo shouted as she spun. She was on the much larger man before anyone else in the room could react, raining open-handed slaps and kicks on him.

While the Sublieutenant was fending off the furious young woman, Zephyr and Maxim made their move, covering the distance in three strides, tackling the brawling pair.

Within seconds, the Sublieutenant was hog-tied next to his still unconscious boss.

After taking the Sublieutenant's wristcomm and making sure any spyware his co-conspirators installed was disabled, Shre' Ta'n placed a call to a friend in the Harrith Guard. The only arm of the Navy she was fairly certain wasn't involved.

After securing the numerous unconscious troopers in the corridors, the team waited until the first Harrith Guard troopers arrived to take over the scene.

The senior-most trooper approached Admiral Shre' Ta'n. "Ma'am." After exchanging salutes, the trooper continued, "Two tens have been taken into custody. I assume a few were not part of the conspiracy, but merely uninformed and misguided officers who saw that the building was under attack and responded."

Shre' Ta'n nodded. "Hopefully. I'd prefer as few traitors as possible."

The man nodded. "There are certainly more than I enjoy thinking about."

She gave him a knowing nod, then turned to see the Dystum, Blu'T'Ohm, and Maxim engaged in a spirited discussion. Wil sidled up next to her, and around his swollen lip, said, "You don't want to go over there."

"What're they arguing about?"

Wil shrugged. "Nothing too serious. The future of the GC."

The woman's eyes grew in size. "Oh no."

Wil nodded.

Bennie reached them. "Hey, losers." He nodded to the trio discussing politics. "What's tha—"

Wil pushed him the opposite direction. "Come on. I think I see Zephyr making *I need you over here* motions."

Shre' Ta'n watched the pair leave, then shook her head. *These people are chaos personified*, she thought to herself. When the news eventually broke, she knew that the entire Harrith Collective would be shaken to its core.

Most Harrith had a fairly low opinion of the Galactic

Commonwealth, but that same number would almost certainly have an equal opinion of members of the government and military working to hasten the interstellar government's collapse.

The next day, the news broke, and it went about as well as the Admiral had expected, except for one thing. As the news agencies breathlessly reported on the veritable who's who of offenders across Harrith society, they were also carrying a story of hope.

She leaned forward, tapping a control on her desk to unmute the large display on the far wall of her office.

The Dystum, with Blu'T'Ohm at his side, was in the press government complex's briefing room. The leader of the Harrith Collective cleared his throat. "Ladies, gentlemen, and those who identify as other. Today you're learning about a despicable cabal that thrived in our midst." After a pause more for dramatic affect than anything else, he continued, "We're not here to talk about that. Our justice system will do its job. We, myself and Blu'T'Ohm Ka-tan, are here to speak on something more hopeful." He stepped to the side, allowing the other man to approach the lectern.

Aboard the *Ghost*, still sitting on the duracrete awaiting departure clearance, everyone leaned forward in their seats.

Wil looked at Maxim. "They're not naming you ruler of Harrith or anything, are they?"

The other man clucked. "I'm here, aren't I?"

Nic, perched on the edge of Bennie's station, said, "What are they going to say?"

Maxim winked at the young woman. "You'll see." He turned to Zephyr. "I think you'll be proud."

On the ship's main display, the Harrith man they'd been keeping safe for the last few weeks began speaking. "Some of you may know me. I've been...outspoken, in my encouragement of GC member societies to leave the organization. In my zeal to encourage more people to see what life can be like without a galactic government telling them how to live, I neglected to realize the potential instability and strife that could follow."

Blu'T'Ohm took a deep breath. He glanced at the Dystum, who nodded.

"So melodramatic," Bennie complained. Everyone shushed him.

Blu'T'Ohm continued, "The Dystum and I have reached out to the Galactic Commonwealth Governing Council, inviting them to come to Harrith Prime to learn more about our system of government and the stability that we've enjoyed for thousands of years."

Zephyr turned to Maxim. "Wow."

His grin was uncharacteristically big. "Right?"

In her office, Shre' Ta'n whistled. "Well, dren. I didn't see that coming." She shook her head. "Despite their penchant for chaos, they certainly seem to leave things better than they found them."

As the Dystum and Blue continued to explain their plan to help the GC reform into a better version of itself versus dissolve into chaos, Cynthia announced, "Finally. We're good to go." She toggled a control on her console, thanking the space traffic controller. She turned to Wil and nodded.

"Imagine if the Admiral hadn't put in a word for us," Wil said.

"Are we sure she did?" Bennie asked. He had been fidgeting at his console since they put in their departure request.

The *Ghost*'s repulsorlifts flared to life, pushing the ship up off the ground. Wil guided the ship up and away from the spaceport, falling in behind a midsized freighter that was burning out of the atmosphere.

Bennie turned. "Wonder what this means for Botrobel?"

Cynthia grunted. "He'll survive. There's always someone somewhere that wants something they can't or shouldn't have."

Nic looked from her mentor to the Tygran woman. "You think the systems that voted to leave the GC will change their minds?"

Bennie rubbed his hands together. "If they don't, they'll need—"

"We are not arms dealers!" Wil shouted.

Bennie turned in his seat. "Yet," he said under his breath.

## THE END

"Good evening, I'm Megan."

"And I'm Xyrzix." The blue-skinned journalist's large compound eyes swiveled from camera to camera.

"And this is GNO News Time," Megan finished. She made a show of visibly collecting herself, then said, "In news that is honestly a surprise, the Galactic Commonwealth Governing Council has announced that they are sending a delegation to the Harrith Collective in order to learn from our neighbors."

Xyrzix blinked several times before continuing, "Certainly, an interesting turn of events. Especially given the timing, as several more Tier 3 and even a few Tier 2 civilizations were set to hold votes in the near future on whether to remain in the GC or not. The council has asked all member societies to pause their votes while the council explores a revamped governing structure that may appeal to a wider cross section of Commonwealth societies."

Megan nodded. "From what we're seeing here in the news room, several proponents of the separatist movement have canceled speaking engagements in those systems."

"Of particular note, Blu'T'Ohm Ka-tan, who if you recall was the victim of several attacks on his life recently, was on stage with the Dystum of the Harrith Collective, inviting the Council to Harrith Prime," her cohost added.

Megan beamed. "I have to say, not as a newscaster, but as a citizen of the Commonwealth, I'm excited to see our leaders proactively working to ensure our society continues."

"With changes," Xyrzix added, smiling to reveal nearly perfectly square white teeth set in an almost straight line.

The pale skin of Megan's audio receptors flushed a deep blue as she nodded. "With changes. Changes that I personally think will be just what the Commonwealth needs to continue on. After all, the Harrith Collective has thrived for thousands of cycles, outside of GC control and involvement. That's not nothing." She took a breath. "Time will tell, of course, and we'll keep you updated as this story unfolds." She tilted her head. "I'm Megan."

"And I'm Xyrzix. Have a pleasant evening."

A month later, the crew was back on Harrith Prime. Standing at the foot of the *Ghost*'s cargo ramp, Wil looked up. "I can't believe this all got sorted out so quickly." He held a hand up over his eyes to shield them from the sun as he watched a gleaming and nearly organic-looking Tarsi-designed shuttle land two spots over from the *Ghost*.

Four Peacekeeper corvettes hovered overhead. The drone of their repulsorlifts required all conversations to be shouted.

Cynthia shrugged, shouting, "When the alternative is the collapse of civil society, speed wins out."

"What?" Bennie shouted. Wil pointed to the shuttle settled on its landing gear. "Oh, yeah. Really hard to steal."

Wil just shook his head.

The *Ghost* was the only nonmilitary craft on the duracrete of the Drotu Municipal Spaceport. A ground vehicle slid up next to the ship. Blu'T'Ohm stepped out. "Hello, my friends." He nodded to the gleaming shuttle nearby. "Who'd have thought?"

Once the GC's Governing Council arrived, it had taken the two groups very little time to realize that the Harrith system of representative government far exceeded what the GC had been using for millennia to less and less effect. While it would take another cycle or so for the reforms to be fully enacted, the GC had been quick to announce the decision and the alliance with the Harrith Collective as consultants on implementing this new governing structure.

"Not me," Nic replied. She was still sad that her friend Gul'P'Ulo had been found guilty of sedition and been sentenced to two cycles of community service for her—limited though it was—part in the cabal. When they received their invitation to the signing ceremony for the alliance between the Harrith Collective and GC, she had reached out to the young Harrith woman. She received no reply.

The team filed into the ground vehicle. Once it began to move, Nic looked at the others. "There's a buffet, right?"

## THANK YOU

Thank you so much for reading this latest Rogues Enterprises adventure

**If you enjoyed it I'd love it if you left a review. Seriously, reviews are a big deal.** They help readers find authors. They help authors show how awesome they are.

Reviews are social proof and go a long way to encouraging other readers to take a chance on an unknown author.

*OFFER*

As they say, there's no harm in asking, so here we go.

If you can help connect me with someone who can get Space Rogues on a screen (Big or Little) I'll cut you in for 10% (Up to $10,000) of whatever advance is paid.

Send me an email and we can discuss.
rights@johnwilker.com

**Want to stay up to date on the happenings in the Galactic Commonwealth?**

Sign up for my newsletter at
johnwilker.com/newsletter
You can also join my Patreon page for all
sorts of awesome goodies!

Visit me online at
johnwilker.com

## ACKNOWLEDGMENTS

I couldn't do this without an amazing group of people who sign up to beta and/or ARC read for me. The Beta readers in particular have to suffer through an early draft to help shape the story.

Below are some of these awesome people (If I missed your name, email me and you'll be in the next one :D )

- Rick Lindsay
- Marcus Zarra
- Chris Boyd
- Roger Gilmartin
- Felix Muller

Thank you so much, all of you!